Advance Prai

Jacobs and Birnbach's YA time-traveling adventure combines SF and elements of classic caper and heist stories.... Fans of classic time-travel narratives will find much to love here. Though the concept of going back into the past to meet younger versions of family members has been done, Jacobs and Birnbach's characters are distinctive enough to keep this work feeling fresh. Tori's unique humor—she refers to summer camp as "New York with mosquitoes"—and the author's smooth prose make this solid, lighter SF yarn a delight.
—Kirkus

What happens when you cross a jewelry heist thriller with time travel? A new take on both genres that is original and entertaining. *Stealing Time* will transport you back to gritty 1980 Manhattan along with protagonist Tori, who finds herself far away from her familiar 2020 to team up with her own teenage father to thwart a crime before her grandfather goes to jail for it. A fresh, fun, authentic must-read for both young adults and those not-so-young who came of age in the 80s.
—R.J. Cadmus, author of *Ordinary Man* and *Mob Guy*

Co-authors Tilia Klebenov Jacobs and Norman Birnbach have crafted a fun and interesting time-travel caper novel, a love letter to New York filled with sharp insights and surprises. A fast, exciting read, and a sure-fire hit.
—Dale Phillips, author of the Zack Taylor mystery series.

Also by Tilia Klebenov Jacobs

Wrong Place, Wrong Time

Second Helpings at the Serve You Right Café

Casper and Jasper and the Terrible Tyrant

Stealing Time

Tilia Klebenov Jacobs

&

Norman Birnbach

First published 2024 in the United States of America by
Linden Tree Press

Copyright © 2024 Tilia Klebenov Jacobs and Norman Birnbach
All rights reserved.

First edition

ISBN: EPUB 979-8-9910249-0-7 (Linden Tree Press)
ISBN: Paperback 979-8-9910249-1-4 (Linden Tree Press)

This is a work of fiction. Names, characters, places, and events appear as the result of the imagination of the authors. Any resemblance to real persons living or dead, places, or events is a matter of coincidence.

Cover design by Asha Hossain Design LLC

To Doug, Nate, and Elwyn:
my own magical gems.
—Tilia

To Deborah, Ben, Fischer, and Rebecca
and
in memory of Maks Birnbach.
—Norman

Chapter 1

New York City, Monday, March 16, 2020

Tori had no way of knowing that the diamond would finish her story, a story begun before she was born.

Through the open door of the study, she heard the click of the keyboard. Her mom, Adina, was securing a rental car for the two of them to drive to Newton, Massachusetts, where they would ride out the pandemic with Adina's sister Simone. Yep, right from one pandemic epicenter to another—Boston's numbers were almost as bad as New York's. Typical, thought Tori. Her folks were such overachievers.

Well, Adina was. Law partner, degrees from Wellesley and Yale, all that. Her dad, Bob, did meh-level cybersecurity, a position he had acquired by going to night school and earning a certificate in Advanced Surly. You never knew what might set him off. Once, years earlier, while visiting Aunt Simone, they had driven past a white, domed building with columns. Tori, who was five at the time, had said, "Look, Daddy—it's Washington!" But Bob had said, "No, that's MIT. I got in there." And then he glowered at the road, hands tight on the wheel, leaving her wondering what she'd done wrong this time.

Classic.

Forget about it, Tori told herself. Right now she had other things on her mind, specifically her parents' impending divorce and the coronavirus that had New York—and the entire world—surfing on waves of terror. Looking out her apartment window at the incongruously bright spring weather, she could almost feel every school shutting and every flight grounding, could almost hear eight million people panic-shopping for toilet paper and clawing the backs of frozen food shelves for every last, leaky bag of peas as every damn door in every building in the city slammed and double-latched shut. How thoughtful of her parents to choose this time to separate.

"Are you packed?" said Adina from the doorway.

Tori gave her mother the side-eye. "Almost."

"Well, finish up. We can't delay."

Tori stared at the empty streets, which ordinarily would have been draped in shamrock bunting for the St. Patrick's Day Parade. Not this year. "I don't think traffic will be much of a problem."

"They might close state borders."

Tori slouched onto the sofa, tucking her shock of purple hair behind one ear. "You should wear a mask."

"Masks are for sick people." Adina yanked on her coat. Her eyes were wide, and the skin of her face looked tight. Even New Yorkers, with their been-there-done-that attitude, weren't prepared for this.

"Dad says to wear gloves." Tori's phone pinged, and she pulled it out of her pocket. The battery was low.

"Your dad's not an expert."

"Neither are you." Tori hated herself, but at that moment she hated her mother even more.

"Gloves are for first responders."

Tori put her sneakers on the sofa because it was a reliable way to make her parents angry. "Wow, Mom. So cool you listen to NPR."

She heard the hiss of Adina exhaling through her teeth. "Be ready to go when I get back." The door banged behind her. It was probably the only one in the building that wasn't welded shut.

Making a face, Tori opened her phone. The ping was a reminder from Barclays Center that the March 21 game was cancelled. Celtics versus Nets. Adina had gotten comps at work, center court seats, and Tori had been looking forward to it for weeks.

Thanks for the memo, guys. As if she needed anyone to jog her memory about the fact that the world was ending. She deleted the notification and skimmed through her messages, hoping she'd missed something earlier. Unlike Barclays Center, her friends weren't texting or even answering her messages. What were they so busy with? They weren't going into exile, like she was.

"Tori?"

Tori jerked her head up. Her father stood in the doorway, shoulders sagging, heavy brows creased, graying hair rumpled as if he'd been pulling at it. Not for the first time, Tori felt a prickle of irritation at his perennially sad eyes and jowly frown. When he wasn't angry, he looked like a bereaved bulldog. "What?"

He crossed the room, proffering a crumpled ball of latex-free gloves. "Take these."

She jammed them into the pocket of her jeans and went back to her phone, thinking, *You can leave now.*

Bob rubbed his ear. "You can visit any time," he said softly.

She swung her legs off the sofa and stomped past him. "Yeah, right."

In a few hours she would be in Massachusetts, land of Boston accents, inferior bagels, lousy pizza, and having to be driven everywhere. She and Adina would flatten the coronavirus curve by staying with Aunt Simone and Papi, the cat Tori was allergic to, and Simone's two young kids Tori would definitely have to babysit even though Adina kept saying she wouldn't. Meanwhile, Bob would stay here, supposedly helping take care of his mother, who lived nearby in a home for the decrepit. Grandma Louise had a beautiful smile but could only breathe with an oxygen tube up her nose. Between wheezes she was always talking about "my Victor," who Tori was named after and who had been dead since before Tori was born. Once when she was little, Bob had showed her the storefront where Victor had worked selling baseball cards and vintage comic books. Now it was a pawn shop, squeezed between a juice bar and a Thai restaurant near Madison Square Garden.

Tori had lived in New York all her life. Well, except for summer camp, but all those kids were from the city too, so it was like New York with mosquitoes. She had grown up in this apartment. Hell, her *father* had grown up in this apartment. And now it would never be home again, thanks to him. His morose silences, his anger that flared and died for no apparent reason, the diamond-hard walls he put up around himself—Adina had stood it as long as she could.

Tori slammed the door to her room and looked around for a charger. The place was a mess, the detritus of her life clumped like trash during a garbage strike. One pile was her schoolbooks for Columbia Grammar and Prep. Most of the neighborhood kids went to PS 142, which was walking distance instead of two subways away, but Bob had gone to CGP and insisted she do the same. Now she'd never go back there.

She shoved the books aside, hoping they were hiding a charger. They weren't.

The yellow walls of her room were naked. Hoping Aunt Simone would let her decorate the attic bedroom that would soon be hers, Tori had taken down her fairy lights and scrunched them into a plastic bag. Ordinarily they sparkled like emeralds and rubies; now they were as dark as her mood. She had rolled up her posters of Billie Eilish and *Hamilton* and secured them with rubber bands, since the pandemic was so dangerous her mom wouldn't let her go to the office store for a poster tube. They leaned against her duffel bag and backpack in a corner. Seeing everything on the floor in a pile of pathos made her feel worse. She wished her lights actually did come from fairies, so they could magically whoosh her away from her multiverse of misery.

After rootling through her bureau, closet, and backpack, none of which held a charger, Tori stomped back to the study. Unlike hers, Bob's posters were still up: one of the starship *Enterprise*, autographed by Leonard Nimoy and William Shatner, and one from *The Empire Strikes Back*. The bookshelf displayed his collection of vinyl, which he rarely played anymore, probably because if he did, he might accidentally enjoy himself. The album facing her had a picture of a guy winding up to hurl a rock through a soaring wall of windows, frozen just before everything shattered. Perfect visual metaphor for this moment.

The phone rang, and she picked up because although it was probably a robocall it might be Grandma Louise. "Hello?"

"Good afternoon." A male voice, unfamiliar. "Is Robert Gold available?"

"Who's calling?" She knew to hang up if they said the words "timeshare" or "extended warranty."

"Tobias Guildersleeve, with the *New York Times*. We're doing a piece on the Desert Sun. The theft more than the gem itself."

The what now? "Hold on." She set the phone down and put it on speaker. "Dad!" she yelled.

"Thanks," said the phone.

"No problem." She pulled out the top drawer, hoping to find a charger lurking among the pens, stamps and Post-it notes.

Bob shuffled in. "What?"

Amazing the way he could sour the air in a room just by entering it, thought Tori. She pulled open a second drawer, nodding at the phone. Her father put it to his ear. "Bob Gold."

"Mr. Gold! Good to meet you at last," the voice blared. Bob jerked the phone away, almost dropping it before setting it back down on the desk and glaring at Tori. She flinched. "Tobias Guildersleeve here, from the *Times*. Don't know if you got my messages, but we're doing a piece on the fortieth anniversary of—"

"I got your messages." Bob's voice was taut.

"Great. So you know I'm hoping to hear what you—"

"No comment." Bob folded his arms, glaring.

Fortieth anniversary of what? thought Tori. *Wedding?* So many errors there.

"Okay, sure. I just want to give you a chance to set the record straight," said the reporter.

Bob gave a short, hard laugh. "I bet you do."

Plus, it seemed unlikely the *Times* would be doing a story about imploding marriages in the Tri-State Area.

"Do you ever feel like a victim too?" said Tobias.

Victim? Tori froze, hoping her dad would forget she was practically touching his elbow.

"Tori, go to your room," said Bob.

Damn. Tori pulled the contents of the drawer forward, peering at them like a lab tech in a bad science fiction movie. "I need a charger."

"I'm sure you know people have formed their own opinions on what happened, which must be so difficult for you." The reporter's voice was liquid sympathy. "Is there something about your father that you'd like them to know? A side of him only you saw?"

Bob's eyes twitched from Tori to the phone and back again. "Out. I mean it."

"Just a sec," said Tori. Two broken staplers, a leatherette diploma cover stamped *PS 142,* a rubber band so brittle it was cracked, and a box of leads for a mechanical pencil. No charger.

"Imagine what a relief it would be to tell your side of the story," said the reporter.

How was it okay that neither of her parents ever had a charger, but they went apeshit if she ever misplaced hers?

"I said, go to your room," snapped Bob.

She looked up from the drawer. "And *I* said, I need a charger."

Bob yanked one out of the wall and thrust it at her, his jaw clenched. She got to her feet.

"Do you think times have changed since then?" said Tobias.

7

"Now you listen to me." Bob leaned over the phone. "Stop calling me at work. Never call me at home. And—"

Tori looked at the charger. "It's the wrong kind."

"Tori—"

"Look." She held up her phone and jabbed the jack fruitlessly at its base.

"Is that your daughter?" said Tobias.

Bob stiffened. "Don't talk to her."

"How has your perspective changed since you became a father? And what does your mother think, all these years down the line?"

Bob slammed his palms down on the desk. "If you speak to my mother—"

"How did this affect your relationship with her?"

"If you contact her, we will sue. My—my wife is an attorney. We will sue. You and the *Times*." Hands shaking, he slammed the phone onto the base as Tori bolted from the study and into her room.

What the genuine hell?

Clearly, something was up; and just as clearly, her father didn't want her to know about it. Well, she had an Internet connection, and she wasn't afraid to use it. What was that guy's name? Tobias Something, at the *Times*.

Several clicks later, she was scrolling through his articles. Mostly local stuff, with headlines like "New York Schoolteacher Faces Perjury Charges" and "How a Cupcake Entrepreneur Spends Her Sundays." Nothing that would enrage her dad.

Her phone buzzed. *R u packing?*

Crap. Why did her mom have to use end punctuation like that? It looked so hostile. Tori thumbed a quick response.

Almost

Don't forget your schoolbooks. Also laptop.

K

She clicked out of Messages and went back to her browser. What had Tobias said? *"We're doing a piece on the Desert Sun."*

Ignoring a new low battery warning, she opened Wikipedia. "Desert Son" yielded nothing, but "Desert Sun" had a lengthy article. About a diamond. The photo with the text was a shot of Gal Gadot at a red-carpet premiere of *Wonder Woman*, wearing a velvet gown. Her only jewelry was a lemon-sized, yellow diamond pendant.

Wow, thought Tori. She saved the photo and enlarged it till the image of the gemstone filled her screen. It was gorgeous, bewitching. It pulled at her in a way she did not understand. She had never seen anything so enchantingly lovely.

With effort, she wrenched herself from the photo to read the article. *The Desert Sun originated in blah and is one of the largest blah blah blah something about carbon and facets.* Tori flicked ahead a few paragraphs.

As famous for its history as for its unusual size and color… flick.

…legends state that the extraordinary diamond yada yada… flick.

…sold to a prominent New York family… flickflick.

…Janna Van der Bleek famously wore it on the occasion of …flickety-flick.

…following which, the family donated it to…. Oh, c'mon, Wikipedia, what about the robbery? Tori drew her finger sharply up the screen, sending the text flying until she reached the header "Theft and Recovery."

The morning of Tuesday, March 18, 1980, the day the exhibit was slated to open to the public, museum security discovered that the diamond and dozens of lesser gems had been stolen in an audacious, overnight robbery. It was later determined that a gang of thieves had scaled the walls of the museum, entering via the windows of the fourth floor where the exhibit was housed. The thieves' evident familiarity with the museum's security systems pointed to an inside job, and suspicion quickly coalesced around then-Chief Gemologist Victor Gold, whose car was spotted near the museum during the robbery. He ultimately served a two-year prison sentence for his role in the crime.

Victor Gold?

Couldn't be. Could it? The footnote at his name took her to an obituary in *The New York Times*.

Victor Gold, Jeweler Turned Jewel Thief,

Dies at 73

Victor Gold, a gemologist and convicted thief connected to one of the biggest jewel heists in New York City history, died July 21 at his home in Manhattan. He was 73. The cause was heart failure, according to his brother, Jacob Gold.

Dr. Gold was a well-respected curator at the American Museum of Natural History, and an assistant professor of gemology and jewelry design at the Fashion Institute of Technology (FIT). But in April 1980, he was charged in connection with the notorious theft a month earlier of the Desert Sun, a storied diamond he had secured as the centerpiece of an exhibit at the museum.

Stealing Time

The daring theft took place over St. Patrick's Day weekend and made front-page news nationwide. The Desert Sun was found within 48 hours, hidden in a Port Authority locker, but some of the smaller gems were never recovered.

Dr. Gold's brother Jacob, initially a suspect, was cleared of any role in the crime. Instead, investigators were quick to pinpoint Dr. Gold as an accessory who coordinated with the Hopewell Gang, a cadre of professional thieves, to steal the famous gem along with others which were part of an exhibit scheduled to open after St. Patrick's Day.

Exploiting his friendship with Janna and Lucas Van der Bleek, the philanthropists who had lent the gemstones and jewelry for the display, Dr. Gold circumvented museum security protocols and convinced them to relinquish the Desert Sun to him, with the understanding that it would be safe under his watchful eye.

Though he maintained his innocence for the rest of his life, Dr. Gold was convicted and sentenced to two years in prison.

Upon his arrest, Dr. Gold was fired by both the museum and FIT. The year after his release from prison, unable to secure employment in his former field, he took over a small shop that sold baseball cards and other sports paraphernalia, renaming it Diamonds to reflect his love of baseball and jewelry. From 1984 to 1995, when he shut down the business, he applied his curatorial discipline to the baseball memorabilia that he sold.

"It's a treasure hunt," explained his wife Louise in a rare interview in 1995, when Dr. Gold retired. "He was in it for the cards and the books, for the art." Mrs. Gold became a Realtor to support the family after her husband's downfall.

Victor Howard Gold was born on June 23, 1930 in New York City to Sidney, an organizer with the International Ladies' Garment Workers' Union (ILGWU), and Frieda (Feldman) Gold, a women's suffragist and factory worker. After graduating from Columbia University with a B.A., Dr. Gold earned a Ph.D. in gemology from Columbia's Department of Earth and Environmental Science.

In addition to his brother, Dr. Gold is survived by his wife, Louise, and their son Robert.

Tori stared at the screen. *His wife Louise and their son Robert?* She read it again. Louise…Victor…Robert….

This was her family.

And…wait…so Grandma Louise's amazing Victor was—a *crook?* Whom she, Tori, was named for! What a way to find out.

Fury bubbled up in her chest. Typical of her parents to keep her in the dark, just as they had about their separation, springing it on her as a done deal. *We're moving to Massachusetts. Pack up. I don't want to hear another word.* Well, they were going to hear plenty of words. Fingers shaking, Tori forwarded both articles to the printer in the study. She would read them aloud to Adina on the drive to Newton. Pull an ambush, just like her parents had done to her.

She nipped through the shared bathroom into the study. Bob stood at the printer, collecting the pages as they came out. A dark flush misted up his neck.

Oh, shit, thought Tori. *Here it comes.* The onslaught of his mood, as unanswerable as an avalanche.

"How dare you?" His voice was loud in the small room.

Tori's gut clenched. "What?"

"Snoop. Into my personal affairs!"

"Right. Snooping. On Wikipedia."

He crushed the papers in his hand. "This is about me and your mother, isn't it?"

"Not everything's about you."

"This sure as hell is." He took a step toward her. "Congratulations on finding such a clever way to hurt us."

Since this was only partly wrong, Tori said, "Obits are public, Dad."

"Oh, sure. The obit and the tabloids and those smug TV comedians," he snapped. "I'm sure you enjoyed your research. Do you want to know what they left out?"

"Bet you're going to tell me."

"What it's like having a father no one will talk to. Hearing your mother crying in the kitchen every night."

Tori, who had awakened that morning to the sound of Adina's soft weeping, folded her arms icily. "Bet that sucks."

"Changing schools and losing all your friends."

"Imagine," said Tori, who had been wondering what Newton schools would be like once they opened again.

Bob waved the crumpled papers at her, his face ruby with anger. "None of these stories—not a goddamn one—says what it's like to be fifteen and have your whole world go straight to hell."

Oh, this was too much. Tori clenched her fists. "News flash, Dad. I know *exactly* how it feels when your father ruins your life!"

She stormed to her room, flinging the door closed behind her. Bob's shadow appeared under it. She glared at the knob as if daring him to turn it. Her eyes stung.

But her father's voice, when it came, was quiet. "Tori?"

"Go away."

Tori's throat grew thick with tears. The floorboards at the threshold creaked as though Bob were shifting from one foot to the other. He spoke again, so softly she could barely hear him. "I hate what I've become."

Makes two of us. Furious, she thumped onto her bed, messing the covers because he might come in and she knew how much he hated a messy bed. She pulled her phone out of her pocket. It opened to the picture of the huge diamond necklace.

Low battery 3%.

Tori stared at the fire-colored gem. Her vision misted, and she swatted tears away with the back of her hand. The back of her throat tasted of salt.

Low battery 2%.

The diamond blurred with Tori's tears, and everything was warm and salty, full of misery and grief and rage. Color swirled from the heart of the gem, filling the room, making images that she understood in the way of a dream.

The Desert Sun. Mrs. Van der Bleek wearing the necklace at the Met Gala. A *New York Times* headline: "'Desert Sun' Diamond Stolen from Museum Here: Thieves Use Window on 4th Floor for Entry to Hall." Shattered display panels. A stone floor thick with broken glass that glittered like the Milky Way. Victor being frog-marched into the police station. A boy with tears streaming down his face. "Mom—the kids at school said—"

Low battery 1%.

Victor's face was lined with torment. "Louise, we've spent his college fund. I can't...." Tori was falling. She cried out, flailing as the battery died.

"Tori?" said Bob from the other side of the door. "Are you all right? Tori?"

Chapter 2

Who's Home in Whose Home?

Tori jerked to a sitting position, shaking her head violently. *What—the hell—was that?* Her hair flopped in her eyes, and she covered her face with her hands, trying to calm the shaking in her limbs. Her stomach churned, and she swallowed hard, hoping to keep everything down.

The door clicked open. *Oh, crap—it's Dad.* She looked up, ready to be angry again.

A boy stood in the doorway. Shaggy brown hair, heavy eyebrows, a Mets sweatshirt. Jeans and sneakers. About her age. They stared, then both spoke at the same time.

"Who are you?"

A heartbeat, and they both spoke again.

"What are you doing in my room?"

Tori gawped at him. She tried again, and so did he.

"This is *my* room. *Your* room? Yeah, *my* room! I *live* here. No, *I* live here!"

The boy goggled. So did Tori. *I know him from somewhere*, she thought. Not school. Camp? Maybe. But how had he gotten into her apartment? And why?

She tried one last time. "Where's my father?"

The boy drew his heavy brows together. "How should I know?"

"He was here, like, a second ago."

"I'm the only one here now."

"Damn right you are." Tori hurtled off the unmade bed and ran past the interloper, down the short hallway and out the front door. The apartment was on the sixth floor, but she wasn't going to wait for the elevator. She skidded down all six flights, barely keeping her feet under her, and burst through the front door. Her foot slipped in a puddle of slush, and a cold wind, thin as a blade, sliced through her tee shirt. She slid to a halt, realizing two things.

One, she didn't have a coat.

Two, she shouldn't have needed one—it had been a warm, sunny day, but now the sidewalk was lumped over with pitted, gray snow.

The weather wasn't the only thing that had gone haywire. The MTA busses were the wrong shape and color. Bulky yellow taxis detailed with black-and-white checker stripes splashed through the slush, and a station wagon with fake wood doors chunked over potholes. The sidewalk was crowded, which it certainly hadn't been earlier in the day. Clumps of school kids, some carrying briefcases instead of backpacks; a young mom, cigarette dangling from her lips, pushing a stroller that didn't look sturdy enough to handle the city streets; and everyone walking around like they'd never heard the words *pandemic* or *lockdown*.

The clothes were all wrong too. Lots of brown cloth coats with wide lapels. Two women wearing fur jackets. *Fur!*

Tori's mind convulsed. Movie set? Hallucination/insanity? Climate change? She took a deep breath of cold air and started walking. In three steps, her sneakers were soaked.

At the corner, a blue newspaper kiosk displayed *The New York Times*. The paper was wider than usual. *Special coronavirus edition?* Hugging her elbows for warmth, she leaned down to see the front page. The photo story in the upper-left corner ("Late Winter Snowfall Snarls Traffic") was in black and white, and the lead headline blared, "CARTER PLAN IS DUE TODAY ON ECONOMY; 10¢ GAS RISE LIKELY; INFLATION CUT IS AIM."

The date on the paper was Friday, March 14, 1980.

Tori stood up fast. Whatever this was, it wasn't funny. She pulled her phone out of her pocket to call home, but the screen was black and unresponsive to either her touch or her whispered curses.

"What are you doing?"

Tori jerked around. It was the crazy boy who claimed to live in her room, wearing a puffy parka, unzipped as though he had pulled it on in a hurry.

"Trying to call my folks."

"What's that?" He pointed to her phone.

"Old 7S." She forced a smile. "They won't get me anything newer. Hey, look, my battery's dead. Can I use your phone?"

"I guess." He turned back to the apartment building, glancing back at her. She followed, stepping around the slush. *Why doesn't he have it with him?*

The boy already had his key in his hand, New Yorker-style. When they reached the entrance, he turned it in the lock while pulling up on the knob and pressing against the door with his hip until it opened.

Tori felt her chest constrict. The building was old, built in the forties, and as Adina said, it had gotten eccentric in its old age. You would have to open that door a hundred times before nailing the knack of it. Which this kid clearly had. How—?

To hide her confusion, she gazed again at the street, trying to pinpoint what was so different besides the weather and the clothes. And the fact that everyone was outside instead of hunkered behind closed doors taping cardboard over the air ducts. The street she had lived on her whole life felt off-kilter. But why? Forgetting that her battery was dead, she reached for her phone to take a picture so she could study it later. She froze, her hand touching the edge of her back pocket.

No one was looking at their phones. No one walked with their hands out and necks bent forward in the telltale sign that they were focused on their screens.

A hideous idea muscled into her mind.

No. Can't be.

"You okay?" The boy slipped the key back into his pocket.

Tori kicked the idea out and gestured at the passersby. "Where are the phones?"

"There's one on the corner, but the cord broke six months ago." He stomped the slush off his sneakers and stepped over the threshold, holding open the door.

Numbly, she followed him inside. Their wet shoes slapped against the thin carpet runner, echoing in the shadows of the tiled hallway. He pressed the elevator button, and the floor indicator moved from 14 to Lobby. Neither spoke. The silence was terrible, tight. What could she possibly say?

"My name's Bobby," said the boy.

Okay, so that was one thing.

"Tori," she said. The elevator doors opened, and they stepped in. It looked the same, maybe a little cleaner than usual. Bobby hit the button. The doors hissed shut, and they clanked up, floor by floor.

"Is that short for Victoria?" he said as the door opened.

"Yeah. Family name."

As they walked down the hall, Tori shuffled data points in her mind, willing the scene to make sense. First off, Bobby was clearly bonkers, thinking he lived in their apartment; but he did know the building and its quirks. Could it be he lived there, and they had somehow never crossed paths?

Nah. Neighborhood teens were easy to spot, hanging at Starbucks and the basketball court and stuff. Unless this guy was Boo Radley, she would have set eyes on him before now.

Second, what about all the weirdness at street level? Everything from the weather to the clothes was nutso.

She kicked off her wet sneakers as Bobby untied his, leaving them next to the mat. The door was ajar, kept in place by the chain. She checked the brass numerals—right number; good, good—and stepped inside.

It was her apartment, all right: same entrance hall, same layout. But now that she had a chance to take it all in—now that she was walking, not Usain-bolting out of her bedroom, tunnel vision on the front door—she saw that everything here was off too. The wood floor was darker, the walls were covered in pale-green, geometric wallpaper instead of yellow paint, and the furniture had a funky, retro-mod look. Weirdest of all, the stink of tobacco hung in the air so thick she could almost chew it.

"My father's named Victor."

Unfairly, Tori found herself irritated by the coincidence. "Well, my father's named Bob, so I guess we're even."

"Didn't know we were keeping score," said the boy. "There's a phone in my dad's study."

"*My* dad's," she snapped, and stomped past him.

Whoever was rearranging things had worked fast. Her dad's big, wooden desk was on the wrong side of the room, and his *Empire Strikes Back* and *Star Trek* paraphernalia were gone. Instead, the walls sparkled with pictures of jewelry: hoop earrings in the shape of leopards' heads; a bracelet that looked like a curved, gold nail; a necklace of amethyst grapes shaded by cloisonné leaves sprouting from curling vines a-glitter with tiny diamonds. Another wall displayed action photos of old-timey baseball players. The big guy was probably Babe Ruth; another one showed a skinny dude in vintage Yankee pinstripes slouching before a teepee of microphones. A Barcalounger and a red, plaid couch took up the center of the room. Either one of them would have given Tori's mother an aneurysm.

"It's on the desk." Bobby gestured at a squat, black phone with a kinked-up cord. Another line led from the base to a plug in the wall.

"Old-school," said Tori, momentarily forgetting to be scared.

Bobby's heavy brows furrowed. "Old-school?"

"In a good way," she assured him. "It's cool." She examined the phone. *Right. I can do this.* She put her finger into the hole next to the number two, pulled it toward the bottom of the dial, and released it. It spun back with a rattling sound. Pleased with herself, she did the same with the number one but forgot to remove her finger, and the dial pulled it back up to the top as it unwound. The whole thing was slower and noisier than she had expected. But by the end of her mother's phone number, she had gotten pretty smooth, and felt a flash of triumph. "Now what?"

Bobby had backed away and was watching her from the doorway as though she might explode. "What do you mean, 'now what'?"

"Like, do I hit send, or what?"

Bobby's look of confusion deepened. "You pick up the receiver."

"Oh, right," Tori chuckled. *I knew that. I just wanted to see if you knew that.* She lifted the handset, and after an awkward moment figured out that the part with the cord must be the mouthpiece, which meant that the upper part was the earpiece, which meant that now it should be dialing.

Which it wasn't.

"Why isn't it dialing?"

Bobby gave up all efforts at politeness. "Have you seriously never used a phone before?"

"Not like this!"

"So you have, what, a party line or something?"

"I—" Tori waved the buzzing receiver around. "Just walk me through it, okay?"

Bobby sighed. "Hang up."

She hung up.

"Now pick it up again."

"But you said —"

"The receiver has to be off the cradle before you dial, or it doesn't go through."

"Well, why didn't you say so?"

"I just did," muttered Bobby.

Furrowing her brows, Tori dialed her mother's number again, this time more smoothly. It didn't go through, and neither did the call to her father. Instead, she got a high-pitched beep and a robo-voice saying, "The number you have dialed is not in service."

"This is so weird," she sighed. "I'm not even getting voicemail."

"Bummer," said Bobby cautiously.

"Think maybe it's a pandemic thing?"

"Sure," said Bobby. "Definitely."

"One more try and I'll...." She paused. What *would* she do if she couldn't reach her parents? "I'll get out of your hair," she said, reaching again for the phone.

This time, she tried the landline that she made fun of her parents for keeping. It was partly for emergencies but mainly so Grandma Louise wouldn't have to learn a new number. Tori whispered the area code, prefix, and the final four digits to herself, and watched the slow turning of the dial.

Busy signal. She groaned and hung up.

"What number did you just call?" said Bobby.

"None of your business," she snapped.

"You said it while you were dialing."

"Then why are you asking me what it was?"

He abandoned the safety of the doorframe to stand next to her. "Did you dial 212-555-1177?"

"Yeah, so?"

"That's our number."

"Just like how my room is your room?"

"You're calling this phone."

"No, I'm not."

"Yes, you are." Bobby pointed to the smudged numbers on the circle in the middle of the dial. Tori peered at them.

212-555-1177.

She felt sick.

"What are you trying to pull?" demanded Bobby. For the first time, he sounded angry.

"I'm not pulling anything," cried Tori. "Something's—wrong." Her knees shook, and she sat down hard on the plaid couch. "I need to call my folks."

Her distress seemed to jolt Bobby back to sympathy. "Did you hit your head or something?"

"What? No."

"You sure?"

"Why do you think I hit my head?"

"Because the number you dialed is our number, and the apartment you say you live in is our apartment."

Tori groaned and hugged herself. Her eyes fell to an ashtray on the desk by a pile of magazines. *TV Guide. Omni*, recommending "Games To Play on Your Calculator." *Time*, with Ronald Reagan on the cover.

"I don't—this is so—" The idea she had thrown out cleared its throat loudly.

"Let's look up your number," suggested Bobby. He pulled a massive paperback out of a bookcase and let it flop open on the desk. "Maybe you're just off by one digit or something."

Tori nodded. "Okay. Yeah. Good idea."

"What's your parents' names?"

"Robert Gold and—"

Bobby looked up from the book, finger still on the page. "Robert Gold?"

"Yeah, Gold like the metal."

"I know how to spell it."

"Well, sometimes people put a U in the middle."

"I know how to spell it because it's my name."

"What?"

"Robert Gold." He pointed to himself. "That's me."

Tori gaped. Brown eyes, heavy brows...images of family photos flashed into her mind: her dad at summer camp, her dad graduating from high school. Back when he had dark, shaggy hair. He looked a lot like—no, he looked *exactly* like this kid.

Whose name was also Bob Gold. And who was staring at her in a way that said at least one of them was whacko.

Tori looked past his shoulder. The window over the desk framed a postcard view of Manhattan, its skyline like a jumble of Lego blocks. It was all familiar...except for two tall, slender towers soaring over everything else, reflecting the cloudy sky.

"Oh, my God," she whispered.

"What?"

Tori pulled her knees to her chest, shaking all over. The ugly idea was pounding on the door. She felt as though her brain had drifted free of its moorings and was spinning slowly and painfully in a whirlpool within her skull. Presently it stopped, presenting her with three options.

First, she was dead.

In a detached way, she saw how reasonable that was. New York was a pandemic cesspool. People were dying every day by the hundreds; she could certainly have been one of them. Maybe she got sick right after she and her dad fought, and the strain of dying had messed with her memory. Yes, that tracked.

But, pointed out her brain, why would the afterlife be her own apartment in 1980?

Second, she had lost her mind.

This, too, made a lot of sense. Being crack-ass bananas would account for everything: maybe she had fabricated her entire previous life.

But just as she was settling into the weirdly reassuring thought that she was one fry short of a Happy Meal, she felt something in her back pocket. Hesitatingly, she pulled out the iPhone. "Do you see this?"

"Sure," said Bobby. "But I don't know what it is."

"Right." Tori slipped the phone back in her pocket. If Bobby could see it, it was real, which meant 2020 was too.

The idea leered in triumph.

Time travel.

She was in her apartment in New York City, with her dad. In 1980.

Chapter 3

Across Town at the Same Time

"So whadda ya think?" said Maeve. The windows around the pool at the Sapphire Ribbon Hotel glowered with the fading light of the March afternoon, but inside the air was bright and steamy. She tossed her head, flipping her hair in a way that had gotten her admission to innumerable nightclubs back when she still needed a fake ID. It was also good for free drinks. The humidity made her chestnut waves even fuller and bouncier than usual, which she liked because guys noticed it. It also made those same guys sweat in their business suits, which she liked even more. Any edge was a good edge. "Ya like it?"

"I like what I see." Dylan Buell looked down his cigarette at Maeve's tanned, athletic form and the bright red swimsuit that covered far too much of it for his liking.

Maeve rotated slowly, giving him the full view. "Good product, huh?"

"Great product."

"You like the design?"

"Baby, if only you knew."

Her teeth flashed in her tanned face. "Sounds like maybe we can do business."

Buell took a long drag on his cigarette. He was not, as a rule, given to bouts of chivalry, and the fact that he was having one weighed on him heavily; but some things are inevitable, and at last he surrendered. "Sorry, honey."

Maeve grinned harder. "I bet we can figure something out."

"Nothing to figure, babe."

She pouted. It was a world-class pout, on a par with the hair flip, and had stood her in good stead for most of her twenty-nine years. "What's the deal? You said yourself it's a good product."

"Decent product," he conceded. "And I like the filling."

"Thanks," called Mike from the other side of the pool. He flexed his biceps, making blurry tattoos of geckoes undulate along his arms. His swimsuit was a companion to Maeve's, trim and red, hugging his hips like spray paint with separation anxiety.

Maeve gave a delighted titter. "Guys. Can't live with 'em, can't shoot 'em." She linked her arm through Buell's and tilted her head toward the door to the hotel. "Let's go upstairs and figure things out. Whadda ya say?"

Again, Buell cursed the instinct that made him disengage from the warm crook of Maeve's elbow. "Not today, sweetheart."

"What's your problem?" Maeve kept smiling, but something else glinted behind her eyes. "You came every day this week, and half the nights."

"Sure," said Buell. "Hell of a show."

"It's not a show."

"It is for me."

"We're serious."

"No, you're not."

"What's that's supposed to mean?"

"You party like a one-girl frat house."

"Thanks."

"It's not a compliment."

"Didn't hear you complaining last night."

"And you won't, hon. But it's not accomplishing anything besides giving the maids a coronary."

Maeve waved an airy hand. "We have business associates over."

"Didn't know there were that many swimsuit retailers in all New York."

"Gotta mix, gotta mingle. It's how deals get made."

"How many deals got made last night, sweetheart?"

"I'm working on one now, if you're interested."

"And the jumping out hotel balconies was what, training for the Olympics?"

Maeve giggled. "The room below said our party was too loud, so me and Gloria went to invite them over."

"Holy God, when I saw you go over that balcony—"

"We know how to handle the ropes."

"Jesus, who do you think you are, fucking Batman and Robin?"

"I'm a bootstrapper."

"You're a huckster."

"We're serious about the business."

"So am I."

"Listen, Jack," said Maeve. "We're looking for investors. You in?"

"Out."

"Why?"

Buell smiled in a way that he thought was confident, bordering on superior. In fact, it was a condescending leer.

"Because baby, other than what's in that swimsuit, you got nothing."

Maeve glared. "Bull."

"I been doing this for twenty years, and I don't stay in business giving money to losers."

"We got a designer, a business manager, and two models."

"Oh, honey." Buell's smile deepened. "You got four stoners, two swimsuits, and delusions of grandeur."

"Me and Mike are both champion surfers."

"Nobody outside Florida's ever heard of you."

"Down there, everyone asks us about the swimwear."

"This is New York."

"What's that supposed to mean?"

"Different ballgame, sweetheart."

Maeve folded her arms. "If you were never gonna invest, why did you come every day?"

"Two reasons." Buell stepped closer to her, but she stood her ground. He held up a finger. "First, like I said—hell of a show." Maeve did not smile, and after a moment, he held up another. "Second, it gave me time to check into you a little. Jesus, what a gang."

"What's that supposed to mean?"

"Arrest records are public, honey."

Maeve looked around the steamy pool room. A family with three toddlers played in the shallow end, but otherwise it was just her, Mike, Teresa, Gloria—and Dylan Buell, the last of their possible investors. Everyone else had gone home.

"Look," she said, "we're making a new chapter, know what I mean? But we need some cash to do it right."

"You're too hot to be a mogul," he said. "Why don't you go back to the beach and get that suit wet?"

"Good idea," she snarled. "It's bone dry around here." She slapped his hand, sending the cigarette into the pool. "Now scram unless you want to go in after it."

Buell's cheeks darkened. He spun on his heel and stormed out the door.

"That went well," remarked Teresa. She was sitting with Gloria at one of the poolside tables. "Whadda ya think? Did I capture him?" She held up her sketch pad, showing a caricature of Buell puffing impotently on a tiny cigarette that drooped sadly from his lips. Gloria giggled.

"Well, shit." Mike sat down to join them, and kicked out a chair for Maeve. "He was the last one."

Chapter 4

Meet the Parents

"Now, let me get this straight," said Bobby for the fifth time. "I'm supposed to believe you're my—"

"Don't make me say it again," moaned Tori. She sat on the sofa, arms wrapped around her shins, head tucked into her knees, breathing into the little cave between her face and her chest, fighting down nausea.

"I don't believe you."

"I don't blame you."

"Am I on *Candid Camera?*"

"What's—never mind."

"I mean, is this a joke?"

"Your name is Robert Ezra Gold," she said to her knees. "Your birthday is February 23, 1965. You go to Columbia Grammar and Prep School, and you've been there since pre-K."

"So?"

She lifted her head. "You're into the Mets—"

"No shit, Sherlock." He pointed at his Mets sweatshirt, which Tori had forgotten he was wearing. She plowed on.

"And the Knicks."

"Not a secret."

"You like *Star Wars* and *Star Trek.*"

"Just like half my class."

"And that British book with the Infinite Improbability Drive."

"Definitely not a secret."

Tori groaned. "You don't follow hockey."

"I think you need to leave."

"You like the Jets more than the Giants."

"Do you want me to call your folks, or what?"

"Yes," she cried, "but you can't, and neither can I." She looked wildly around the familiar-yet-different room, then sat up straight, pointing in triumph to a photo on a bookshelf, next to a brass clock. "That's your parents. On their honeymoon." Bobby opened his mouth, but she cut him off. "They were at a rooftop restaurant overlooking the Acropolis, and they asked the waiter to take a picture of them with it. But the way he did it, we can see them but not the Acropolis. They didn't know till they got home and got the pictures developed, and they got it framed because they thought it was funny."

"You know what isn't funny?" Bobby folded his arms and looked at her coldly. "This."

"No kidding." She drew her knees up to her chest again, thinking hard.

"My parents are coming home soon."

"Lucky you."

"Seriously. You need to go," said Bobby.

"Go where?"

"Wherever you came from."

"Here?"

"I mean, before you were in my room."

"Before I was in your room, I was in *my* room, which is what *your* room will be forty years from now!" she said wildly. "If

I've never been here before, how come I know so much about it?"

"Everything you've said is stuff a hundred other people know." He stood up. "Look, I'm sorry, but if you don't leave, I'm gonna call the cops."

"Jellybeans," she said suddenly.

"What?"

"You have a bag of licorice jellybeans in your room."

Bobby froze. "No, I don't."

"Hidden."

"Who said you could go through my stuff?"

"Sometimes it's in your suitcase, and sometimes it's under the liner of your laundry hamper."

"That's private!"

"A friend of yours gets them for you every year—"

"You know Nichelle?"

"You eat them with dark chocolate."

"What? No!"

"You never told your friends, because you were afraid they'd think it was weird. You never told your mom, because the jellybeans are Easter candy and she'd freak. But you told me when I was seven and you found me eating Froot Loops and Cheddar cheese. And I was, like, really embarrassed, but you said it was okay and you told me about the jellybeans and the dark chocolate, and how you never told anyone about it, *ever*."

Her toes curled in her wet socks, and her heart beat so hard she could feel it in her arms. She could see her father's face in the face of this boy. The eyes, the brows. The way he held his head, the way he tightened his lips when he was thinking, as he was now. She was afraid to turn away. Finally, Bobby spoke, his voice shaking.

"Froot Loops and Cheddar cheese?"

"Licorice and chocolate?" she snapped back.

Bobby sighed and rubbed his ear. "I believe you."

Tori whooshed out a gale of pent-up breath as she collapsed back on the sofa. "Thank God."

He looked at her, shaking his head. "I have a daughter?"

"I know, I know," groaned Tori. "It's crazy. Why am I here?"

"Well." Bobby seemed to consider this. "That part's not so crazy."

"Seems pretty whacko to me."

"Having a daughter who's my age." Bobby rubbed his ear again. "That's the crazy part."

"But the time travel makes perfect sense?"

He shrugged. "It's in all the science fiction books and movies."

"Good to know." She rolled her eyes.

"How did you get here?"

"I don't know."

"Do you have a machine or something?"

"No."

"Did you touch something?"

"No."

"Or say something?"

"No."

"Did you slay a young goat and study its entrails?"

"*No.*"

"You must have done something."

"I didn't do anything, and I don't know why I'm here."

"Weird."

"Not super helpful."

"Sorry. I'm a little out of my depth here."

The front door clicked open and closed. "Bobby?" called a voice.

"That's my mom," whispered Bobby. "Oh, my God. What are we going to tell her?"

The door to the study opened, and a woman in a gray jersey dress leaned in as if to turn off the light. Her dark hair was parted down the middle, held back with combs in a soft style that accented her high cheekbones and strong jawline. She arched her eyebrows in surprise. "Bobby? You didn't say you were having a friend over."

Tori scrambled to her feet and held out her hand. "Hi, Gra—Mrs. Gold. My name's Tori."

"Nice to meet you, Tori." Louise's shake was firm, her hand nothing like the tremulous, papery one Tori knew. And she wasn't wheeling around an oxygen tank either. "How do you know Bobby?"

"From Camp Ramah."

Louise turned to Bobby with a smile. "Will Tori be joining us for Shabbat dinner?"

"That would be great," said Tori before Bobby could answer. "Actually, I was wondering if I could stay for maybe a couple of days, if that's okay."

"Are you in some sort of trouble, dear?"

"Kind of." Tori gave what she hoped was a chuckle and not a desperate cackle. "I was supposed to be visiting friends here for the weekend —"

"Because there's no school Monday," chimed in Bobby.

"Right," said Tori, wondering why there was no school Monday. "But the airline lost my luggage from Boston and then it turns out my friends are having a family emergency, so I can't stay with them."

"I'm the only other person she knows in New York," said Bobby.

"Good heavens. You poor dear."

"She used her last dime calling me."

"The last one," agreed Tori. "So, I, like, hate to impose, but is it okay if I stay here?"

"We wouldn't have it any other way," said Louise.

"Thanks. That's super-nice of you."

"Nonsense, dear, it's a mitzvah. That couch is a pullout, so really it's no problem. Do you need to call your parents to let them know where you are?"

"Nah," said Tori. "I already told my dad."

Chapter 5

Enter the Snake

"Snake's here," said Mike.

"Don't call me that," said the man in the doorway.

"Hey, Snake," called Maeve. "Come on in."

Mike stepped aside, holding open the door to the suite. Their visitor was short and slight, with dark hair and deep-set, brown eyes above a prominent nose and pointy chin. His mouth was up at one corner, giving the impression he was in on some joke no one else could hear. "Jesus," he said, surveying the room. "Did you have a party or an apocalypse?"

"Good to see you too," said Maeve from her perch on the sofa. She was wearing jeans and a gauze peasant blouse, and smoking. Her feet were bare, the toes sporting a pedicure in a shade of red that was loud enough to warn ships away from submerged rocks. "Drink?"

"Whatcha got?"

She waved. "Whatcha can find. Food's gone, though."

"My kind of joint." He stooped to pick up a bottle from the floor. It sloshed with amber liquid. "Glass?" At Maeve's dark look he amended, "Never mind—I like mine neat." He settled on the love seat opposite her, put his feet on the coffee table, and took a swig. "Any luck?"

Maeve leaned forward, stabbing her cigarette butt into a silver ashtray rolling with stained filters. "Do I look like we got lucky?"

"Sorry, babe."

"This is crap, man." She flopped back on the sofa, arms wide across the back cushions. "Sears gives frickin' Cheryl Tiegs a whole sportswear line, and I bet she's never been on a surfboard in her life."

"Mmm."

"And frickin' Christie Brinkley probably gets a million dollars for standing under some palm tree for *Sports Illustrated*, lipstick and all."

"Probably," agreed Snake, who had procured the issue in question because of his deep love of palm trees.

"But does anyone care about a swimwear line that you can actually surf in? Hell, no."

"Did you tell them that?"

"Assholes just came to stare."

"Hard to blame them, baby." Despite his mocking words, his tone was warm, and Maeve relaxed as he took another chug. "So what did they say?"

"Like, besides 'You're no Cheryl Tiegs' or whatever?"

"They're right." He set the bottle down next to the ashtray. "You're ten times hotter, and don't you forget it."

"Smarter too." Mike was leaning against the wall by the door, arms folded across his massive chest.

Snake smirked at him. "Did they tell you you're no Christie Brinkley?"

"Watch it, asshole."

"Sorry, sorry." He picked up the bottle again. "You're just as cute as her, I swear."

Mike's face tightened. He took a single step forward, indicating with that brief, fluid motion that he outweighed Snake by sixty pounds and would be happy to demonstrate the advantage this gave him.

"Don't be a spaz, man." Maeve smiled as she lit a fresh cigarette.

"Who you calling a spaz?" said Snake indignantly.

"Both of you." She blew out the match and dropped it in the ashtray. "Mike, can you get me a beer? There's one in the minibar."

Lips compressed, Mike retrieved the can and handed it to Maeve from over her shoulder. As she opened it, he straightened up and, glaring at Snake, employed a series of increasingly detailed gestures to illustrate what he, Mike, would do to him, Snake, should the two of them ever happen to find themselves together in an ill-lit venue devoid of witnesses. Snake beamed at him, bottle dangling from his fingers. "Hey, where's the other lovely ladies?"

"Getting change so Gloria can call her caseworker." Maeve took a swallow of beer. "Mind leaving us alone for a minute, Mike?"

Mike's scowl deepened. "Why?"

"Because I want to talk to Snake, and I can't concentrate if you're standing behind me waving your hands around telling him you're going to shove his face up his ass and tie his ears around his balls." She gave him a seraphic smile. "Okay, hon?"

"We'll miss you," called Snake as Mike stomped away and slammed a bedroom door behind himself.

"You crack me up." Maeve took a drag and blew the smoke out her nostrils.

"What's his damage, anyway?"

She waved her cigarette dismissively. "The girlfriend, the kid. The usual."

"Whew. For a second I was afraid maybe he didn't like me."

Maeve chuckled. "Hey. Can you be serious for a moment?"

"For you? Anything."

"How about for a job?"

"Now, there I can be very serious." He put the bottle on the table and leaned forward, fingers clasped between his knees.

"Good, because there is no way I'm going home like this." She took a gulp of her beer. "You in?"

"You bet. I like my thumbs attached to my hands."

"That what whatsisname told you?"

"No-Name Nicky. Yeah, he was very specific."

"No-Name Nicky?"

"You heard me."

"Why's he called that?"

"He didn't like the first three nicknames he had."

"For real?"

"To the max."

Maeve shook her head. "After this job, you can call him whatever you like."

"Details, please." Snake took another swig.

"We scoped out a gotrocks couple two floors above. Talked to them a few times already, so it'll look natural when I invite them to our next party. Me and Mike will host. Big group."

Snake nodded. Maeve would keep the gentlemen preoccupied, and Mike would enthrall the ladies. "Go on."

"Terri and Gloria get the key and go upstairs. They pass you the loot, which you keep till the heat dies down. You pay off Nicky. Couple weeks later you go on vacation in Florida. I'll meet you at the bus station." She gave a triumphant grin.

Snake waited. When no further details emerged he said, "That it?"

"Sure."

He shook his head. "I don't like it."

"Why the hell not?"

"For starters, you don't know how much loot Mr. and Mrs. Gotrocks even have in the room."

"Kidding me? She's got a tennis bracelet Chris Evert would kill for. With earrings to match."

"Which she'd likely wear to the party, or leave in the hotel safe." Snake stood and paced the expanse of carpet. "What if they leave early?"

"We make sure they don't."

"How you gonna get the key from him?"

"Have one of the girls get real close."

"Which he'll probably remember, don't you think?"

"So what?"

"It's the kind of detail hotel detectives ask about. Not to mention cops."

"Doesn't prove anything."

"Plus, you never invited Mr. and Mrs. Gotrocks till that night their room got broke into, which is the same evening only half your gang's got an alibi."

"That's why we give everything to you, genius."

"And then I sit on the loot for, what, twenty hours on a bus and hope no one asks what's in the bag? Or lifts it?" Snake shook his head. "Plus, this is the third time this week I been here. The girls at the front desk all say hi. The cops connect the dots, and next thing you know I'm in front of a judge. No, thanks."

A sour fleer slid across Maeve's lips. "You got a better plan?"

"Not yet," admitted Snake. The living room was not quite as vast as Yankee Stadium, so he had reached the window. He slouched against the frame, hands in pockets, surveying the streetscape below with a weary eye.

Snake's New York contacts were as vast and varied as the metropolis itself. He had played poker with bestselling writers, and done shots with tabloid journalists. He knew thugs and gamblers; he knew high-end call girls who bedded investment bankers, and starlets who were turning tricks till they got their big break. He had a table at Elaine's—sort of; Elaine had thrown him out when Mia Farrow complained about him, but let him back in when Breslin and Mailer put in a good word. Yeah, this was his town all right.

And now the city he loved was letting him down.

A bus trundled down the broad avenue, and even from here Snake recognized the banner ornamenting its side. He had seen several on his way over, and a few posters on the subway as well. *See Your World Differently after You See Our Jewelry*; and *Diamonds Are Forever, but This Exhibit Is Temporary*; and *At the Museum of Natural History, Rock Beats Paper. Also Gold and Silver and...*. Each one had twisted his guts. To think of all that swag just sitting there so tourists could veg out in front of it, collecting talking points for the folks back home in Smileyberg. *"Aunt Prudence, out there in the Big Apple they got a necklace worth more than your sweet taters and corncob pipe put together!"* Damn, life was so unfair.

Just sitting there...

...where anyone could....

He turned from the window. "I got an idea."

"Yeah?" She lit a new cigarette. "Is it brilliant?"
"Oh, baby," breathed Snake. "It's a gem."

Chapter 6

Shabbat Shalom

The dining room was the only spot that looked right to Tori: same table and chairs, same candlesticks, even the same tablecloth, China, and flatware. The breakfront was the same, but it held several new silver platters. Of course, they weren't new; she was.

"I mean, my life's the reboot here," she said.

"What do you mean, 'reboot'?" Bobby took silverware from a drawer.

"A restart." She set candlesticks on the table. "Like with a movie or TV show where you recognize some of it, but the rest is new. Candles?"

"I'll get them. So like when they switched Dick York with Dick Sargent in *Bewitched?*" He circled the table, setting forks and knives in the wrong places.

"Uh, more like a do-over." She followed him, rearranging the flatware. "So it's more modern, usually."

"For TV?"

"And movies."

"Why not just do something new?" He took a box of stumpy, white candles out of a drawer in the breakfront, and set it down by the candlesticks.

"To make money, I guess." She shrugged. "It's usually with stuff that's already popular, so they know people will watch."

"Does it work?" Bobby twisted a candle into one of the candlesticks.

"Sure. They rebooted Spider-Man like, fifty times."

"Spider-Man's still around?" He put down the candlestick and loaded the second one.

"Still swinging around. New one's really good."

Bobby shook his head, smiling. "So, Hollywood's basically run out of story ideas in your day?"

Tori felt a surge of protective indignation. "In my day, people your age run the studios."

"So?"

"So they like watching the same things they've always watched."

"If one of them is a decent Spider-Man, I'm okay with that." He surveyed the table. "Did you change the way I set the places?"

"Yes."

"You're bossy."

"I blame bad parenting."

Bobby put the box of candles back in the drawer and shut it. "Nowadays, 'reboot' is a computer term."

"It still is."

"So you use computers in two thousand twenty?"

"Oh, God, yes. Not so much with old people, but pretty much everyone else. So Gran—" She lowered her voice. "Your mom doesn't, but the kids I babysit for, they've got computers, and they're in kindergarten and third grade." She let her voice return to normal. "And we say twenty-twenty, not two thousand twenty."

"I will endeavor to remember that when the time comes," said Bobby solemnly.

"Well, when it does, I need to be there." She had been having so much fun comparing notes with Bobby that home had started to feel like a place she was on vacation from, not a time that hadn't happened yet. "How do I get back?"

"Right." Bobby became brisk. "I've got some ideas. First off, what's your mission?"

"My what?"

"In science fiction, time travelers usually have a mission. Also, they're always right about stuff."

"Like setting the table correctly?"

"Har. Har."

"Sorry. Go on."

"I mean stuff that people in the time they're visiting don't know about. Usually they came to keep it from happening. Like, stopping Lincoln from being shot."

"I'm a smidge late to keep Lincoln from being shot."

"Or else to keep a future thing from happening." Bobby was in his element now. "On *Outer Limits* there was this guy from the future who time-travels to keep a mutating virus from destroying humanity. You said there was a virus in 2020, right?"

Tori felt swimmy. "You think I could stop the coronavirus from happening?"

"Why not?"

"It's global."

"So was the one in *Outer Limits*."

It didn't feel right. "How does he do it?"

"He decides to kill the scientist who creates the virus but he lands in the wrong year and the scientist hasn't been born yet, so instead he tries to keep the guy's parents from getting married, and that doesn't work so he figures he'll kill the guy's father, and when *that* doesn't work he runs away in his spaceship with the guy's mother, who's fallen in love with him, and they blast off but he disappears because he's created a time convulsion, which means he was never born, and it ends with the scientist's mother crying in the dark because she's all alone in the future and oh, crap, I'm sorry—"

Tori shuddered, her eyes stinging. "I'm *not* here to stop the pandemic from happening."

Bobby patted her back awkwardly. "Okay."

"I'm not," she insisted, even though he was agreeing with her.

"Okay, okay."

"The time traveler is always right!"

"Of course."

Bobby's eyes were dark with concern. He was so distressed for her that she felt sorry for him. She stood up straight. "Look. Having a mission makes sense. And if you're right, we need to figure out what mine is, because it sounds like until we do, I can't go home."

Bobby nodded. "We'll figure it out."

"Thanks." She smiled at him, tucking her purple hair behind her ear, and he smiled back.

They walked back into the kitchen, with its white Formica counters and cabinets and black-and-white vinyl floor. From a boxy, little radio shoved back on the counter, a choir sang something ethereal full of thees and thous. Louise crooned along softly as she diced carrots into perfect cubes. Tori had never seen her grandmother look so comfortable.

"Mrs. Gold? Is there anything I can do?"

"You don't mind?" Louise stirred the rice while turning down the flame under a pot of soup.

"It's fun. I used to help my grandma make Friday night dinner."

Bobby made a choking sound. If Louise heard, she ignored it. "It's sweet of you to be so helpful. Bobby must have told you a lot about our apartment."

Tori blinked. "He did?"

"Well, you seem to know just where everything is."

"Oh. Right, yes. He did."

"We talked a lot at camp," said Bobby quickly.

"I can see that. Well, Tori, since you can't have Shabbat dinner with your own family, we'll just do our best to make you feel at home here. You can wash the things in the sink. Thanks for pitching in."

Bobby and Tori were putting the last bowl in the dish drain when Victor walked in ten minutes later, a challah in one hand and flowers in another. Louise leaned away from the stovetop so he could kiss her on the cheek, and Bobby took the bread into the dining room.

"Who's our guest?" said Victor, smiling at Tori. He was dressed formally, in a way her own father rarely was: white shirt, wide tie, and a blue suit with creases still sharp after working all day. Very respectable. Exactly how a criminal mastermind would look.

"My name's Tori." She held out her hand, resolved not to show she was on to him. "I know Bobby—"

"—from Camp Ramah," called Bobby from the dining room, and once again they were speaking in unison.

Victor shook her hand, chuckling. "From Camp Ramah. Got it." His grip was firm but not overly so, and unlike some adults who paid scant attention to their children's friends, Victor focused on her when they spoke. He had a tidy mustache, and his eyes were sapphire, like hers. Oh, hell, they were *exactly* like hers. Why hadn't anyone ever told her she had her grandfather's eyes?

"Tori had a travel snafu, and she's spending the weekend with us," said Louise. "Tori, dear, my hands are full. Would you mind putting the flowers in the vase? It's by the radar range."

"Sure." Tori filled the cut-glass carafe with water and arranged the stems of chrysanthemums and baby's breath. "Is it your anniversary or something?"

Louise smiled till her eyes crinkled, and Tori sucked in her breath because at that moment she saw her grandmother, the same way she caught glimpses of her father in Bobby's smooth face and dark hair.

"Always marry a man who brings you flowers on Shabbat," said Louise. "Mr. Gold has surprised me that way every Friday since we got engaged."

"You'd think she'd have spotted a pattern by now," said Victor, loosening his tie. "Dinner soon?"

"About ten minutes."

Louise invited Tori to join her in lighting the candles, and they stood side by side, chanting the blessing over the twin flames. All four of them sanctified the bread and wine, and Victor sang *Eshet Chail* to Louise. That wasn't something Tori's own family did, which was the biggest difference.

Well, that and the general mood. Sometimes lately Tori had trouble eating because of the tension between her parents; the last few months, the only time the three of them had eaten together was Friday nights, and even that was edgy. She couldn't imagine her father plowing through twenty-two

Hebrew verses about how great his wife was when days would pass with them barely talking to each other.

How had Bobby started here, and ended up the fault-finding crab she knew?

After they were done with the chicken soup, Bobby and Tori cleared the bowls. "Quit staring at my parents," he whispered as soon as they were in the kitchen.

"What?" She assessed the dishwasher, wondering how to open it.

Bobby nudged her out of the way, and pulled the door down. "My parents. You've been, like, *gawking* at them all through dinner."

"Give me a break. This is uber-weird for me." Tori rinsed the bowls and handed them to him along with the spoons. "Your mom is so young."

"Young? She's forty-five."

"When I saw her last week, she was eighty-five."

Bobby hesitated. "Okay—I've been trying not to ask this, but…how are my folks?"

"How are they?"

"Yeah. I mean, obviously, I'm alive, I mean in 2020, and I have a," he gulped, "*daughter*, so I guess I'm married—"

Tori felt her cheeks grow hot. "You're married." For now, anyway.

"But in forty years? How are my folks? You said you saw my mom, so how is she?"

"She's—" Tori fumbled.

"She's what?"

"Well, she's—" *Breathing through a tube and wheezing like Darth Vader….*

"Are you two ever coming back?" called Louise.

Tori wiped her hands off with a dish towel. "Tell you later," she whispered.

"What part of Boston do you live in?" asked Victor as they sat down.

"Outside of Boston, actually. Newton." Tori hastily marshaled every recollection she had of Aunt Simone's neighborhood, hoping to filter out anything that might have changed since 1980.

"Does that mean you're a Red Sox fan?" Victor passed her the plate of chicken.

"No, no. My dad's a Mets fan—it's kind of the family religion."

"Your father sounds like a sterling fellow."

"Are you all right, Bobby?" said Louise.

"Sure," coughed Bobby, reaching for a glass of water. "Just swallowed wrong."

"I'm a Mets fan too," went on Victor. "So's Bobby."

"Yeah, he keeps telling me."

"Anything you want to see while you're in town?" Louise asked.

Yikes. What did tourists do in New York in 1980? "Go to, um, the top of the Empire State Building, or Central Park, or a museum or something."

"Ah," Victor said, his handsome face lighting up. "Have you been to the Museum of Natural History? That's where I work." Pushing his chair back, he rose from the table. "I'll be right back." He walked out of the room and returned with a blue Tiffany box. With a flourish, he removed the contents for all to admire. Tori gave a squeak, and her hand flew to her mouth.

"Are you all right, dear?" Louise asked.

"That's—" She lowered her hand, clenching her fists under the table. "Is that the Desert Sun?"

"It surely is," laughed Victor. "I'm impressed, Tori. How did you know that?"

Don't throw up don't throw up don't throw up. "Isn't it super-valuable?"

"The real one is." He casually tossed it in the air. "This is a replica."

"A replica?" Tori's pulse slowed by a few clicks, down into the low hundreds.

"Or stunt double, if you prefer." Victor handed it to her.

Tori reached out automatically, grasping the massive stone. The candlelight flickered through it, creating a flutter of rainbows in its heart. Had Victor already lifted the Desert Sun? "Stunt double?"

"It's CZ."

"CZ?"

"Cubic zirconia."

"Cubic—"

"Yeah, Tori, it's a fake," said Bobby. "Do you work part-time as an echo?"

Tori forced herself to smile as she handed the glittering ball of sunlight back to Victor. "Why do you have a fake Desert Sun?"

"We're prepping a new exhibit, and I had this made so we can see the best spot for the real one. You know, figure out the lighting and everything." Victor sat down again, leaning the ersatz gemstone against his wineglass. "If you think this is arresting, you should see the real one. We're installing it Monday, and the gala's Tuesday night. Big affair. Bess Myerson is coming with Ed Koch."

"I have to wear a suit," grumbled Bobby.

"It's coming on St. Patrick's Day?" said Louise in surprise.

Tori was surprised too. The St. Patrick's Day Parade drew hundreds of thousands of marchers plus millions of spectators, confounding traffic—and everything else—for blocks around. The caterwaul of bagpipes pulsed in the air, hairy legs in kilts pounded the pavement, step dancers with shamrocks embroidered on their blouses pranced down Fifth Avenue, and beer flowed like the Hudson River. On St. Patrick's Day, New York was more Irish than Ireland.

"Security's idea," said Victor. "They figure no one could pull off a heist in that crowd."

"True," said Bobby. "Someone would throw up on them before they got three feet."

"Bobby, dear. Not at the table."

"I bet it's amazing," Tori said. "The real one, I mean."

"I don't think I've ever seen anything so beautiful." Victor's eyes drifted to the fist-sized bauble that was scattering bands of color across the tablecloth.

Tori stared at Victor staring at the diamond until Bobby jumped up and grabbed his mother's plates. "C'mon, Tori, let's wash up," he said, backing into the kitchen with his arms laden.

Louise gave a delighted chuckle. "Tori, you are a *wonderful* influence on our son. Feel free to visit any time."

Bobby turned on the water and leaned close to Tori, speaking in a low voice. "What was *that* all about?"

"Sorry, sorry." Tori yanked on a pair of rubber gloves from the edge of the sink. "For a second, I thought—I thought—"

"Thought what?"

I thought he was brazen enough to just stroll out of the museum with that diamond and I was in the presence of a criminal genius and any second the cops would kick in the door. But hold up, that's not what the article said. It said....

What had it said?

"Wait a sec," she said abruptly. "What's today's date?"

"March fourteenth."

"For me, it's March sixteenth."

"So?"

"So why would I go back forty years and two days?"

"Why would you go back at all?"

"It's so specific."

"That's your sticking point? Two more days?"

"It doesn't make sense."

"None of this makes sense."

"Yeah, but exactly forty years is kind of symmetrical. Why two extra days?"

"Leap days?"

"Let me think." She squeezed her eyes shut, wishing she could remember the details of the Wikipedia article, wishing she could pull it up on her phone.

"I notice while you're thinking, I'm doing the dishes," muttered Bobby.

Tori's eyes flew open. "It's the diamond."

Chapter 7

Dishing over the Dishes

"No kidding." Bobby was impressed. "How much do they steal?"

"Lots."

"And get away with it?"

"No." She swallowed, but the ball of acid at the back of her throat would not budge.

He looked at her with concern. "Hey, you all right? You look sick."

She wiped her forehead with the back of her wrist. A stream of bubbles dripped from her rubber-gloved fingers into the sink. "Guess I'm not used to time travel."

"Want to sit down?"

"I want to figure out what we're doing."

"What we're doing about *what*?"

"Stopping the robbery."

Bobby folded his arms. "Whadda ya mean 'we,' Kemo Sabe?"

She blinked at him. "You said you'd help me."

"I meant help you figure out why you're here."

"Well, now I need help with the next part."

"I didn't sign up for this."

"Neither did I!" She groaned, thinking of Victor bringing flowers to Louise and talking with Bobby about the Mets' new general manager. "But it's why I'm here."

"Are you sure?"

"Yes!" she almost shouted, then lowered her voice again. "Look. I've been trying to think of something that makes sense—"

"I think we've already established that none of this makes any—"

She waved her hand, and a clump of greasy suds splatted onto the counter. "You know how it feels when you're trying to remember something, then you do and it just—lands right?"

"But you're not remembering. You're guessing."

"I'm not." She felt more certain with every passing second. "I need to stop them. Somehow. And I don't know how, because I've never been to New York in 1980!"

Bobby pulled a dish from the sink and set it in the rack. Droplets pattered onto the rubber mat, pooling in grooves that led to the sink. "There's like a million and a half robberies in New York every year. What's so special about this one?"

Tori swallowed. "Look—you were asking me about your folks."

"Yeah?" Bobby perked up.

"The exhibit they steal is one your dad's in charge of."

"That would be all of them."

"The one with the Desert Sun."

Bobby reached for the bottle of Dawn. "So that's why you recognized it."

Tori's knees quivered. Words swirled inside her head like plastic bags on a windy sidewalk. *Convicted thief Victor Gold…investigators were quick to… notorious… sentenced…years in prison*.... "Look," she said finally, "I don't think I should tell you anything about your future, you know? It seems like a Monkey's Paw-Oedipus Rex kind of thing. But—I think if I stop that heist, I'll get home." She held up her hand as he started to speak. "I know, I know. But I sure can't think of anything else. And if I don't do it, maybe I'll be trapped here forever. Or never born. I don't know."

Bobby's eyebrows furrowed. He rubbed his ear. "Wow."

"Go on," said Tori. She felt defensive, exhausted. "Tell me I'm nuts."

He shook his head. "I don't think you're nuts."

"You don't?"

"I think you've figured out your mission." He rinsed his dish towel and wrung it out before spreading it on the edge of the sink to dry. "So, Future Girl. Ever foiled a heist before?"

Tori felt her shoulders relax. She hadn't realized she'd been clenching them. "You're gonna help me?"

"I guess." Bobby rubbed his ear again. "Soon as we figure out how."

"Should we tell your dad? It's his rock."

Bobby considered this, then shook his head. "He'd never believe us. He's, you know, a color-inside-the-lines guy."

"Know any experts on time travel or museum heists?" sighed Tori.

Bobby snapped his fingers. "Uncle Jacob."

"Uncle...." *Dr. Gold's brother Jacob, initially a suspect, was cleared of any role in the crime....* "He knows about heists?"

Bobby laughed. "Of course not. But he's a push-the-envelope guy. He makes things happen."

"What kind of things?"

"Well, like, ever heard of Tom Seaver?"

"Tom Terrific?"

"So you *do* know him."

"He's your fave." Still.

"The whole team started playing better when he joined," said Bobby.

"So I hear."

"He threw a no-hitter two years ago."

"Uh-huh."

"No way would they have won the '69 World Series without him."

"You were four," said Tori impatiently. "What does this have to do with the robbery?"

"This is about my uncle," said Bobby. "Three years ago, he takes me to Shea Stadium to see Seaver pitch against the Braves—Mets won, by the way—and afterwards he goes, 'I got a surprise for you.' So we go down to the dugout, and Tom Seaver is *waiting* there for me—with an autographed ball!" Bobby looked nearly aswoon from the memory. "I mean, it wasn't my birthday or anything. He just knew how much it meant to me, so he made it happen."

"And he can apply this can-do attitude to foiling a museum robbery?"

"He'll have some ideas, anyway." He picked up the kitchen phone and dialed. "He always does."

As Bobby told his parents they were going out and scrounged for an extra coat for her, Tori tried to force a feeling of optimism. They were going to see Uncle Jacob. Uncle Jacob was a smart guy, Bobby assured her. Uncle Jacob would fix everything.

But a nervous wiggle jumped in her stomach as they headed out the door. She had heard the Seaver story before, many times. But her father had never told her that his uncle was behind it.

In fact, he had never told her he had an uncle.

Chapter 8

The Great Uncle

"Hope you don't mind I started without you." Jacob spoke around his cheeseburger as Tori and Bobby slid into his booth at the Western-themed diner he had chosen for their rendezvous. "Late meeting. I'm starving, kid. What's your friend want? My treat."

Tori tried not to stare at her great-uncle, a previously unknown twig on her family tree. He looked like Victor, but with quick, brown eyes and a foxy smile. Plus, his sideburns were longer. He wore dark slacks and a matching jacket over a white dress shirt that was partly unbuttoned so that some of his chest hair showed.

"Tori, you want a milkshake?" said Bobby.

"I don't need anything," she said.

"Hey, no problem, little lady." Jacob twisted around to signal a waitress. "Two milkshakes. Chocolate good? Yeah, chocolate. Thanks, hon." He turned back to Bobby and handed him a laminated menu featuring a Southwest burger (topped with guacamole) and an English burger (on an English muffin instead of a bun). "Better than that kosher crap your mom makes you eat, huh, kid?"

"Thanks for meeting us, Uncle Jacob."

"Always available for my favorite nephew. So what's the big emergency, Mysterio?"

"I'm your only nephew."

"Don't try to change the subject, kid. You were very cagey on the phone. So what do you need from your Uncle Jacob?"

Bobby put down the menu and nudged Tori. "You tell him."

She took a deep breath. "Mr. Gold—"

"Call me Jacob, kid. Everybody does. And hey, before we go any further, what's your name?"

"Tori."

"Tori what?"

"Gold."

"No kiddin'." Jacob chuckled as he lifted his cheeseburger. "Wonder if we're related."

"Super-common name," said Tori.

"Probably from Ellis Island," said Bobby at the same time.

Jacob regarded them over his burger. "Definitely not related," he said. "Got it."

"I know Bobby from Camp Ramah."

"Lots of Golds there, no doubt," said Jacob.

"Tori has something really important to tell you," said Bobby. "Go on, Tori."

She took another deep breath, and poured out a cataract of words. "There's going to be a robbery at the Museum of Natural History this weekend, and the target is the jewels that Bobby's dad is in charge of, so if they disappear it's going to look like he's involved."

Jacob's smile vanished. He put down his cheeseburger and looked from Tori to Bobby and back again. Around them, forks chinkled and waitresses took orders while diners asked about the Friday special. "Go on."

His warm, brown eyes were steady on hers, and Tori realized with a jolt that he was taking her seriously. Despite Bobby's ringing endorsement of his uncle, she had been prepared for a lot of spadework involving phrases such as, "Sure, it *sounds* crazy," and "No, I don't do drugs." But against all expectations, Jacob trusted her. No wonder his nephew—his only nephew—valued his judgment. So she told him everything she had told Bobby, minus the bits she figured he would never swallow. When she was done, Jacob leaned back in his seat. "Okay, Tori Not-Related-Gold. I have some questions."

"Shoot."

"First off, how do you know about all this?"

"I told you. I saw the plans." So to speak.

"Where?"

Online. "I can't say."

"And you can't show me."

"No." That part was definitely true.

"Fair enough, kid. We all have secrets." He took a sip of water, and the ice cubes rattled as he set his glass down. "Next question. Are you in danger?"

"I—I don't know."

"Is my nephew in danger?"

"I don't think so."

"I can take care of myself," said Bobby.

"Same," said Tori, hoping it was true.

"Hey, no offense." Jacob held up his hands in an attitude of surrender, then leaned across the table at Tori. "But here's the thing, and I'm going to be very honest with you. I run with a sketchy crowd—I mean, I used to. Mended my ways, one hundred percent. But I still know people, and I gotta tell you, if this was on the radar it's likely I would have heard about it before now."

"Maybe it's under the radar," said Tori.

"Plus, you're hearing about it now," said Bobby.

"That I am," said Jacob. He rubbed his thumb on his glass of water. A droplet tumbled from the rim and meandered down the side on a silver trail. "Last question. Let's say you're right. What do you want me to do about it?"

Tori glanced at Bobby. They had worried over that very issue on the way over. And really, there was only one answer.

"Call my dad," said Bobby. "He'd never believe us, but if it comes from you—"

"Hold up, hold up." Jacob leaned back again. "I do not think that is such a first-prize idea, kid."

"Why not?" said Bobby.

"Well, for starters, your mom is not a founding member of the Jacob Gold fan club, if you know what I mean."

"Just ask for my dad if she picks up."

"Or call him directly," said Tori.

"What? No, this can't wait till Monday," said Bobby impatiently. "And anyway, his office is closed for St. Patrick's Day."

"No, I mean just call him on his phone," said Tori.

Jacob cocked his head at her. "How many phone lines does your family have, kid?"

Tori's mind flashed to the rotary phone in the apartment. *Oops.* "We—I mean—"

"Never mind," said Bobby. "Just call. My mom will put him on."

"It's after sundown," said Jacob. "I know what your mom's like."

Bobby slid out of the booth. "We'll coach you. Come on."

The phone booth was at the back of the diner, near bathroom doors marked "John Waynes" and "Calamity Janes." Bobby and Tori stood in the doorway, Tori watching in fascination as Jacob clinked a dime into the slot and punched the square buttons. He didn't even have to dial 212. But when the phone rang at the other end, she could barely hear it.

"Tell him to put it on speaker," she whispered to Bobby.

"What?"

Jacob stuck his finger in his ear and frowned at her. "Hey, Louise, it's Jacob. Can you put Vic on?"

"I said, if he puts it on speaker—"

"What speaker?"

"The phone's! What else?"

"What are you *talking*—"

Jacob twitched the mouthpiece against his chest, scowling. "You guys mind? Trying to—hey, Victor!" He flipped the phone up to his ear and broke into a grin as though his brother could see him. "Yeah, Shabbat sha-frickin'-lom. You got a minute?"

Whenever he wasn't speaking, Jacob covered the mouthpiece with his hand and tilted the listening end so Tori and Bobby could sort of hear. They hissed reminders and details to him, and he relayed them casually, as though he had just thought of them, adding a few of his own as he went along. "Yeah, over the weekend, that's right.... Well, it sounds serious to me.... When's the rock coming in?.... I dunno, Vic. Maybe hire a couple extra guards?" Bobby beamed at her and flashed a thumbs-up, and she beamed back. This man was a master. Typical of her dad never to have even mentioned his name. Good thing she had Bobby for that.

Finally, Jacob hung up and turned to them. "There you go, kid. Extra security for the world's biggest diamond, faster than shit through a goose."

Bobby hugged him, his elbows bumping the sides of the cramped booth. "Thanks, Uncle Jacob. You're the best."

"No worries, kid. You know I got your back. Now get the hell out of here so I can finish my burger in peace, okay?"

Chapter 9

Who Can You Trust?

Victor put down the phone as Louise walked in, arms full of bed linens and pillows.

"I'm expecting one more call. Sorry." Victor stood up. "Need a hand?"

"Thanks." Louise set the sheets and pillows down on the table. "I hope she'll be comfortable."

"You say that any time anyone sleeps in here." He bent to remove the sofa cushions, stacking them against the wall. "And so far, no complaints."

"That we know of."

"I'll check our AAA rating on Monday."

Louise's smile softened, and she handed him her last cushion. "Does she seem a little odd to you?"

Victor bent to unfold the couch. "You mean besides the purple hair?"

"She says she's from Boston, but doesn't have a Boston accent."

"You're from New York, and you don't have a New York accent."

"I went to Bryn Mawr."

"Maybe her mother went to Bryn Mawr too." Victor pulled the couch open, kicking down the folding legs. "Maybe you were classmates."

"She's here without a suitcase or a jacket," persisted Louise.

"I thought you said the airline lost her luggage."

"And her jacket?"

Victor paused while reaching for the pillow. "That does seem odd, now that you mention it."

"Also, she's been here before."

"To New York?"

"To this apartment."

"Really?"

"She knows where we keep things. Silverware, kitchen utensils." Louise took a sheet and unfurled it over the bed.

Victor knelt, knitting his brows as he secured the sheet with a hospital corner. "So what are you saying?"

She knelt at the opposite bed corner and lifted her eyes to his. "Have you noticed how eager to please she is?"

"You mean polite?"

"I mean scared."

"Scared of what?"

"How many times did she jump like a rabbit at dinner?" Louise stood up, tugging the sheet smooth. "And Bobby's always leaping in to cover for her."

"Are you saying he's doing something wrong?"

"I think he's protecting her from something."

"Like what?"

"Who knows? He's always taking in some wounded soul. Half his friends are from broken homes."

"Well, that's about the average," said Victor. "And thank you kindly, Governor Reagan. You'd think he'd be tired of running for president by now."

"Vic, are you listening to me?"

"Mr. Family Values and his no-fault divorce law," he fumed. "Funny how the Moral Majority glides right over that."

"Can we not talk about politics, please?"

"Sorry, love. Go on."

Louise took a breath. "I think she's a runaway."

Victor's eyes widened over the pillow he was shoving into its case. "You do?"

"I heard her tell Bobby she can't go home."

"Good Lord."

"It all fits, doesn't it? Showing up here like that, with a pretty thin story and not needing to call anyone—she said she did, but I never saw it."

Victor set the pillow down. "She said Newton, right? Bet we can find her folks pretty quickly."

Louise shook her head as she settled the pillow at the head of the bed. "Kids don't run away for no reason."

"Look, if Bobby went missing, we'd—"

"Bobby's the one she turned to for help," said Louise.

Victor rubbed his chin. "So?"

"So maybe she needs a safe harbor for a few days."

"Look, Louise, that sounds very noble, but we're talking about a kid we don't even—"

The phone rang. Victor grabbed it. "Hello?"

"Hey, it's Todd."

"Tell you more later," Louise whispered, putting down the last pillow. She left the room as he nodded his thanks to her.

"Thanks for getting back to me so fast," said Victor into the phone. "We have a problem."

"What?"

"There's going to be an attempt on the Desert Sun exhibit."

"*What?*"

"You heard me."

"When?"

"This weekend."

"You sure?" Todd's voice was gravelly. Victor wondered if he were taking notes in his tight, blocky script.

"Sure as I can be."

In the pause that followed, Victor imagined he could hear the head of museum security putting down his pen and leaning back in his chair. "That doesn't match anything we've heard," said Todd finally.

"I just heard it myself."

"From who?"

"A reliable source."

"Again, Vic, who?"

"I can't say."

"Is it the FBI?"

"No."

"The guys at the Twentieth Precinct?"

"No."

"The NYPD's art theft squad?"

"Todd—"

"Because those are *my* sources, and no one's reported anything."

"I told you, I just found out about it myself." Victor's voice rose.

"I heard you. And a few more details would be nice."

"This is a reliable source."

"Does the reliable source have a name?"

"Not at the moment, no."

"But you're asking me to trust it."

Victor sighed. "I'm asking you to trust *me*."

"Why are you being so cagey?"

"I gave my word to the Van der Bleeks that their gems would be safe. I gave my word."

"My name's on this too."

"We need to beef up security."

"We have all the latest security features."

"We need more."

Todd's voice was still pleasant, but it had a thin edge to it. "Remind me, Vic. Which one of us is Chief Security Officer?"

"All I'm asking is some additional safeguards for the exhibit."

"I've got a budget to think about."

"And I've got priceless gemstones to think about."

Todd clucked his tongue. "What were the details of this threat?"

"All I can say is, it was credible."

"Look, Victor, all this cloak-and-dagger stuff is fun, but it doesn't tell me where to station guards."

"I was hoping you could hire one or two more," said Victor.

"Like, for the pm shift?"

"Perfect. My source tells me the plan is for one of the nights."

"Give me some time to shuffle the budget," said Todd. "Should be able to do it, though."

"Thanks, Todd."

"Totally how I wanted to spend my Friday night."

Victor grimaced. "I'm really sorry."

"Nah, just messing with you. Gets me out of some of the Girl Scout crap my daughter's doing."

"Well—I really appreciate it."

"Hey, we're a team. You and me. Not me and the Girl Scouts." He chuckled, and after a heartbeat, Victor joined him. "And look, likely you're worrying over nothing."

"You think so?"

"There's a ton of publicity around the exhibit. Somebody's bound to talk about it. But if no one from the FBI or the NYPD has heard anything—well, one random wingnut probably doesn't rise to the level of serious threat, you know?"

"I hope you're right," said Victor. "But extra guards sound pretty good to me."

"Me, too."

"I'll be in tomorrow to look around."

"Seriously?"

"Yes. And if you can come too, I'd appreciate it."

"Yeah, sure," said Todd after a pause.

"Thanks."

"No sweat," he said wearily. "It's why they pay me the big bucks."

He hung up. Victor spun his chair around, replaced the handset, and saw Louise in the doorway.

"You heard a rumor." Her voice was cold.

"That's right."

"From Jacob?"

Victor exhaled. "Yes."

"Jacob said someone's planning to steal the Desert Sun."

"Yes."

"And where did he hear this?" She rubbed her forehead. "From the goons he gambles with? Or one of his current harem?"

"I don't know."

"He hasn't had a real job since the day I met him," she grumbled. "Just one shady deal after another. I bet that's why he knows about this—if he's even right about it."

"Oh, come, now," said Victor. "I think you're being a bit harsh."

Louise snorted. "Name me once, just *once* that man has ever done anything for you that didn't benefit him more."

"He's done more for me than you know."

"When you were boys," she said. "What has he done in the past, oh, twenty years or so?"

"Tonight he told me that a diamond whose safety is in my hands might be in danger," snapped Victor. "And if he did hear it from his usual crowd, then he took a hell of a chance by talking to me about it."

Louise folded her arms and stared stonily at him. Victor's expression softened. "Go easy on him," he said gently. "He wasn't lucky enough to find a Louise."

She shook her head. "You'd have been fine without me."

"I'm not so sure of that."

"And yet you're sure he's got your back."

"Yes. And I have his." Victor stood and clicked off the lamp on his desk.

Chapter 10

Time Travel Tourist

Bobby grabbed Tori's elbow and steered her around the third signpost she had almost walked into. "Watch out."

"Sorry." She pulled her arm free and gazed about her. Crowds thronged the sidewalks, spattered with neon colors from the shop windows' lights.

"You're rubbernecking like a tourist from East Bucksnort."

"I've lived here my whole life!"

"Then start acting like it. You want to get mugged?"

"Well, everything's different now."

"Different how?"

"I mean, like, the streets are the same, so my feet know where to go," said Tori. "But the—I guess, the atmosphere. It's, um, changed."

"How so?"

Tori hunched her shoulders in the jacket Bobby had lent her, and stepped over a pile in the middle of the sidewalk. "Well, like that."

"The dog crap?"

"Yeah. How come no one's cleaning it up?"

"It's a shitty job."

"And the walk signals." She waved at the corner. "Ours don't say 'DONT WALK' with the stupid missing apostrophe—"

"My English teacher hates that."

"Now there's a red hand for Don't Walk and a walking guy for Walk."

"Progress," said Bobby with a sigh.

"You seem disappointed."

"I always thought the future would be more futuristic."

"Anyway, that's different." As were the cigarette filters rolling along the concrete. People walked and smoked at the same time, gesturing with their cigarettes or leaving them clinging to their lips and talking around them. Tori saw one man with a Ned Flanders-style mustache and newsboy cap light a fresh cigarette with his old one before flicking the butt aside, squishing it with a twist of his shoe almost like a dance step—what, so the sidewalk wouldn't catch fire? Empty cigarette packs and crumpled food wrappers clung to the undersides of the curbs, exuding a miasma of smoke, poop, and rotting food. A storefront Tori knew as a dog groomer's was topped with a sign reading, "Super Sex-O-Rama! Books—Novelties—Video Cassettes! Now with Air Conditioning." Every wall was a pastiche of posters that either obscured graffiti or provided a new canvas for it. The cars were clunkier than the ones she was used to, rackety and more angular; some even backfired, making a noise like a shot. And where were the bikes and scooters, the food trucks, the SUVs, the food carts so expansive they needed several umbrellas to shelter them?

"I want to go home," she said.

"We're working on it."

"How? By telling Uncle Jacob about the heist? Because in case you didn't notice, I'm still here."

"Look, don't worry," said Bobby. "In science fiction stories, time travelers almost always get back home."

"*Almost?*"

"Almost."

"Great." Tori angled her body to weave past a stack of cardboard boxes full of oranges in front of a store whose sign read, "Oasis Nuts and Fruits Now Open Sundays." Wooden stands full of pears and melons took up half the sidewalk before giving way to a jumble of splintered fruit crates shoved up against the wall.

"There's a lot of science in science fiction," said Bobby.

"Like what?"

"Like time travel, Future Girl. Einstein says it's possible."

Tori grabbed his arm. "Let's call him. Maybe he could figure out how to get me home. I'm an actual time traveler. I bet he'd love that!"

Bobby hesitated, then awkwardly patted Tori's hand. "Einstein died in 1955."

Tori's cheeks flushed. She dropped his sleeve and kept walking. "I knew that."

"Did you?"

"No." Tori wanted to stomp instead of walk. She always felt so dumb around him. And he never cared. Why was he always so—

"Don't feel bad." Bobby kept abreast of her as they threaded their way along the sidewalk. "I mean, he wasn't even a real person."

"What?"

"Einstein. He never existed."

Tori stopped walking so abruptly Bobby nearly shot past her. "I'm not stupid," she snapped. "He's in the history books."

"Nope." Bobby shook his head, his face a painting of innocence. "Turns out he was only a theoretical physicist."

Tori snorted into the collar of the jacket Bobby had given her.

"Made you laugh," he said quietly.

She lifted her head. "Yeah. You did."

"Full disclosure: Einstein was real. And he said time travel is possible."

"Well, he was right about that."

"He was a regular Einstein."

"Did he say how to undo it?"

"Not that I know of."

"I'll—" She reached for her phone to look up "Einstein and Time Travel" before remembering her battery was dead. "Never mind."

"One thing that's worrying me, though."

"Only one?"

"This isn't the past."

"It is for me."

"Sure. But it's the present for everyone else." Bobby gazed at the New York City nightscape as a siren wailed in the distance.

"So what?"

"Well—for us, your time isn't real. It hasn't happened, so it doesn't exist." He looked at her, eyes anxious. "How can you go somewhere that isn't there yet?"

Tori gasped, stomach churning. "So you're saying—"

"Don't panic," Bobby cut her off. "If you got here, you can go back. Stands to reason."

"Right." The deep breath she tried to take stuck in her throat. She started walking again, almost running, telling herself that her pounding heart rate was due to her rapid stride, not the panic boiling up inside her like vapor from a sidewalk steam vent.

Bobby matched his pace to hers. "We need to find a way to go forward in time."

"I'm doing that right now," said Tori. "Just not quick enough."

"Try running really fast," Bobby panted. "The closer you can get—to the speed of light—the better."

"I don't have a spaceship." She stopped at a corner, breathing hard, and jabbed the walk signal. Bobby's New York had fewer vehicles than hers, but traffic flow was somehow worse. "And excuse me for not packing my dilithium crystals!"

Bobby's eyes lit with joy. "You know about dilithium crystals?"

Tori shoved her chilly fingers into the pockets of Bobby's old jacket, feeling a mishmash of loose change, paper clips, and the corner of what she guessed was a bus pass. "You showed me."

"I did?"

She turned to him, keeping half an eye on the signal. "When I was ten, I got really sick and I was out of school for a week. Mom—my mom had a thing at work, so you stayed home with me and we watched *Star Trek*. All of it."

Bobby looked like a saint having an ecstatic vision. "*Star Trek* is still on TV?"

"On—oh, I don't know." Tori felt oddly embarrassed for him. "We own it."

The light changed, and they crossed the street. "How?" said Bobby.

"On disc."

"LaserDisc?"

"Sort of. Or you can stream it."

"I don't know what that means."

"Anyway, it's pretty common."

They stepped onto the opposite curb and continued down the street. "So we watched the whole thing?" said Bobby.

"All three seasons."

He shook his head, a smile lifting his cheeks. "I must be an *amazing* father."

"Absolutely." Tori's own smile felt tight.

He turned and waved at a doorway. The sign over the door read "Vinyl Countdown." The Os in "Countdown" were pictures of records, and the side portions of the Ns were arrows pointing to stairs that descended below the sidewalk. "Hey, let's go in here. There's an album I want."

Chapter 11

Still Rock and Roll

～◆～

The clerk, a young Black man with dark, shiny curls, sat behind a cash register by the door. He nodded as they came in, then returned to reading a copy of *The National Enquirer* whose headline blared, "FDA Warns over Half of US Hookers Are Space Aliens!" Tori nodded back and rubbed her hands, grateful to be out of the March night's sting. "Cool," she said, gazing at the bright, crowded room. A rack of albums ran down the center, and bins of records lined the walls. Cassettes and LPs faced cover-out on the shelves, and a mosaic of multichromatic albums undulated just below the ceiling. From speakers high in the corners, a honeyed contralto crooned that we can never know about the days to come.

Bobby beelined to a section labeled "Spoken Word." Some of the albums were new, still in their shiny plastic wrap; others were worn, and gave puffs of musty air as he flipped through them. "My friends and I come here a lot. Like, meet up if we're going to a movie or something. Much better than Crazy Eddie."

"What's that?" The name conjured up images of a guy with skittish eyes selling bootlegs on a folding table in Washington Square Park.

"Local chain. Great commercials, but their selection is pretty mainstream."

The clerk spoke without looking up. "That's 'cause their buyer sucks."

Tori leaned on the rack next to Bobby. "This is more vinyl than I've ever seen in one place," she marveled.

"Yeah? Is it all cassette," he glanced at the clerk, and shifted his voice slightly, "where you're from?"

"Oh, God, no."

"Then how do you listen to albums?"

"I don't."

Bobby stopped, one finger marking his place in the rack. "But there's still *music*, right?"

"Oh, sure. And albums too, but you don't have to buy the whole thing."

"You don't?"

"You just get the part you want."

"How?" He picked up a record whose cover showed a white man, lips pursed, adorned with balloon animals, Groucho Marx glasses with a false nose, and what Tori could only presume was a fake arrow through his head. Diminutive capitals spelled out the title: *LET'S GET SMALL*. Bobby waved one hand over it and made an extracting motion with his fingers. "Wooo*oooo*! Nope, not working."

She giggled. "Not like that."

Bobby replaced the record and continued flipping through the stack. "Seems like you wouldn't get the whole experience if you only pick your favorite tracks."

With a flash of aha, Tori realized why songs on Apple Music and iTunes were called "tracks." Funny how she'd never wondered about it before. "I don't see what difference it makes," she said. "You can always shuffle the music anyway."

"Shuffle?" Bobby looked up. "Like, play the tracks in a different order? No, you can't."

Tori stared around the cavern of albums, silent music yet to be played. "You mean you listen to the songs in the same order every time?"

"Yes."

"No."

Bobby tilted his head. "C'mere." She followed him to a section marked "Today's Best Rock," where, after a quick search, he handed her a beige album adorned with a black-and-white photo of a man and a woman posed about a footstool. "Turn it over. Don't show me."

The top third of the back was taken up with fanciful script declaring *Rumours Fleetwood Mac*, below which was a list of the songs and their running times. "And?"

"'Second Hand News,'" said Bobby. "'Dreams,' 'Never Going Back Again.'"

He was listing the tracks, in order. "Okay. You can stop."

"'Don't Stop,'" said Bobby. "'Go Your Own Way'—"

"I'm trying to!"

"Don't interrupt," he said. "Uh—'Go Your Own Way,' 'Songbird,' 'The Chain,' 'You Make Loving Fun,' 'I Don't Want to Know'—"

"'Oh Daddy,'" giggled Tori.

"'Oh Daddy,'" repeated Bobby. "'Gold Dust Woman.'"

She slid the album back. "So what you're saying is, 1980 music listening is a series of endless, rote repetitions."

"Better believe it," he said. "What's yours?"

"Digital, with streaming services. And you can access your music anywhere."

Bobby shook his head as they headed back to the Spoken Word section. "Sometimes when you talk, I understand every word but none of the sentences."

"Same," said Tori. "What are you looking for, anyway?"

"*The Restaurant at the End of the Universe*," he said. "They haven't released it here yet."

"Then why are you looking for it?"

"It's out in England. Nichelle heard it when she was there over vacation. Used copy might turn up."

"Try the import section," called the clerk.

While Bobby browsed, Tori meandered over to the Qs in the rock section. *A Day at the Races. Live Killers.* A single of "Crazy Little Thing Called Love." She picked up the little record. Damn, it had only been out for a few months! The classics of her day were the big hits of today. So strange. Near the beginning of the alphabet, she found *A Hard Day's Night. The White Album. Yellow Submarine.* Well, at least those were old for both of them.

Bobby was at her shoulder, eyes alight with hope. "Hey. Do the Beatles ever get back together?"

Tori flinched inwardly. When did that thing with John Lennon happen? "I told you, I can't tell you."

Bobby sighed. "I guess they're too old for a reunion by your time anyway. I mean, they're almost forty now."

"For my generation, all rockers are old."

Bobby clutched the rack. "Seriously?"

"Seriously. A lot older than forty."

Bobby released the rack. "So tell me more about music. Or some pop culture thing. That should be okay, right?"

Tori chewed her lip. "I guess."

"Hit me." He looked as eager as a puppy.

What would be safe? Tori's eyes drifted to a bin whose hand-lettered label read, "NEW RELEASES." The top album showed a guy winding up to hurl a rock through a soaring wall of windows.

Whoa. Early Father's Day present! She handed it to him. "Here."

"Billy Joel?"

"You're gonna love it." She remembered him playing it when she was little, and she had to admit the music was solid.

"'You May Be Right,'" he said, glancing at the back of the cover.

"Duh. The time traveler knows stuff."

Bobby chuckled. "That's the name of the first song."

"Ah—but maybe not all the stuff."

The clerk turned the page of his tabloid. "Forget the science fiction and listen to the lady, bud," he said. "She's got taste."

A few minutes later, they walked back into the night with Bobby carrying his new record in a bag. "So now what?" said Tori.

Bobby looked at his watch. "We better get back. I'll call Nichelle in the morning."

"Because she's into science fiction?"

"Because she's my smartest friend."

"Like Uncle Jacob?"

"Different kind of smart," said Bobby. "But she will have ideas. Guaranteed."

The bag bumped Tori's leg, prompting a monstrous thought. At her urging, Bobby had purchased an album she knew from home—which meant that as of right now, her actions in 1980 were likely affecting 2020.

Stealing Time

Had she just made her era-of-origin happen, warts and all? Or had she just created a time convulsion, and would her story end with her crying alone in the dark—if she even existed?

She jammed her cold hands into the pockets of her jeans. One brushed her phone; the other found the rubber gloves Bob had given her to keep her safe. They were oddly comforting, these relics of the future, and she held onto them the rest of the walk home.

Chapter 12

Securing Security

~ ◆ ~

Todd Dixon sat at his tidy desk and smiled at the candidates. Somehow, he had two applicants this morning for a job that hadn't existed the day before. Talk about luck! Still, it was past nine, and his next meeting started at eleven. Oh, God, that next meeting. He picked up the first application. "Your name's Mike?"

"Mike Maliah, that's right."

Maliah? Todd wondered what kind of a name that was. Mike's skin and close-cropped hair were dark, even under the fluorescent lights, and his eyes looked like Kato's on *The Green Hornet*. His cheekbones were high, his nose was small, and his jaw was square, giving his face a flat, rectangular look. More to the point, though, his résumé said ex-military, and so did the big shoulders and the upright way he carried himself. Todd glanced surreptitiously at the wall clock. Nine-fifteen. If he could wrap this up by 9:45, he'd be in good time to join Erin and Daphne and Daphne's Girl Scout Troop 523, whose numbers seemed to exceed the population of Burma.

"I see you've been in the service." Todd took a sip of coffee.

"Yes, sir. I was a SEAL."

"Impressive." He put his mug down. An identical mug at the top, right-hand corner of his blotter held pens and pencils and a staple remover. The stapler sat precisely midway between the mugs. Security operated out of two cramped offices carved out of the Department of Herpetology, and every iota of space counted. Todd's Out Box was well-kept, the papers lined up and nothing slopping over the edges. His In Box was empty. "And then you moved on to bouncing."

Mike nodded at the résumé. "You can call any of those former employers. They'll all vouch for me."

"Good to know. Now—"

"Hey," said the other candidate. "What's a girl got to do to get a word in edgewise around here?"

Todd glanced at her. If he got to the meeting late, his wife wouldn't let him hear the end of it. Daphne needed help with her St. Patrick's Day patch, and like a damn fool he'd said yes without asking what that entailed. "She can wait her turn, Miss," he looked down at her application, which was next to Mike's. "DeMarco?"

"Yeah, that's right," said the girl, in a tone that indicated that everyone knew that, or should. "Teresa DeMarco."

She was pretty, thought Todd. Petite, fine-boned, with a nose so aquiline as to be almost daunting. Might make a good docent. He turned back to Mike. "I'll be honest—something just came up, and we need a guy right away."

"Great," said Mike.

"Oh, that's rich," said Teresa.

Todd gave her his best Chief Security Officer look. "What's that supposed to mean?"

The look bounced harmlessly off her. "It means you're ready to hire him without even looking at my application, that's what." She folded her arms and glared.

Todd's irritation felt like spiders scuttling through his veins. Spiders who needed to be somewhere else in half an hour. He studied the girl's résumé. "Rhode Island School of Design?"

"Majored in illustration, but I also did art history plus coursework in design and spatial dynamics." Out of the corner of her eye, she flashed a smug look at Mike.

"This doesn't say you finished."

"Money ran out my senior year."

"And now you're a…cartoonist?"

"Caricature artist. You know, for tourists on the boardwalk."

Funny, thought Todd, how both of them happened to be from Florida. "Miss, I'm not sure this is the skill set we're looking for."

Teresa's confident look melted into a lour. "So you're not looking for someone with a fine arts background and an extensive history of working with the public?"

"I can start whenever you need me," said Mike.

"So can I," said Teresa.

"Miss DeMarco," began Todd. "Museum guards need to be ready for all kinds of situations." He glanced again at the clock. Nine-twenty. Damn Saint Patrick, damn his day, and especially damn his Girl Scout patch. Why all the unholy enthusiasm around it? Wouldn't it have been enough to dance a jig while wearing green socks? Maybe bake some soda bread that he and Erin could pretend to enjoy? But no, Daphne had decided to organize a walkabout cookie sale for Monday, meaning that she and the other girls would weave up and down the sidewalk during Monday's parade, peddling cookies under the yowl of bagpipes while sidestepping pools of chartreuse vomit. Junior feminism for the win!

"So Mr. Dixon here might prefer someone with actual combat experience," pointed out Mike.

Teresa, who in Todd's estimation might have weighed ninety pounds soaking wet, blazed with the fury of a small woman scorned. "How do you know I wasn't in the Navy too?"

"Heh," said Mike. "Heheh."

"If you were, you forgot to put it on your application," said Todd, picking it up. It might have been his imagination, but when he and Daphne had announced the plan for the walkabout cookie sale at the last Girl Scout meeting, the grins on the moms' faces had looked a bit too shiny for his taste.

"*Sorry*," said Teresa. "Didn't know I was applying to Mensa."

"I bet they forgot too." Todd's eyes flicked back to the clock on the white wall above Teresa's head. That minute hand was flying along. He needed to get home, to a living room that was floor-to-ceiling cookie cartons and would soon be wall-to-wall Girl Scouts, their moms all smiling at him like Norman Bates reaching for his favorite kitchen knife.

Teresa snapped her fingers at him. "Hey. Am I keeping you from something?"

"Huh?" said Todd.

"You keep looking at that clock. I came in here to get a job, not to have somebody use his body language to tell me he's got someplace else to be."

"We should be able to wrap this up pretty quick," said Todd, smothering his annoyance. Damn, there must be about a squillion cookies to organize. And you couldn't just divide the tonnage by the number of girls in the troop. Nope, it had to be by order of "incentivized enthusiasm," as the troop leader called it, meaning that each kid decided how many cookies she planned to sell. Also, two-thirds of them needed to be Thin Mints.

"Thing is, I have a kid," said Mike, glancing at the backs of the photos on the desk.

Todd brightened. "Oh, yeah?"

Mike nodded. "Back in Florida. He's almost three. I call on weekends, but it's not the same, you know?"

"Cry me a river," muttered Teresa.

"Does he live down there?"

"With his mom," said Mike. "It's hard being away from the little guy, but there's more jobs here."

"A family man needs a paycheck," said Todd. His eyes flicked to his desk photo of Daphne smiling, gap-toothed, in her green uniform, her sash shingled over with patches. Todd had spent half the night before helping her make an alphabetized, color-coded graph showing who would get this many boxes, who would get that many, and who would get half again as many as the first girl, which would definitely streamline things, assuming, that is, that everyone showed up for the meeting. Which was starting in less than an hour and a half.

"And how," said Mike. "I got to do what I can for him."

"Well, that makes my decision a lot easier," said Todd.

"Waitaminute," said Teresa. "So you're going to give him this job just because he has a kid?"

"Why not?" said Todd.

"That's discrimination!"

Todd sighed and picked up his mug of rapidly cooling coffee. "Do you have any children, Miss DeMarco?"

"Not that I know of."

Well, that settled that. Tens of thousands of families visited the museum every year. During school vacations, the place was packed tighter than a subway car at rush hour. Unless you had kids, you couldn't truly appreciate that every family has its own little quirks, its own ways of doing things, like defying the laws of physics and compressing ten boxes of cookies into a backpack that should only hold six. That was for the girls. The moms (it was mostly moms) got more. Way more. Because they would have to follow their daughters the day of the parade, replenishing each Girl Scout's store of cookies from their own whenever the kids sold out. Outdoors, in March. During one of the biggest parades of the year. He put his mug down. "Then please tell me why you're better for this job than a father and a bouncer who used to be a SEAL."

"Does he know anything about art?"

"Miss," said Todd with a patience he did not feel, "I'm trying to choose the right candidate to work at one of the best museums in the world, and right now my choice is between a college dropout and a military man. So if there's anything that you can add to your list of qualifications that's not on your resumé, please tell me about it."

Teresa paused. "I...like uniforms," she said finally.

Mike snorted. "Didn't you get tired of them when you was in the Navy all those years?"

Teresa half-rose from her chair, every sinew tight. "Goddamn it. Are you calling me a liar?"

"We're done here." Todd tapped Teresa's papers together and handed them to her. "You can see yourself out. Mike, welcome to the American Museum of Natural History."

At 9:45 precisely, Todd exited by the back door as Teresa stomped down the front steps, application and résumé bunched in her fist.

"Hey," said Maeve. "How'd it go?"

Teresa glanced back at the building before tossing the paper wad into a trash can. "Mike got the job."

"Bitchin'," said Maeve as they turned and walked down the street. "I'll tell Snake."

"Chief Rent-a-Cop didn't like me," confided Teresa.

"He wasn't supposed to."

"He sure liked Mike." She glared at the sidewalk.

"Mike looks the part," pointed out Maeve. "Brick shithouse."

"And just as smart." Teresa hunched her shoulders against a thin wind that blew off the sidewalk. "I got most of an art degree, and he doesn't know which end of a paintbrush to hold."

"What's he doing now?"

"Uniform and orientation. He'll be back tonight." A thread of bitterness ran through her voice.

Maeve gave a half-chuckle. "You took a hit for the team, Terri. It takes a bright girl to play a dim bulb."

Chapter 13
What Now?

―◇―

Tori drifted awake to the ever-present street song of New York: dogs barking, sirens blaring, people cursing in different languages. She squeezed her eyes shut, hoping she was back home, but as she rolled over, a metal support bar jabbed her through the thin mattress. No, this was not her bed. Or her decade. She winced and sat up, pulled on her jeans, and checked the analog brass clock on the shelf: quarter past nine. The bathroom connected the study and her—Bobby's—bedroom, so she went in and knocked on his (her?) door. He was sitting on the bed, dressed, and reading the sports section of the *New York Times*. "Wasn't sure when you'd wake up, slugabed," he said.

"Yeah, well, I'm up now." Tori had slept poorly—maybe it was the mattress, maybe time travel was tiring—and it did not bring out the best in her. Plus, it was hard to be simultaneously home and not home. Even if the home she wanted to get back to wasn't a particularly happy place at the moment, and the moment wouldn't happen for another forty years.

Bobby appeared not to notice her crankiness. "Mom's cooking."

"Oh, she doesn't have to do anything special for me." With one of the cognitive dissonance moments that characterized her present existence, Tori was suddenly aware of being a guest in the apartment she had lived in her whole life.

"Nah, it's one of her Shabbat things," said Bobby. "Along with not smoking till sundown. Hey, what do people do for breakfast in 2020?"

"Eat it, usually."

"No, I mean, how do you do it? Pop a couple pills with a glass of Tang?"

"Only when we visit Willy Wonka," she giggled.

Bobby sighed and turned the page of his newspaper. "Another illusion goes belly-up."

"What's Tang?"

"Powdered orange juice." Bobby straightened the pages, folding them together for easier reading.

"Seriously?"

"It's pretty gross," he admitted. "NASA sent it to the moon with the astronauts."

"Maybe they should've left it there. Hey, do you have an extra toothbrush? We keep them over there." She waved at the pedestal sink in the bathroom behind her. "In the cabinet that's not under the sink yet."

"Cabinet under the sink, eh?" he mused. "That's a good idea."

"So's a toothbrush."

"I'll ask my mom." He put the paper down and left her alone.

Tori looked around the room. The biggest wall held a poster of Tom Seaver deep into a windup, face creased with determination. She squatted to look at the bookcase under the window. *The Lord of the Rings* and *The Hitch-Hiker's Guide to the Galaxy* leaned up against *Roots*, *All the President's Men*, a bunch of *Star Wars* novels, and some books by Alexander Key. The lowest shelf had titles that had clearly been there the longest: *From the Mixed-Up Files of Mrs. Basil E. Frankweiler*, some Dr. Seuss, *The Dark is Rising*, and a battered copy of *Mrs. Frisby and the Rats of NIMH*. On the middle shelf, a small, plastic Darth Vader, light saber raised, faced off against a small, plastic, and hopelessly blonde Luke Skywalker. Leia, Han, and a tiny R2-D2 offered moral support from the sidelines.

Bobby walked back in with the toothbrush. "She's making challah French toast. So good."

"Thanks," she said, taking the toothbrush. "Hey, those *Star Wars* figurines you have? Get a bunch, and leave them in the packaging."

"Why?"

"They'll be worth a lot later."

"Seriously?"

"Seriously. But only in the original packaging."

"The next movie's coming out this summer," protested Bobby, who clearly wanted to populate his middle shelf with as many thrilling tableaux as it would accommodate. "What if there's some cool new character?"

"Get two sets then. But keep one in the—"

"Packaging."

"Right."

"I got that the first two times you said it."

"It's the only way they're worth anything," said Tori icily.

"People in 2020 are weird," said Bobby. But he smiled as he spoke, and Tori felt herself smile back. She liked this kid. He had a way of finding the funny, of knowing when she started to feel bad then turning things around with a deft touch, even though he'd only known her a few hours. Whereas her father, no matter the situation, always managed to make everything worse.

What had happened to Bobby to make him so…not Bobby?

Breakfast was every bit as good as her future father had promised. Friday's leftover challah made beautiful French toast, creamy and eggy on the inside, redolent of cinnamon, nutmeg, and vanilla. Tori delighted Louise by having thirds.

Victor was in the study, having promised to join them shortly. While Louise was at the table, Tori and Bobby entertained her with tales of hijinks at Camp Ramah. Apparently very little about it had changed in forty years, so Tori was able to chime in convincingly with details about how cold the lake was, and how the girls in her cabin had freaked out when a bat had gotten in one night, except for one kid whose mom was a wildlife biologist and who had thus known what to do (open the door). As soon as Louise left to do the dishes, though, they switched topics.

"Who wins the election?" said Bobby. "I'd vote Anderson if I could."

"Who?"

"Well, that answers that."

"Oops."

"Technology, then. Flying cars?" he implored her. "Jetpacks?"

"Well, no. But there are electric cars now."

Bobby stopped, a dripping forkful of French toast halfway to his mouth. "You're kidding me."

Tori shone with satisfaction. "Nope. For real."

Bobby set down his fork and burst out laughing.

"What's so funny?" said Tori.

"Those have been around since the 1800s."

"What? No, they haven't."

"Yeah, they have. The *early* 1800s. I did a history report on it." Bobby picked up his fork again, shaking his head. "Man. So the big advance of 2020 is two hundred years old?"

Tori blushed furiously, reaching for her back pocket to look up "Electric Vehicles" on her phone, then remembering she couldn't. "Well, we also have the Internet."

"Which is what?" said Bobby with his mouth full.

What indeed? Tori thought hard. "It's like...a network," she said finally.

"What kind?"

"Say you want to look something up."

"Okay," said Bobby in a way that indicated this was not unpleasant to imagine.

"Instead of going to the library, you just open Safari or Chrome or whatever, type the thing you want into the search bar, and it comes up." She felt triumphant. "Anything. I looked up coyote pee on eBay once. And you can do it on your phone."

Bobby looked bored. "English, please."

"What?"

"I have no idea what you're talking about."

Tori took a final corner of French toast and chewed it while she thought. "Sorry," she said finally. "Lemmee start over again. Say you want to look something up."

"'Kay."

"Jellybeans, let's say."

"Okay."

"And chocolate."

"Ha. Ha."

"So you go to the library."

"That reminds me. I have to call Nichelle."

"Focus. You're going to the biggest library in the world, where all the information is. Everything."

"New York Public Library. Gotcha."

"So you go to the—what's that thing called with all the little cards in it?"

"The card catalog?"

"I guess. So you go over to it and tip it over, and spill all the cards onto the floor. You're knee-deep in cards. But it's okay, because you have a magic magnet, and it's been programmed—like a computer—with the word 'jellybean.' So you just wave it over the mess of cards on the floor, and any card with the word 'jellybean' on it jumps onto the magnet. So now you have all the information in the world about jellybeans on your magnet." She smiled at him triumphantly. "Any topic, any time."

"Really?" Bobby leaned back in his chair. "What if I wanted to look up stuff about 'Nights in White Satin'?"

"The song?"

"Yeah. I never got why the knights are wearing satin."

"It's not knights, it's nights."

"Well, that clears that right up."

"With an N. The time of day when it gets dark."

Bobby considered this, then shook his head. "Nah. I think it's about good-guy knights, and satin is a metaphor for how shiny their armor is."

Tori moaned. This was very high on the list of things she did not want to explain to a boy, especially not this one. And yet, do so she clearly must. "It's about a time when the singer's girlfriend gave him…satin sheets."

"Sheets?"

"I looked it up."

"With your magic wand?"

"With the Internet, yes."

Bobby's eyes widened. "It's about *sex?*"

Tori did a facepalm. "How did you ever get together with Mom?"

"Guess we'll find out." Bobby leaned forward. "So people look up stuff like that on their phones? How?"

For the hundredth time, Tori reached for her back pocket, then stopped again. "Damn!" Her fingers flew to her mouth, and she glanced at the kitchen door.

"The water's running," Bobby reassured her. "She can't hear us."

Tori nodded. "It's just that I wanted to show you. It's pretty cool if you've never seen one."

"The phone thingie?"

"It's also a camera and a writing tablet and a record store and a movie theater, all in one. It—eliminates boredom."

"Then why do they call it a phone?"

"Because it's a phone too."

"It's so weird that you just carry one around with you."

"Everyone does."

"Including me?"

"Definitely including you." Bob complained about screenagers, but in reality he was on his phone just as much as she was on hers. "You keep telling me it's more powerful than the computers you had in high school."

"So why do you even bother going to school, if you literally have all that in your back pocket?"

"That's what I keep saying!"

"I take it we've had this conversation before?"

"And you *still* make me go."

Bobby hung his head in mock shame. "I think I just lost a few cool points."

"The Internet's awesome. And I do love my phone."

"So is that how you traveled through time? With your phone? Does everyone have time travel?"

She tried not to laugh. "Definitely not."

"Then how did you get here?"

"I keep telling you, I don't know." Sighing, she looked down at her plate, where the butter and maple syrup swirled together in fragrant ribbons.

"Do you think it's because of that plague you were telling me about?" Bobby leaned forward, his shaggy hair falling into his eyes.

"I don't think pandemics cause time travel, no."

"Probably not." Bobby sat up and pushed his hair away. "Or there would have been a lot of it in 1918."

"They say ours is the same kind of virus as that one. Related, anyway."

"Damn. And no vaccine for it?"

"You can't have medicine for a disease that didn't exist a few months ago."

Bobby shook his head. "Your life sounds like a cross between *Star Wars* and *The Seventh Seal*."

"Be it ever so dystopian, there's no place like home."

"Funny."

"You think this is funny?" roared Victor. His office door slammed shut, muffling the rest of his angry words.

Tori and Bobby jerked in surprise. "Does he always shout like that?" she whispered.

Bobby shook his head. "Almost never."

"Wish we could hear what's going on."

"We can." Bobby stood, beckoning her to follow. With an anxious glance at the kitchen, Tori trailed him into the master bedroom. "Watch and learn, young grasshopper." Bobby unplugged the cord to the trim, white phone on the bedside table. "But be quiet." He lifted the handset, covered the mouthpiece, and carefully replaced the plug. Tori tilted her head toward his as Victor's voice filled her ears.

"You're holding out on me." Victor's voice had a harsh, almost guttural quality Tori had not heard before.

"I told ya everything I know." Jacob's voice.

"Now, why don't I believe that?"

"Relax, bro."

"Sure, relax. Do you know how long it took to put this exhibit together?"

"Bet you worked real hard on it."

"These people trust me!"

"You're a very trustworthy guy."

"If anything goes wrong, I'll get the blame."

"No way. You, the Boy Scout of the museum world?"

"Hilarious, Jacob."

"You're not the only one with problems."

"I'm the one with this problem, thanks to you."

"Thanks to me? That's rich. I'm the one who told you about the heist. Know what that could cost me?"

"Who are these people?" snarled Victor.

"Now, that I can't tell you."

"Are you in cahoots with them?"

Jacob gave a short, hard laugh. "'Cahoots'? Seriously, Vic?"

"You still think this is funny?"

"Hell, no. Cahoots is a very serious matter for me."

"Cut the—"

"It means that you're in league with someone."

"I know what it means."

"Do you? Because I always figured that if two people are working together—in cahoots, you might say—then no trustworthy person would ever, ever cut out at the last minute and leave the other person holding the bag. Is that what it means to you, Vic?"

Victor slammed the phone down. In the bedroom, Bobby dropped the handset back onto the bedside table as with one accord he and Tori bounded back to the dining room and plunked, wild-eyed, into their chairs.

The study door flew open. Victor stalked out, his jaw tight. "Louise?" he called. "I'm going to the museum."

Chapter 14

Nailing Down the Details

"Great work, man. Catch you on the flip side." Maeve hung up the phone and set it back on the end table. She grinned at Gloria, who was curled up at the far end of the deeply luxurious hotel sofa, flipping through the current issue of *Mademoiselle*. "Snake has a line on a car for Monday night. He's gonna drive."

"Beats taking the subway." Gloria turned the page.

"Wouldn't wanna get mugged with what we'll be carrying," agreed Maeve. She let out a whoop and punched the air. "Snake, you are the *man*."

"He doesn't like being called Snake."

Maeve bounced onto the other end of the sofa, sinking into its rust-colored cushions. Light washed through the tall windows, setting the metallic wallpaper aglow and illuminating the dark-gold carpet. "I was starting to wonder how we'd pay for this joint."

Gloria did not look up. "Think the front desk will take diamonds?"

"We'll fence a few before we check out."

"Monday's a holiday."

"So we wait till Tuesday."

"The same day the cops discover the heist? Brilliant."

Maeve sat up straight. "What's eating you?"

Gloria turned a page with exaggerated precision. "Nothing."

"Bull."

Gloria turned another page. Just as Maeve opened her lips to speak, she said, "They keep asking me questions."

"Who? The cops?" Maeve jerked her head in alarm, eyes wide.

Gloria rolled her eyes. "Yeah, they're onto us. Because they're psychic."

"Well, who, then?"

"The Village."

Maeve flumped back on the cushions with a sharp exhale. "You had me worried for a second."

A year before, Gloria had appeared before a judge who had explained that no matter how far behind one was on the rent, charging for one's intimate companionship was still a felony in the state of Florida, as was the act of lightening a gentleman's wallet in anticipation of his refusal to tip. The judge had given her a choice between jail and the Magdalene Village, an experimental home for reforming ladies of transactional virtue. The decision had not been difficult.

Gloria's hands balled into fists, scrunching her magazine. "Easy for you to say."

"Kid, after Sunday night you won't need group therapy and voc-tech and lights out at ten."

"I don't know if I still have a job, even."

"You won't need that, either."

"I like my job." The Magdalene Village had secured Gloria a position at the Coco Beach Fashion Bug, a florescent nook whose only color came from its racks of polyester clothing. To her astonishment, Gloria found that she enjoyed working there, and was cheerful and competent with the customers.

"Just hang tight, OK?" Maeve reached for a pack of cigarettes next to the phone and tapped it against her palm.

"You said I'd be selling the swimwear line."

"The swimwear line didn't pan out, remember?" Maeve shook loose a cigarette and placed it between her lips. She patted the pockets of her jeans, frowning.

"I have to get back." Gloria pulled a lighter from her own pocket and handed it to Maeve. "I keep calling them, but they're getting mad at me."

"So screw 'em," said Maeve as she accepted the lighter.

"Jesus Christ, Maeve, easy for you to say! I don't show up soon, the judge'll put a bench warrant out on me."

Maeve lit the cigarette and took a deep pull, then exhaled slowly. Smoke poured from her lips. "Tell them you're having a family emergency."

"I did. Two weeks ago."

"Tell them it got worse." She handed back the lighter.

"I did." Gloria lifted her hips to shove the lighter back into her pocket. "A week ago."

"What did you say?"

"I said she died."

"Who?"

"My *tía*. They think I'm in Miami."

"You have an aunt in Miami?"

"They think every Cubana has an aunt in Miami."

"So you told them she's dead?"

"First I said she was sick. Then I told them she died. Now they're wondering how long a Cuban funeral takes."

Maeve chuckled and took another drag on the cigarette. "See? That was smart. You're worrying about nothing."

"I didn't sign up for this, Maeve." Gloria's brows drew together, making an omega-shaped crease above her nose.

"Chill. Mike's in like Flynn, and Terri's almost done with the maps. Another day and a half, and you can tell those goody-goodies to kiss your ass."

"Maybe." Gloria frowned at the crumpled magazine in her lap. Her dark curls tumbled forward, hiding her eyes.

"Plus, you and me get the fun part." Maeve extended one leg, poking Gloria in the thigh with her toe. "Don't tell me you're not psyched for it."

Gloria raised her head, a reluctant smile lifting her cheeks. "Maybe."

"That's my girl." Maeve pulled her knees to her chest, and pursed her lips. "The only thing that I can't figure is how some snot-nosed kids tumbled to it."

"Why do you care?"

"What if there's another gang planning to hit the place? Or did they somehow find out about us? But how? That could really screw things up."

"You said it didn't matter." Gloria's voice was tinged with alarm.

Maeve sighed and stretched her legs out again. "I'll call Snake back. See what he thinks."

"He doesn't like being called Snake."

"Maybe." She picked up the phone. "But it suits him."

Chapter 15
Feeling Secure

Victor marched into the exhibition hall, brows furrowed. "Where's Todd?"

"He had a family thing." Dana, the Deputy Security Officer, trotted half a step behind Victor, who was six inches taller than she.

"He told me he'd be here this morning."

"He was."

"He's not now."

"*I'm* here," Dana pointed out.

Victor's steps lengthened until he stopped at a roped-off area a third of the way down the room where a huge banner announced, "The Desert Sun: Timeless Beauty from the Van der Bleek Collection." Surrounded by cordons stood a maze of display cases, clear as air, each holding a special treasure: a lantern made of jade, carved like the head of an ibex, its horns curving gracefully back from its forehead to form the handle; a gilded chess set, each piece studded with rubies, arranged on a chessboard as if halfway through a game; a pearl-and-diamond necklace, looped casually around the neck of an onyx bust. The cases were unlit, poised for their moment, like a Broadway star waiting for the curtain to go up.

A young woman sat on a padded bench nearby, busying herself with a sketchbook. Her hand made quick, deft movements as her eyes darted from the room to the paper and back again.

"Good morning," half-panted Dana to the young woman.

"Morning."

"The exhibit isn't open yet."

The woman's smile dazzled in her tanned face. "I'm loving the light and shadows from the windows."

"If you think that's special, come back next week," said Victor. "This will be the most spectacular exhibit in the museum."

Dana, who had by this time regained her breath, joined Victor at the ropes. "More spectacular than the *Tyrannosaurus*? Or the meteorite?"

Victor pursed his lips in the manner of one not speaking his mind.

"I know," sighed Dana. "Uglies."

"Nobody spends more than a few seconds in front of that piece of space junk," said Victor. "They check it off the to-do list, and move on. And where do they come?"

"Here."

"And where do they stay?"

"Here."

"That's right. Here. The Hall of Gems and Minerals."

"And do you know why?" muttered Dana under her breath.

"And do you know why?" said Victor. "It's the diamonds, rubies, sapphires, and what people have done with them—it's the genius, the legends, the *artistry* of the jewelry that keeps our visitors enchanted."

"So I hear."

"Masterpieces that reflect the highest aesthetic capability of their culture, whose beauty exists only to give people pleasure. That's what brings visitors to this museum."

"Yup."

"Todd doesn't get that."

"He gets it enough to hire a new guard."

"Yes, good. Nothing like a fresh set of eyes."

"You're worried about nothing."

"This exhibit isn't nothing."

"Professional thieves don't hit museums."

"Let's not be the exception that tests the rule."

"Know what they like?" said Dana. "Jewelry stores. Private homes like your friends the Van der Bleeks'."

"I told them the collection would be safer here."

"Safer here than anywhere else."

"I hope so."

"Crooks like places with lower defenses, higher rewards. Like cathedrals."

"Tell you what," said Victor. "You cover the museum, and we'll let the churches hope for divine protection." He rubbed his chin, assessing the display. Only one case, the one in the center, was empty.

"If you eliminate opportunity, you eliminate theft," said Dana. "Was it a risk when the Met let people see King Tut?"

"Point taken," said Victor. "Tell me about the new guard."

"Former military."

"Nice."

"He's meeting us here right after his orientation."

Victor glanced around the room. "What about the windows?"

"On the fourth floor?"

"Well, how about—"

"Victor, I'm telling you, we are cutting-edge." Dana puffed up her chest and gestured around them, pointing out each feature, her voice resonating in the all-but-empty hall. "There, there, and there—cameras, and the feed goes straight to the command center."

"Any sound detectors?" asked Victor.

Dana shook her head. "The vibrations could damage the displays."

"How about alarms?"

"Hundreds, and they're wired to the Mosler panel. Ever seen it?"

"That wall of lights? Todd showed me once."

"Yeah, and each one corresponds to a number. Green means all systems are go, see? So if a light turns red, we know there's a problem and we can look up where it is."

"How about security lights? For nighttime, I mean."

"About a third of the displays have floor lights that trip with a motion detector."

"Why only a third?"

"Gotta pay for the Honeywell somehow."

"I heard about that."

"Plus, anything we can't handle, we call 911 and it automatically gets routed to the Twentieth Precinct."

"No kidding. That's amazing."

"You find the gems, we keep 'em safe."

Victor mulled this over. In the silence, the woman on the bench turned to a fresh page in her sketchbook and bent over it, drawing with brisk strokes.

"Keep them safe," said Victor, half to himself. He turned and smiled at Dana. "Maybe we can bring in the Desert Sun early."

Dana chuckled, then stopped as she realized he was serious. "Todd would pitch a fit."

"You said yourself this is the safest place for it."

Footsteps sounded behind them. "You wanted to see me?" said Mike. He was wearing his new uniform, but the shirt collar would not button around his neck, so part of his chest tattoo showed at the gap. As he would have happily explained to Dana and Victor, it depicted a rising wave full of sharks, which it reminded him of surfing in Hawaii. However, since the only part they could see was a squiggly blue line, they did not ask.

"It's Mike, isn't it?" said Dana with a smile. "Right, good. Mike, this is Dr. Gold. The exhibit is his baby. Victor, Mike's working nights starting tomorrow. Fred's showing him the ropes."

Victor extended his hand and watched as it disappeared into Mike's. "Between you, the cameras, and computer, I suddenly feel a lot safer," he chuckled.

"Wait here." Dana disappeared into the hallway, reappearing moments later with a broom which she handed to the new guard. "Good to keep busy, right? Victor, come on down to the office. See you later, Mike."

After Victor and Dana had left, Mike pushed the broom past the woman on the bench. "Cameras, computer," he said softly. "Me and one other guy tomorrow. Did you get all that?"

Teresa closed her sketchpad. "All that and more, buddy. All that and more."

Chapter 16

Yellow Ribbons

"No," said Louise for the fourth time.

"But *Mom*—"

Louise smiled brightly at Tori. "Would you excuse us for a moment, dear?" She rose from her seat at the table, and held open the kitchen door. Scowling, Bobby followed her in. As the door swung shut, Tori jumped up next to it, straining to hear and poised to spring back to the table.

"Now, you listen to me, young man." The words were muffled but audible. "Your dad's very busy with that new exhibit, and he doesn't need you underfoot."

"Underfoot? The museum's huge."

"And then there's Tori."

"What about her?" Bobby's voice was suddenly wary.

Louise sighed. "Sweetheart, put yourself in her shoes for a minute. It's obvious she doesn't want to ask for help, and I admire that, really I do, but you're going to have to find a way to give her a hand anyway."

"Give her…?"

"Bobby. Her luggage disappears, she fetches up here with only the clothes on her back—and she's a *girl*."

"I know she's a—"

"Have you asked if she has extra underwear?"

"*Mom!*"

"I think you see my point, dear. Boys can live in the same stinky socks for three weeks and never tell their parents—"

"That was just the one time!"

"—but it's different for girls. Does she have antiperspirant? A clean bra?"

"I'm all out of bras, Mom."

"Don't be fresh."

"I lent her my antiperspirant."

This was true. Bobby's spray deodorant delivered its load in an icy blast that had made Tori screech like brakes on a subway car. Plus, she hadn't been sure how long to press the button, and between that and aiming wrong a few times, she had swathed the bathroom with drifting plumes of chemical mist. Also, Bobby's toothpaste tube was aluminum. He had squished it in the middle, and tendrils of Crest curled from pinprick holes on either side of his fistprint. Twentieth-century toiletries were not for the faint of heart.

"I'm not going to argue about this. That girl needs a few things so she can be comfortable the rest of the weekend. And you're going to make sure she gets them without embarrassing her."

A few minutes later, Tori and Bobby headed out. "I'm an '80s fashion icon," she said, rolling up the cuffs of her sleeves. This time, Bobby had lent her his Camp Ramah sweatshirt to go with his old winter jacket. Both were too big on her, and flapped in the March breeze.

"Better believe it," said Bobby.

"And we're going shopping together." She jammed her hands into the pockets of the jacket and tightened her shoulders against the cold. "Weird."

"Why weird?"

"I always go shopping with Mom."

"My mom does most of the shopping too." Bobby shrugged. "Not feminist, but true."

Tori bit her lip. How many times had she and her mother fabricated an errand just to escape her dad's sullen moods, his silences that filled the apartment? "Where are we going?"

"Drug store, then Gap."

"In my time, there's a drug store every few blocks." They strolled past a sign that proclaimed, "IT'S THE LAW clean up after your dog," illustrated with a stick figure crouched behind a dog, shovel and dustpan in hand.

"Why? Is everyone sick in 2020?" He emphasized pronouncing it *twenty-twenty*. "Besides that pandemic, I mean."

"In a way, I guess."

"How so?"

"Well, like allergies."

"Everyone has allergies?"

"Not everyone. But it's really common." She stepped around the shards of a glass Coke bottle on the sidewalk. "Like peanuts."

"Peanut allergies?"

"Yeah. Most schools are nut-free. You can't even bring in a PBJ."

"Sounds nutty."

"Ha. Ha."

They stopped at a corner and waited for the light to change. "I have a PBJ pretty much every day at school," said Bobby.

"I know."

"I told you?"

"Over and over." But she smiled.

The pedestrian light came on, and they crossed the street. "So what do you think of New York by daylight?" said Bobby.

Two MTA busses rumbled past, festooned with graffiti as if taggers had all the time in the world. The one in the lead was blue and white, with a sleek, convex windshield and an electric destination sign. The one trundling behind it was boxy and studded with bolts, looking like something Rosie the Riveter might have put together for fun after the war. In their wake, a burger wrapper twirled into the air before dropping to the concrete as though exhausted by the effort. Trash bags lined the sidewalks, overflowing with torn magazines and crushed cans oozing disreputable liquids. Mounds of cigarette butts formed rings around them, like the foothills of a carcinogenic mountain range. The combined stench of litter and car exhaust rasped in her throat, and she tried not to cough. "It's great," she managed.

"What's the most different?"

As Tori pondered where to begin, a man in torn, splotchy jeans leaped to a car at a red light. He sprayed the windshield with a squirt bottle, covering it in gray bubbles. His shirt hung in tatters from his shoulders, swaying with his movements, and a rip across his backside gave a glimpse of grimy underwear. The driver, who clearly thought her windshield looked better when she could see through it, semaphored furiously. Ignoring her, he shoved a squeegee across the glass, leaving uneven trails through the suds. The driver shouted through the closed window and turned on her windshield wipers, spritzing him. He threw down his squeegee, and spat on her windshield. The light changed. As the car rolled forward, wipers slapping, the man stomped past Tori and Bobby, the outer sole of one of his shoes flapping.

"They don't usually spit," said Bobby, as if in apology.

Tori nodded, not wanting to insult him or his city. She pointed at an anemic-looking tree in a cage on the sidewalk, a yellow streamer hanging limply from its trunk. Many others were similarly adorned. "What's with the ribbons?"

"They're for the hostages."

"What hostages?"

"In Iran." Bobby glanced at her in surprise. "It's a pretty big deal."

"Let's pretend for a minute that my US history course only went to Watergate."

"Watergate." Bobby shook his head. "That was horrible."

"So I hear."

"You'd come home from school, and the only thing on TV was the hearings. Every channel, even PBS."

"My God. The suffering."

"Channel Nine would play some black-and-white movie, and Eleven had cooking shows."

"You always told me you watched the hearings every day."

"I did." Bobby grinned. "There was nothing else on."

Tori looked at the boy who would be her father, and grinned back. "So, the ribbons?"

"Right. So last year—it was in the fall some time—a bunch of students in Iran stormed the embassy, our embassy, and captured a bunch of people working there. They've been holding them hostage ever since."

"Why?"

"The old ruler of Iran was getting cancer treatments in the States. The students wanted us to send him back so they could...I don't know what they wanted to do to him, actually."

"Nothing healthy, from the sound of it."

"Probably not. And of course the US doesn't negotiate with terrorists, so it's been a standoff ever since." He sighed.

"So, wait—are they terrorists or students?"

"Everyone says students."

"Maybe they're student terrorists and this is a terrorist internship program."

"Anyway, the ribbons are to remind you about the hostages."

"I guess it works."

The Genovese Drug Store was squished between a retail carpet seller and a muffin shop, and the G in the name over the door was enclosed by the outline of a mortar and pestle. The aisles were narrow, and a poster behind the cash register showed a sporty-looking blonde lady, cigarette in hand, under the words, "Virginia Slims Lights—When he offers you a low tar cigarette, tell him you've got one of your own."

"Seriously?" squawked Tori.

"My God. Now what?"

She pointed. "'In the crush-proof purse pack'? And it's *trademarked?*"

Bobby pulled her hand down. "Please don't tell me you've never seen a cigarette ad before."

Tori decided not to tell him that every time she clicked on a video, YouTube sent her an anti-vaping PSA, prompted by her I'm-obviously-a-teenager browser history. "But—I mean, they're acting like it's this, I don't know, girl-power thing to smoke, even though it'll *kill* you, but they also think all women wear purses—"

"Tell you what," said Bobby. "We won't buy any, okay?"

Tori goggled. "You can just *buy* cigarettes?"

"Sure. I do it for my mom sometimes."

"Are you *kidding* me?"

"You have to be eighteen, but no one asks. Do you want a hairbrush or not?"

They found a brush and comb and some emerald-green shampoo in a clear, plastic tube. Most of the deodorants were aerosols. Tori held one up. "Right Guard? Is there a Left Guard?"

"You're a riot."

She put it back and picked up another one. "Ooh, here's your fave. But why is it extra dry? Isn't Arrid dry enough?"

"Catch." Bobby tossed her a travel-sized toothpaste, which she caught with one hand. "Good thing you didn't drop it."

"Why?"

"'Cause then you'd be crestfallen."

Tori found herself giggling. "That is so *dumb*."

"I love Tom Swifties."

"I know—you still do!"

"That freaks me out," Bobby said.

"Nah, you're just consistent."

"That's what I mean. You know stuff about me from a life I haven't lived yet."

"Freaky," agreed Tori. But she was thinking, *Know what's really weird? This is the most I've spoken with you in years.*

As they headed to the cashier, she stopped.

"What's wrong?" Bobby asked.

She pulled him close. "My credit card is on my phone," she hissed, "and my phone doesn't work, and Apple Pay doesn't exist yet."

"Got any cash?"

She shook her head. "I usually pay electronically." She turned back to replace the items. "Except in freakin' 1980."

"I got this." He pulled out his wallet. "My mom gave me money. Not electronic, so it'll work in freakin' 1980."

"But I can't pay you back."

"Consider it an advance on your allowance."

While Bobby paid and the cashier put their purchases in bags, Tori scanned the tabloids at the checkout counter. Her favorite headline was a dead heat between "Hitler and Elvis Spotted Rescuing Lost Kittens," and "I Was Bigfoot's Dominatrix." What would they say if they knew about her? "Time-Travel Teen in Midtown Museum Mix-Up"? Well, that didn't make any sense at all—the museum was on the Upper West Side.

As they left, Bobby said, "If you don't use cash, do they still call them cashiers?"

"Huh. I never thought about that. Yeah, they do."

"And what's Apple Pay?"

Tori sighed. "It started with the great apple famine. Now we're reduced to bartering for essential goods with Granny Smiths."

"No way."

"It was a lot like the Irish Potato Famine of the 1840s."

"Seriously?" Bobby's eyes widened.

Tori laughed. "No."

"Har. Har."

"Apple's a tech company."

"Tech like technology?"

"Yeah. They make—credit cards and—things for the Internet."

"I think I've heard of them. Any relation to Apple Records?"

"Dunno. Hey, where are we going? I still need socks and stuff." She had borrowed a pair of his tube socks, and although they kept her feet warm, the thick terry cloth crunched her toes inside her sneakers.

"The Gap. There's one on 14th. Know it?"

"Yeah, we have those."

"And then we're meeting Nichelle at Gray's Papaya. She's really cool—you'll like her."

Tori took a sidelong glance at Bobby. He wasn't talking like he had a crush on this girl or anything; it sounded like they were just friends. The dad she knew never talked like that. He seldom mentioned anyone from high school, or anywhere else for that matter.

The dad she knew had her and Adina. He had clients, maybe a few colleagues. But no friends.

Until now, she had never stopped to wonder why.

Chapter 17

At Home with the Van der Bleeks

    Victor had first met the Van der Bleeks on a bright, June afternoon several years earlier. Their townhouse was six stories tall and occupied almost half the block, giving it more frontage on Park Avenue than any other private residence. Indeed, only the Swedish consulate across the street and the Italian one up the block were larger. That day, Victor had skipped his office hours at the Fashion Institute of Technology to be there, and now he worried he was at the wrong address, since neither the recessed double doors nor the marble pillars flanking them displayed a street number. Nonplussed, he glanced down the sidewalk. Next door was a red-brick building, narrower than this one but still impressive. Victor trotted up the steps and knocked, using a heavy, bronze knocker shaped like a pineapple. The door opened immediately, revealing a tall gentleman dabbing his lips with a napkin. His salt-and-pepper hair was combed straight back from his high forehead, and the pocket square in his dark suit matched his tie. "Yes?"

    Dapper, thought Victor. There was no other word. "Sorry to disturb you. I'm looking for the Van der Bleeks."

    "One house over." He smiled, pointed back where Victor had come from, and shut the door.

    "But there's no—" Realizing he was talking to a pineapple, Victor hurried back to the first house, and rapped with one hand. It made no sound at all; the door seemed to swallow the impact of his knuckles. He scanned the entryway in increasing agitation. The pillars supported a semicircular balcony whose underside boasted a mural of fluffy clouds drifting in a serene, indigo firmament. It did not match his mood. He pulled back his cuff and looked at his watch. One minute late. He sighed sharply, shifting his weight from one foot to the other, cursing Fate and doorways lavished with pillars and murals but not house numbers. Or knockers. Or bells. Or intercoms. Or—

The door opened. "Good to meet you, Professor Gold," said the dapper gentleman.

Victor's jaw dropped. The gentleman chuckled and extended his hand. "Lucas Van der Bleek. Forgive me, and do come in—the other door leads to the kitchen, and I happened to be making a quick snack."

He held open the door. Victor stepped over the threshold onto a marble floor veined with gold. Chatting easily, Van der Bleek led him alongside tall windows whose panes rippled with hand-blown glass, past a soaring staircase bisected by a brilliant blue carpet that flowed down the steps like the mighty Mississippi, and under a chandelier that could have passed for the Rockefeller Christmas Tree's adolescent cousin. After what seemed like a half-hour stroll, they arrived at a library lined with floor-to-ceiling mahogany bookshelves gleaming discreetly on every wall. It was larger than Victor's first apartment, and he suspected that the books and artifacts on the shelves could have formed the core of any self-respecting museum.

Lucas plopped down at a carved wooden desk, double-pressed a button by his phone, and gestured Victor to a chair opposite him. "I appreciate your making a house call, Professor, at a time when doctors no longer do so." His accent was so slight that it registered mainly as a meticulous way of speaking.

"You don't have to call me Professor, Mr. Van der Bleek." Victor nestled into his seat. It was soft as whipped cream.

They stood as the door opened. A woman entered, dressed in a colorful Lilly Pulitzer dress and kitten heels. Her shoulder-length hair was silver, not a strand out of place. She wore a Cartier Tank Watch, just like Jackie O's, and a gold wedding band. Pearly button earrings mirrored her smile and highlighted the lines of her neck. She shook Victor's hand. "I've been looking forward to meeting you, Professor Gold."

Lucas pulled a chair over for his wife, and trotted from the room. She sat, and Victor settled back again. "It's my pleasure, Mrs. Van der Bleek."

"Oh, please. My friends call me Janna. And we're so thrilled to have you here to help—we barely know what half these things are."

"I'm flattered. But wouldn't you prefer someone from Van Cleef, or Harry Winston?"

"We looked at them," she said. "Briefly."

"Briefly?"

Lucas returned and set down a tray of boxes: blue Tiffany, red Cartier, brown Bulgari, and others. "Quite briefly," he said. "How do you like the Fashion Institute of Technology?"

"Very much." Serving as an adjunct professor was a change of pace from Victor's museum job, and gave him the chance to pass his love of artistry to a new generation.

"Then you'll be pleased to know that President Garcia personally recommended you for this project."

"She said you were looking for someone to help you grow your collection," said Victor.

"That we are. And as for Tiffany's and their ilk, well, we got the sense that Ostrow—" a name Victor recognized as a top Tiffany executive— "was just trying to push us toward his designs." Lucas waved at the boxes. "We wanted someone with a little less skin in the game, if you see what I mean."

"A gemologist with a background with vintage design," said Janna. "Without the jewelry empire."

"We have a few nice pieces already," said Lucas, "but we don't want them to get lonely, now do we?"

"I suppose not."

"Then let's get started," said Janna.

Together, the Van der Bleeks unpacked the boxes, setting out the contents for Victor's appraisal. A gold ring of two panthers twined around a sapphire. A Victorian pearl choker. Diamond earrings, ruby bracelets. The Van der Bleeks might have been amateurs, but their instincts were flawless. Victor felt almost tipsy from the sheer, giddy brilliance before him.

"These are stunning," he said. "I hope you have a good security system."

"It's a very safe neighborhood, for New York," said Janna. "Between the two consulates, we have more gendarmes than we know what to do with."

"That reminds me," said Lucas. "Didn't you say that nice young man on the Tuesday shift just became a father?"

"Edgar, yes. Twins."

"Good heavens. Remind me to give him a box of cigars. Oh, look—the one that started it all." He handed his wife a bracelet, and she slipped it onto her wrist. "Queen Wilhelmina presented this to my mother in recognition of her services rendered during the war." He pronounced it the Dutch way: Vil-hel-*meen*-ah.

"Lovely," said Victor, admiring the gold lions encircling Janna's wrist. They looked familiar.

"My parents were on opposite sides politically," said Lucas. "My father enthusiastically supported the German invasion. He only found out after the Allied victory that my mother had been running a spy network out of our kitchen the whole time."

"Good Lord." Victor felt as though his chest were full of fluttering shadows. His grandparents had left Europe long before the war, maintaining a robust correspondence with the family back home—until the letters stopped coming. Lucas's mother had fought against the darkness that had stilled those voices and millions more.

"I loved my father, but my values are my mother's, I assure you," said Lucas, apparently noticing Victor's shock. "It's what fuels our philanthropy. I'm eternally proud of what she did."

"I suppose you had no idea?"

"Oh, none whatsoever. It would have put me in terrible danger, so she never said a word. But the queen was very grateful, and she gave my mother this gift. After returning from London, of course."

"Did Wilhelmina design it, by any chance?"

"She did," said Lucas in surprise. "How did you know?"

"May I?" Victor gently lifted Janna's wrist, rotating the bracelet link by link. "Wilhelmina updated the national crest of the Netherlands around the turn of the century, and these lions match her design. But if I'm correct—ah, here we go." He tapped the clasp with one finger. "The fastener is two lionesses. So I assume the queen's intent with this bracelet was to represent Dutch lions keeping the Nazis at bay, yes? But it only becomes a circle—a protective circle—when the lionesses link paws. They are the ones keeping it together." He smiled at Lucas. "Your mother and the queen, joining hands to save their country."

Lucas's jaw dropped, and Janna burst into startled laughter. "Professor, you are a marvel!" she exclaimed.

"No, no. Just a gemologist with a background in vintage design."

"And an astonishing eye for detail," said Lucas. "We thought about giving it to a museum. For the history, you know. But then we found out, well—"

"No one's interested in modern Dutch," said Janna.

"It is underrated," Victor had to admit.

"Which makes our little hobby a bit easier," said Lucas.

"But not all these pieces are Dutch," said Victor, surveying the *objets d'art* luminating Lucas's desk.

"Quite right," said Janna. "My favorite is from oceans away." She opened one of the last boxes and raised her cupped hands for his inspection.

Victor caught his breath. The golden gem fluttered with flecks of light, starshine and moonglow and sunlight whirling together in an eternal dance. It was like gazing at an invitation to the birth of time.

∼ ◇ ∼

By the time Victor reached the Van der Bleeks' elegant corner of town, the Saint Patrick's Day bunting had largely petered out. The butler showed him to the library. "Mr. Van der Bleek will be downstairs momentarily. Would you like some Perrier while you wait?"

"Thank you, Jasper. That would be great."

As the head servant departed, Victor settled into his usual chair, his fingers thrumming on its upholstered arms. Van der Bleek walked in, holding a glass of fizzy water. "This is yours, I believe."

Victor stood, taking it. "Thanks, Lucas."

"All set for Tuesday?" Van der Bleek sat down, but Victor remained standing. "Victor? Everything all right?"

Victor lowered himself to the edge of his chair, setting his drink on a glass-topped end table. For everything to come off flawlessly, the diamond needed to be installed today. "We're actually ahead of schedule, if you can believe it," he said with forced cheer.

"Good, good."

Otherwise, the entire endeavor might be compromised. He could see that now.

"And we've installed sensors in every vitrine," Victor went on.

Pilsner, the Van der Bleek's Siamese cat, slinked over to Lucas, who placed her on his lap and rubbed her under the chin. "Sounds like a reasonable precaution."

"With plenty more in the hall—more than the rest of the museum put together." Victor found he was talking fast.

Bored with being petted, Pilsner darted up Lucas's wingback chair and onto the bookcase, where he strolled along tracts by or about Dutch scientists such as Leeuwenhoek, Lorentz, de Sitter, and Huygens. Lucas had shown Victor the entire collection, including a Dutch-language first edition of Einstein's theory of relativity. Translated by Lorentz, it contained his signature along with that of "A. Einstein." The binding was cheap because, Lucas had explained, the publisher thought no one would ever read it.

"Plus, I had Todd hire an extra guard, just in case. Retired Navy SEAL. He looks like he could take out a crew of burglars with a broom."

Pilsner moved on to the Van der Bleeks' trove of miniature statues and carvings from the sub-Sahara. Thousands of years old, Victor knew. Some were from Picasso's private collection. Not for the first time, he found himself thinking that any one of them was worth enough to send Bobby to MIT and anywhere else he wanted to go.

"Most reassuring," said Lucas.

Pilsner twined through sculptures whose forms expressed the deepest convictions of ancient societies. Centuries later they had given rise to Cubism. Victor tried not to imagine what one misplaced flick of the cat's tail might do. "Todd's confident we've got everything covered. So is Dana."

"But you're not."

Victor slumped back in his chair. "You know me too well."

"I should hope so, by this point."

"Well, then—how would you feel about moving the Desert Sun today?"

Lucas's eyes widened. "Today?"

"Your call, obviously. And Janna's."

"You said security was all set."

"Even so."

"Is there scuttlebutt on the street? I watch *Starsky and Hutch*," he added by way of explanation. "Or did, before it was cancelled."

As Pilsner jumped back onto Lucas's chair, her tail hooked around one of the statues. It wobbled. Victor found he was gripping the arms of his chair, as he always did when the cat sauntered through the collection. Lucas appeared not to have noticed. The statue righted itself like one of Bobby's old Weebles, and Victor breathed again. "It's safer at the museum than anywhere else," he said.

Lucas picked up his glass and moved his hand in little circles, staring down into the swirling liquid inside. "Janna would be devastated if anything happened to that piece," he said quietly.

"I know."

"It means so much to her."

"I know, Lucas. I know."

He looked up. "You really think this is the best way?"

Victor swallowed. "I'll be honest, Lucas. There has been some...scuttlebutt."

"I suppose it would be odd if there weren't, given the publicity. Did I tell you *The New Yorker* interviewed us for a 'Talk of the Town' piece?"

"And if they know that diamond is here, who else does?" said Victor.

"I hadn't thought of it that way." Lucas glanced around the room at the pieces he and Janna had accumulated over a lifetime. His eyes were anxious.

"Sudden fame is a mixed blessing." The Van der Bleeks had been well-known within certain circles for their philanthropy, but the exhibit had put them on the map—literally. "If you give me the okay to move the Desert Sun today, I can have a runner here in twenty minutes. You and Janna won't have to give it another thought till you're ordering cocktails at the opening."

"That wasn't the plan," said Lucas.

"No, it wasn't."

"But if you think it's best—"
"I do," said Victor. "Best for everyone."

Chapter 18

Wonder Woman

~⟨◇⟩~

"Is this some cruel jest?" Tori shivered under the marquee of Gray's Papaya, which blared, "Drink our vitamin packed energy giving PAPAYA nature's own revitalizer." Bobby's old jacket was too big, and puffs of wind drifted around her torso and right through the Wonder Woman tee shirt they'd gotten her at the Gap. Her old one, which had gotten a little gamey, was in the bag under her new toiletries.

"She loves this place," said Bobby.

Taking the 1980 subway to get here had been an experience. They had found what Bobby called the "Goldilocks car"—not too full, not too empty—and had remained standing for the trip rather than risk an encounter with the mystery liquid clearly visible on several of the contoured, plastic seats. The floors were sticky, the air reeked of pee and French fries, and the cars were so loud and janky compared to the ones Tori knew that it seemed the only thing holding them together was the graffiti.

"There's no indoor seating." Tori tilted her head toward the big windows, indicating customers placing orders, moving down the counter, picking up overloaded dogs and drinks, and dribbling back out into the chilly March day.

"So I keep telling her."

Tori shifted her bags from her left hand to her right. The toiletries made it heavy. "She's in luck. This place is still a thing in my day."

"Sorry to hear it."

"Me too."

"In 2020, do I still say I don't like their papaya juice?"

"Oh, yeah." They smiled at each other.

An old man in a patched coat stood next to a red trash can, talking loudly. His face was so tanned it looked like leather. A woman pushing a stroller made a wide berth around him. Her toddler thrashed his booted feet in the air, one hand waving a single-serving box of Cheerios he had evidently just finished. With a deft swoop, the woman plucked the empty box from his fingers and tossed it at the trash can. It hit the pagoda-like top and bounced off, landing at Tori's feet. She picked it up, glad to take a few steps, and wedged it into the overflowing barrel. "You also say their hot dogs are—"

"Don't mess with my stuff!" The old man lurched at Tori, his face scrunched into angry lines.

Bobby grabbed her arm and pulled her back. She whirled to face him as they trotted back at the entrance to the restaurant, the bags bumping between them. At the same time they both said, "What are you *doing?*"

"You can't get that close to crazy people," he said, letting go of her sleeve.

Tori rubbed her arm. "How do you know he's crazy?"

"He's talking to a trash can!"

Bobby was right: the old man had resumed his monologue, though to judge by the nasty looks that flitted from the corners of his eyes, some of it was now about her. She felt her cheeks grow hot. "I didn't notice."

"How can you not *notice* something like that?"

"When I'm from, people talk on their phones when they're walking."

"He doesn't have a phone. Obviously."

"Well, they usually use AirPods—wireless headphones—so you don't see the actual—"

"Tori." Bobby rolled his eyes. "All of our phones—*all* of them—are connected to cords, and the cords are connected to walls."

"I know that! I just forgot."

"This is 1980. Can you try to remember *that?*"

Tori flinched. Here he was again. The Bobby who spoke to her so condescendingly, who had yanked her away from the guy by the trash can, was unpleasantly like her father.

Worse, he was right. Back home, she could always tell the difference between pedestrians on the phone and randos who thought squirrels were Jesus. Here in Bobby's New York, she'd had a brain fart at the wrong moment.

Keep it together, he's your only ally, maybe the only way to get home. "I'm sorry. Everything's—different, you know?"

"Forget it," said Bobby. He lifted his arms, then let them flop to his sides. "Just got scared there. Sorry."

Now that, thought Tori, was more like Bobby than her dad. "No problem."

Bobby brightened. "Oh, hey, there's Nichelle." He waved as a pretty Black girl in a tan coat approached. "Listen, don't tell her you're my daughter. It would freak her out."

"So what are we going to tell her?"

"That you're an accidental time traveler from 2020, and we need to figure out how to bend the space-time continuum to get you home."

"Good thing we're not going to freak her out."

"Hey." Under her coat, Nichelle wore jeans and Keds. Her tight curls cascaded from under a bright-red, knit hat, and bounced against her cheeks. She held out her hand with a sunny smile. "I'm Nichelle."

"Tori." She grasped Nichelle's hand.

Nichelle regarded her. "Have we met? You look familiar."

"No."

"Oh. Love your hair, though. Radical." She smiled approvingly at Tori's purple streak. "I'd love to do that, but my mom would not approve, if you catch my drift."

"Parents. What can you do?" Tori smiled at Bobby's dirty look as he held open the door for them. "I've never met a Nichelle before," she went on. "Super-cool name."

"So far as I know, there's only one other." Nichelle got in line. "Ever seen *Star Trek?*"

"Sure. My dad is, like, in *love* with that show. Geeze, Bobby, quit shoving."

"Bet mine loves it more."

"Oh?"

"I was named after the actress who played Lieutenant Uhura." She chuckled and shook her head.

"Seriously?"

"Well, he liked her before *Star Trek*," admitted Nichelle. "Tori's a neat name, though. Bet you don't have to keep spelling it for people."

"I always have to say it's with an I, not a Y."

"What's your last name?"

"Gold," she said without thinking.

Nichelle brightened. "Are you cousins or something?"

"No," they said together.

"Because you look a lot alike, now that I'm looking."

"No, we don't," they said in unison.

"Hold up," said Nichelle to Bobby. "What's going on?"

"Nothing."

"Then why are you acting so weird? Both of you."

"You wouldn't believe us if we told you," said Bobby. So they did.

Chapter 19

A Visit from Nicky

～◇～

The buzzer for the front door growled, paused, then growled again. Snake caught the speaker button on the third ring. "Yeah?"

"Let me in."

Snake jerked away from the wall, his finger slipping from the button. The buzzer sounded. He pressed the little knob again in mechanical horror. "Nicky?"

"No one else."

"No one?" said Snake hopefully.

"Buzz me in, dipshit."

"Gimme a sec." Snake glanced wildly around his apartment. Sunlight streamed through the dirty windows, illuminating the uneven floorboards and the nicked plaster of dun-colored walls. The buzzer rattled again, and Snake stabbed the button, fingers shaking.

"Snake," rumbled Nicky, "do not be anserine. Open the door."

"Sure, Nicky, sure," panted Snake. "It's just—I was asleep. I need a minute to get dressed."

"I'll walk nice and slow on my way up. Now open the fucking door."

Snake groaned and pressed the admit button. By the time two sharp knocks sounded at his entryway, he was fully dressed and had brushed his teeth. Still, a bitter taste bubbled in the back of his throat as he slid open his two door chains and flipped the switch for the deadbolt. "Nicky. Good to see you. Coffee?"

"Cut the crap." Nicky stomped in, scowling. "And I got a guy at the stairs, so don't even think about it."

Snake shut the door. His mouth was dry, his hands were wet, and his gut churned like a washing machine full of bowling balls. He waited.

Nature, in designing No-Name Nicky, had favored expediency over aesthetics. He was just under six and a half feet tall, and just over three hundred pounds. His mouth was wide, his jaw was narrow, and his nose was flat and asymmetrical. His beady eyes squinted from within rings of scar tissue, and his hair came halfway down his forehead in a spiky carpet. He stood in the center of the sunlit living room, his shadow seeming to take up half the floor. "Know what brings me here on a Saturday morning?"

"Yes."

No-Name surged toward Snake and slapped a meaty hand on his shoulder. Snake sagged under its weight. "You're a fuckup."

Snake nodded. It was not the first time he had heard this assessment.

Nicky's other hand smacked Snake's other shoulder. His eyes glittered. "Where. Is. The. Money?"

"It's coming."

"When?"

"Soon!"

"Now." He leaned forward, his oblate nose almost touching Snake's face.

"Tuesday," gasped Snake. "I'll have it Tuesday."

"Now, why do I not believe that?" Nicky tightened his grip.

"It's true."

"It was also true the other times you didn't pay."

"I got a job lined up."

"Sure you do."

"I do. I swear!"

Nicky straightened up, sighing the sigh of one who is about to explain the obvious. "How many times have you put me off, Snake?"

"Ah…."

"I count twice."

"And I appreciate it, Nicky. I really do."

"This being the third time."

"Third and last."

"Still having trouble believing that."

"I'm telling you, after this weekend I'll be flush."

"Or flushed." Nicky chuckled, but when Snake joined him in a watery imitation, he stopped and glared at the smaller man whom he still gripped in his enormous paws. His fingers tightened.

"My boss trusts me," said Nicky. "I don't want to disappoint him, especially not on behalf of a gutless weasel such as yourself. No offense." He gave a final squeeze and released Snake, stepping back and flexing his sausage-like fingers.

Snake rubbed his bruised shoulders. No-Name Nicky worked for an organization that paid witnesses not to speak, and journalists not to write. Instead of socializing over golf, the CEOs met at stripholes where they played cards, drank beer, and planned murders. "Tell him if he waits till Tuesday, I can make good," he managed finally. "Whole thing. No more payment plans."

"You said the job's this weekend."

"It is."

"So pay Monday."

"Monday's a holiday."

"You in a fucking union now?"

"Look, I—"

"Got your health insurance and dental wrapped up in this?"

"The job's Monday night."

"You said it was this weekend."

"It is."

"Then why is it suddenly on Monday?"

"Because Monday's a holiday. It's part of the weekend."

"Don't shit me, asshole." Nicky's right hand curled into a soft fist.

"Of course not." Snake's attempt at a smile sent his lips into spasm, so he stopped. "Job's Monday night."

"Change it."

"I can't."

Nicky looked at him. His mouth did not move, and his eyes were expressionless. "I like you," he said finally.

"Thanks," said Snake after a heartbeat. The statement might very well be true. It was also irrelevant, because if No-Name Nicky had ever had a conscience, he had long since squelched it. He had killed people with whom he had shared meals. He had maimed men who trusted him.

"The thing is," went on Nicky, as if he hadn't heard, "that we, I and my boss that is, we have a real problem with you right now."

"I know, Nicky, I know. And I take full responsibility for that."

"Do you?"

"I'm telling you, after this job you'll never have to see me again."

"That would be nice. Know why?"

"Why?" said Snake, who knew perfectly well why.

"Because my organization, we work our own way. We do not have legal recourse. Know what I'm sayin'?"

"Sure, Nicky. Sure."

"This is not a situation where I can turn to the courts for redress."

Snake, who was similarly constrained, stayed silent.

"My boss is not a patient man. And my own job security is far from guaranteed."

"I'll make good."

"Economy's in the crapper."

"Sure is," agreed Snake helpfully.

"Jesus Christ, they're even talking about gas rationing. Again."

"Assholes."

"Fucking peanut farmer."

"Hell, I didn't vote for him."

"Me neither." Nicky shook his massive head. "Anyway, sorry, Snake. Business is business." He pulled open the lapel of his enormous, tan jacket and reached in with his free hand.

Snake stumbled backward. The door hit his shoulder blades. "Double," he croaked.

Nicky's hand stopped, and his eyebrows lifted by a fraction of a millimeter. "Double?"

"Tell him if he waits till Tuesday, I'll pay double."

Nicky dropped the lapel. He appeared to think. It was not a speedy process, but it was thorough. Snake waited, taking shallow breaths. "He might go for that," said Nicky finally.

"Great!"

"Or he might not," said Nicky. "Between you and I, you have not given him much reason to trust you."

It was true. "Tell him I'll do full on Monday or double on Tuesday."

Again, he waited as thoughts made their way across the vast, featureless expanse that was No-Name Nicky's mind. Finally, the big man nodded. "Deal."

Snake let out his breath in a whoosh, and his body sagged. He smiled. "You won't regret it."

"I know." Nicky stepped close, grabbing Snake's shirtfront with one hand. His other hand curled into an anvil-like fist, and smashed into Snake's gut. Snake doubled over, eyes squeezed shut, mouth opening and shutting impotently. Nicky dropped the shirt, and Snake slid to the floor. Nicky towered over him. "Because if you welsh this time, you're fuckin' buried, pal."

Nicky let himself out. Facedown on the dark floorboards, Snake curled around himself, whimpering convulsively.

Chapter 20

A Matter of Time

"Time travel?" Nichelle's eyes were wide. They had grabbed a table at Nico's, a coffee shop down the street where they could talk and Tori could stop shivering. "Like, seriously. *Time travel?*"

"Bobby said it would freak you out," chattered Tori.

"He was right."

"Sorry," said Bobby.

"And, well, I need help." Tori sipped the cocoa Bobby had bought her, relaxing as the hot liquid fanned through her insides. She set the mug back on its coaster and rubbed her chilly fingers.

"So there's a, like, plague happening? Here?" Ignoring her banana muffin, a chaser for the papaya juice she'd finished on the way over, Nichelle pointed at the table in a way that paradoxically indicated all of New York.

"Everywhere," said Tori. "They shut down Italy."

"No way."

"No joke."

"How do you shut down a whole freakin' country?"

"You close the borders and you don't let anyone in or out."

"Damn." Nichelle shook her head. "What causes it?"

"A virus. New kind."

"Why?" said Bobby.

"I'm just wondering if it's from the hole in the ozone layer," said Nichelle.

"The what?" said Tori.

"Maybe," said Bobby. "Or some other environmental thing. You know, like Love Canal, only bigger."

"What's a Love Canal?" said Tori.

"But that causes birth defects and stuff. Tori's disease doesn't sound like that," said Nichelle.

"It's not *my* disease."

"Or acid rain, maybe?" said Bobby.

"It's everyone's disease," said Tori. In her day, Planet Earth was unified by terror, socially distanced yet stumbling forward as one. "Together, apart," as politicians, reporters, and TikTokers proclaimed in a mighty chorus. Except for her parents, of course, who had chosen this moment of global unity to disunite.

"Or the wrong river caught on fire," went on Nichelle.

"Save the whales, man," said Bobby.

"Or smog. You know, from gas-guzzlers." Nichelle's face was unalloyed innocence except for a gleam in her dark eyes. "I mean, who even owns a car in the city?"

"We don't." Tori thought about her mother braving the terrors of the pandemic to rent a car. God, she missed her mom.

"We do." Bobby blew his straw-paper at Nichelle

"Eco-criminal." She swatted it out of the air.

"Jealousy is an ugly color on you, Little Miss Greenpeace McTreeHugger."

"Of the Long Island McTreeHuggers," said Nichelle.

"Can we get back to the fact that I'm stuck in the wrong millennium?" said Tori.

"Right, right," said Nichelle.

"Got any ideas?" said Tori. "Bobby says you're his smartest friend."

"For real?" Nichelle gave Bobby a dazzling grin.

"Don't get swell-headed," he said.

"I won't." Her smile faded. "This one's a stumper."

"Tell me about it," said Tori.

"I mean, I'm smart, not magical."

"Poppycock," said Bobby. "Magic is just science we don't have the math for yet."

"Poppycock?" said Tori.

"Something wrong with poppycock?"

Her chin trembled with suppressed giggles. "I always figured you for a fiddlesticks or balderdash kind of guy."

"When I say poppycock, I mean poppycock, dammit."

Nichelle crinkled her lips, thinking. "So you know about the speed-of-light thing?"

"Sure," said Bobby.

"No," said Tori.

"Basically, there's no such thing as universal time," said Bobby briskly. "It runs differently for everyone."

"What? No, it doesn't." Tori lifted her mug for another sip. The coaster came along for the ride. "A second for me is a second for everyone else."

"Says the time traveler," chuckled Nichelle.

Bobby peeled the coaster from the underside of Tori's mug. Taking a pen from his pocket, he made two dots on the paper circle, one on the rim and one near the center. "Look. Let's say these are two guys named, um, Wolfgang and Pickles."

"Which one's which?" Tori set down her cocoa.

"This one's Pickles." He tapped the one on the rim. Then he stabbed the center with the tip of his pen, and spun the coaster with his finger. "Both of them make a complete circle in the same amount of time, right?"

Tori watched the circle rotate. "Right."

"But Pickles here has to make a bigger circle in the same amount of time, which means he goes faster than Wolfgang. So the points on the coaster move at two different speeds, even though they make the same number of revolutions per minute."

Tori stared as contradictory ideas brawled inside her head. "But—wait—"

"So cool, right?" said Nichelle.

"But they're just dots," she protested.

Bobby covered the coaster with his palm. "Shh. They'll hear you."

"No, I mean—that's not real. It's like one of those optical illusions that's a vase or two faces, depending on how you look at it."

"Nope." Nichelle slid the coaster away from Bobby and, using his pen, drew a tiny clock face next to each dot. She spun it again. "If those were real clocks and not just my fantabulous artwork, the one at the rim would keep time slower than the one near the center."

"No," said Tori.

"Yes."

Tori clutched her hair. "Argh!"

"You think you've got it rough," said Nichelle. "Pickles is prone to motion sickness." She rocked the coaster back and forth, a sadistic chuckle rolling deep in her throat.

"I know how he feels," said Tori. "My brain hurts."

"Sorry." Bobby nudged her mug toward her. "Have some more hot chocolate."

"Which brings us to the speed-of-light thing," said Nichelle. She picked up the straw-paper Bobby had blown at her and tore it, squidging the halves into little wads. "Let's say these are twins."

"They do look alike," said Tori. "I think this one's named Hagatha."

"This one's Lady Odette Hightower III," said Nichelle.

"Ooh, fancy."

"Now, the closer you get to the speed of light, the more time slows, relative to everything else." Nichelle lifted her straw.

"Why?"

"Because time runs differently for everyone, remember?"

"Okay, but what's that got to do with the speed of light?"

"Einstein said to imagine you were riding on a beam of light," said Nichelle. "You're moving as fast as it is, right? But the rest of the world seems fixed as you go past. The world's time would be different from yours, so time would end for you."

Tori took a moment to absorb this. "But not for them," she said finally.

"Right. Their time and yours are different. So now let's say you shoot one twin into space at *near* the speed of light." Nichelle put the straw to her lips and directed a violent poof at Lady Odette Hightower III, sending her skittering across the table. "Let's say she travels at that speed for a few years. Her time doesn't stop, but it slows down. When she gets back, she'll be younger than Hagatha, so long as Hagatha stays on Earth."

"Holy crap," said Tori.

"Ready for another mind-bender?" said Bobby. "Time and space are the same thing."

"No, they're not."

"Yes, they are."

"Not in real life."

"Yes in real life." Bobby rubbed his ear. "Look. The Air Force has this thing called Navstar. It's a bunch of satellites that—"

"It is *so* cool," interrupted Nichelle. "My aunt did some of the math for it."

"—that can find anything on Earth," said Bobby. "Just pinpoint your position anywhere. And without Einsteinian physics, it doesn't work. The chronometers on the satellites run thirty-eight millionths of a second per day slower than on Earth, and the systems need to accommodate for that time loss, which means that the wrong time would put you in the wrong place."

Tori's mental fog lifted. "So it's a GPS."

"What's that stand for?"

"Global Position Satellite. Positioning. I think. OMG. We use that all the time."

"How do you use satellite positioning? And I swear, if you say 'phone,' I will—"

"Phone?" said Nichelle.

Tori unzipped the pocket of Bobby's old jacket and pulled out her phone, popping it out of its case so Nichelle could see its sleek and, for her, futuristic lines. The other girl took it hesitantly, her fingers tracing the blank, black screen. "This is a *phone?*"

"Yeah."

"And a Walkman and a digital watch and a computer and pretty much everything else," said Bobby. "Or so I hear."

Nichelle turned it around, shaking her head in amazement. "How does it work?"

"Right now it doesn't."

"How come?"

"Guess there aren't enough satellites yet."

"So it's a communicator."

"Yeah. Well, no. Sometimes your call drops—hangs up. Randomly."

"Captain Kirk has that problem all the time," said Nichelle in sympathy. "And these little circles here?"

"Camera lenses. You can take photos or videos. Um, little movies."

"Any good?"

"Good enough to make TV commercials, sometimes."

"Where do you put the film?"

"There isn't any."

"That's so cool." Nichelle handed her the phone. "You really are from tomorrow."

"Thanks." Tori put the phone back in its case and slipped it into her pocket. "I'd like to get back there." Had 2020 frozen while she rocketed past on a beam of whatever the hell had happened to her? She took another sip of hot chocolate, and, feeling more than warmed up, pulled off her sweatshirt, revealing her new Wonder Woman tee. Nichelle waved at it. "Nice."

"You like Wonder Woman?"

"Love, love Lynda Carter. I don't know why they cancelled it."

"They came out with this awesome Wonder Woman movie when I was in middle school," said Tori. "The actress is Israeli."

"So Israel still exists," said Bobby.

Crap, thought Tori. This kid was sharp. What if he remembered some tiny detail she mentioned, and butterfly-effected the world out of existence? Stick to pop culture and tech, she reminded herself. That should be OK, right? "Her name is Gal Gadot, and…" she stopped.

"What?" said Bobby.

"I just remembered. Before I—came here, I was reading about her, about that actress. And she was wearing the Desert Sun."

"Is that why you freaked out when you saw my dad's fake?" said Bobby.

"Partly."

"Fake what?" Nichelle asked.

"Desert Sun. Huge diamond for my dad's exhibit," said Bobby.

"The one on all the posters?" said Nichelle.

"Yeah. And it's going to be stolen," said Tori.

"Really?"

"Really."

Nichelle sat up straight, her curls bobbing. "This mondo diamond is in danger?"

Tori winced, thinking about how much damage the theft would cause. "It is."

"And it went to you for help."

"What? No, it didn't."

"I think it did." Nichelle drummed her fingers on the table. "Look, matter interrupts light, right?"

"Well—I guess so." Tori forced her mind down yet another alleyway that Nichelle and Bobby clearly waltzed through on the regular. "If it didn't, we couldn't see it."

"You got it, Future Girl. So now think about the relationship between matter and light."

"Um...are they living together, or just friends?"

Bobby's face shone. "Nish, you're a genius."

"Yeah, but I'm humble about it."

"What did I miss?" said Tori.

"Energy and mass are equivalent," said Bobby.

"Is that the E=mc2 thing?" said Tori.

"Right, exactly," said Bobby.

"Hold on, hold on, let me think." Nichelle rumpled her brow. "We're all mass, which means we're all energy—and energy can be refracted."

"Go on." Bobby leaned over the table at her.

"Like how white light turns into rainbows when it goes through a prism." Nichelle squeezed her eyes shut, clearly forming thoughts and words at the same time. "And what's your diamond? A ginormous prism." She opened her eyes, her face gleaming with triumph.

"But I've never even seen the real thing," said Tori.

"No, but you time-traveled, and diamonds are freaking old." Excitement misted Bobby's cheeks.

"Lots of things are old," said Tori. "Dinosaurs and stuff."

He shook his head. "Dinosaurs are hundreds of millions of years old. Diamonds are billions."

"Billions?" said Tori.

Bobby's eyes were bright. "Ordinary diamonds can be three billion years old or more."

"Dang," said Nichelle. "That's more than some stars. So how old is this desert diamond?"

"No idea," said Bobby. "You can't date them without destroying them."

"So this one could be...." Nichelle's voice trailed off.

"Really, really freakin' old," said Bobby.

The three of them digested this. "So the diamond is a time portal," said Tori finally.

"Maybe," said Nichelle. "Look, you're a physical being. Matter is energy. Energy is light. And somehow, that diamond refracted you and put you back again somewhere—sometime—else."

"Light and energy and time and space," said Bobby. "My God, it all works."

"Beam me up, Scotty," breathed Nichelle.

Chapter 21

Picture Perfect?

"So maybe the Desert Sun is, like, leaking or something?" said Tori.

"Why not?" said Nichelle.

"How so?" said Bobby.

"No clue," said Nichelle. "But if I'm a diamond, ancient-ancient-*ancient*, maybe I can mess with time in ways science doesn't understand. Yet. Maybe I know when shit's about to hit the fan. So I pick the one person who can save me, and I put her where she can do it."

"But why me? I'm not special."

The other girl shrugged. "Maybe you get special later. Maybe you have superpowers you haven't discovered yet. Who knows? But the constant in all this is that diamond. So far as I can tell, it picked you out of four and a half billion people to come here, at this moment."

They paused to let her words sink in.

"Well," said Tori finally, "then maybe I need to have a chat with it."

"How?"

"Go to the museum. Slip under the ropes while Bobby creates a diversion." She waved her hands. "Can't be that hard."

"Yeah, it can," said Bobby.

"Oh, come on. Don't tell me a resourceful guy like you can't come up with some way to distract a museum guard."

"You could pretend to faint," said Nichelle.

"Or puke," said Tori. "Do you guys say 'puke'?"

"Sure," said Nichelle. "Puke, barf, upchuck, blow chunks, do the technicolor yawn—"

"It's not at the museum," said Bobby.

"Wait. What?" said Tori. "Yes, it is."

He shook his head. "Remember? My dad said they were bringing it Monday."

Tori pinched the skin between her eyebrows. Had the Wikipedia article said the diamond was stolen Tuesday, or that the theft was discovered Tuesday? Why, oh why hadn't she grabbed the printout before running to her room? Because her father was yelling at her, that's why. Typical.

Bobby leaned over and patted her shoulder. "Hey, don't worry. You said the Desert Sun gets stolen from the museum, right?"

"Yeah," she muttered.

"So it's safe. It can't get stolen from a place it isn't in yet."

Tori lifted her head. A lightness briefly filled her chest before growing brick-heavy. "Then how am I supposed to protect it?"

"Maybe you already have," said Nichelle. "Maybe your quest is done."

"But I'm still here."

"True." Nichelle considered this as she nibbled her muffin. "You were reading about the diamond when you got beamed here?" she said finally.

"Looking at a picture, yeah."

"Do you have the picture?"

"On my phone."

"How can a picture be on your—"

"Never mind," said Bobby hastily. "What's your point, Nish?"

"I guess I'm thinking if a picture is the trigger that sends her here when the diamond's in danger, maybe it can send her back now that the diamond's safe."

"But that picture doesn't exist yet," said Tori.

"Does it have to be the same one?"

"How should I know?"

"I know where there's a picture of it," said Bobby. He stood up. "You were right, Tori. Let's go to the museum."

Chapter 22

Tell Your Uncle Jacob

"You seriously have to check in with her?" Halfway to the museum, and Bobby insisted on stopping to make a call. Naturally.

"You seriously walk around with a phone in your pocket?" said Bobby. Nichelle tossed a look from him to Tori, eyebrows raised.

"What's that got to do with anything?" said Tori. Her life hung in the balance, and her dad insisted on following some stupid rule.

"Well, this is what I have in mine." He pulled out a dime. "Your mom ever call you when you're out?"

"Well, usually she texts, but—"

"Texts?" said Nichelle.

"Great," said Bobby. He pushed the accordion-hinged door of the booth with one hand. "Look, maybe in 2020 New York is super-safe. Or maybe it doesn't have to be, since it sounds like every kid is basically LoJacked."

"You don't have to get all—"

"This isn't 1950, you know. It's dangerous."

"How do you text?" said Nichelle.

"How dangerous?" said Tori. With a prick of alarm, she looked over her shoulder at the cityscape that seduced her with its familiarity and confounded her with a thousand reminders that she was not, appearances to the contrary, home.

"Kids disappear," said Bobby. "All the time."

"And?" said Tori. You couldn't grow up in New York and not know that kids vanished sometimes. Nobody she knew, of course. Other kids, the kind who only existed in headlines and Missing posters and true crime TV.

"Last year a six-year-old walked to a bus stop and never came home," said Nichelle.

Six? That was different. Tori thought of the kids she sat for at home, who weren't born yet. She could see why Bobby was being—protective, kind of. "Jeeze. They ever find him?"

"Still looking," said Bobby. "Anyway, my folks like me to phone when I'm out."

"Getting back to the main point," said Nichelle, "is text even a verb?"

"Look, I don't call my mom much, okay? It's different." Tori hunched her shoulders against the puffs of wintry breath capering down the sidewalk.

"Guess it's a 1980 thing." Bobby's expression softened. "You cold?"

"Yeah." The day was still raw, and Bobby's coat was still too big.

He held open the door for her, and punched in the number as she stepped inside. Tori left her shopping bags with Nichelle, who waved from the other side of the graffiti-slashed glass. "Hi, Mom," said Bobby. Pause. "We got Tori some stuff at the Gap, and hung out with Nichelle."

Tori found that in the absence of speakerphone, everything Bobby said prompted a question for her. "He did?" *Who did what?* "You shouldn't call him that." *Call who what?* "Yeah, I'll call him now." *How many freaking dimes do you carry around with you?* "Love you too, Mom." *Aw. That's so sweet.*

He hung up, blushing. "Don't say a damn thing."

"Wasn't going to." When was the last time she had told either of her parents she loved them?

"She'll be your grandmother."

"Chill." It came out more sharply than she had intended, and she softened her tone. "Someone called?"

"Jacob." Bobby fished another dime from his pocket, and dropped it into the slot.

"She calls him something else?"

"Yeah, Uncle Lars."

"Is that his middle name?"

"Short for Larceny." He barely looked at the pad as he dialed, but his face lit up when a voice buzzed at the other end. "Hi, it's Bobby. My mom said you called. Yeah, she's still here." He glanced at Tori. "For the weekend.... No.... Of course not. Okay, we can be there in, like, fifteen minutes. Okay, forty. Forty is fine."

"And?" said Tori when he had hung up again.

Radiating triumph, Bobby opened the door and they spilled onto the sidewalk. "Jacob wants us to meet him at Popover's," he told her and Nichelle. "He's bringing someone from the museum to talk to us. Someone really high up."

"Hey, that's great!" said Tori.

"I knew he'd come through."

"Where's Popover's?"

"Fifteen blocks." Nichelle pointed uptown.

"Hold on a second." Bobby screwed his face up and started muttering. "One-point-six-one times .75—carry the three—"

"What are you doing?"

"Converting to kilometers." His eyes were still squinched shut. "Is five, plus three is eight—"

"Why?"

"So you'll know how far it is."

"Fifteen blocks is three-quarters of a mile." She hoisted her shopping bags.

Bobby's eyes flew open. "You mean we *still* haven't switched to metric?" he wailed.

◇

"Specialty is the giant popovers," Nichelle said as they sat at a table by the window.

"Kinda got that from the name." Tori glanced at the menu, her foot drumming on the floor next to her shopping bags. It was their third eatery that day, and she was hungrier for action than food. "Shouldn't we get to the museum?"

"After we talk to Jacob," said Bobby.

"I need to talk to the diamond."

"I thought you needed to foil the heist."

"Maybe I was wrong. Maybe the Desert Sun and I can have a chat and work everything out."

"We'll get there."

"When?"

"What's the rush?"

"What's the *rush?* That thing is my only way home!"

"If you need to foil the heist, telling the museum about it might be just as important," said Nichelle.

"Maybe." She glanced at the window. "Does Jacob have a girlfriend?"

"Often," said Bobby.

"Looks like he has one now."

Jacob was walking across the street, holding hands with a woman in a brown leather coat and matching boots whose stacked heels made her taller than him. She was slender, but her style choices were big: billows of tawny hair, tinted glasses in square frames, gold hoop earrings brushing her shoulders. She leaned her head to his to say something, and they laughed.

As the adults reached the table, the woman's eyes widened behind her big glasses. She stopped with one hand in her pocket, the other on the purse hanging from her shoulder. It matched the coat and boots.

"Hey, Bobby, Tori. And Nichelle! Didn't know you were joining us." Jacob's grin was like sunshine. "How's the music going?"

"Got a gig this afternoon," smiled Nichelle.

"Cool." He beamed at Bobby. "Kid, like you to meet Dr. Hopewell. She's that security expert I—"

"Charmed," snapped the woman. "Jacob, a word?"

"Sure thing." He pulled out a chair for her.

Dr. Hopewell remained standing. Her cheery mood had evaporated. "You said informant, not teenybopper."

"Bobby's smarter than you and me plus all those initials after your name, Doctor." Jacob indicated the chair. The woman glanced at the teenagers, and back to Jacob. Her lips tightened, and with a sharp sigh she unbuckled her coat and draped it over the back of the chair before sitting and letting Jacob push her in.

"So who are you?" she said, turning to Tori. Her breath was a smother of tobacco, and Tori could smell the fumes wafting off her coat as well.

"Tori." She held out her hand. "Bobby and I go to the same summer camp."

"And you're the smart one." Dr. Hopewell had already dropped Tori's hand, and was focused on Bobby, who smiled at the compliment.

"I get good grades," he said modestly.

"This isn't school." Dr. Hopewell dug a cigarette pack out of her purse and lit one. "Hope you don't mind if I smoke," she said as the vapors drifted from her nose and lips.

My God, this whole generation grew up on an oxygen deficit. "Do you work with Bobby's dad?" said Tori.

Dr. Hopewell chuckled. "Let's just say I—"

"Dang, Uncle Jacob are you okay?" said Bobby.

For the first time, Tori noticed that Jacob was a mess. His cheeks sagged, and his eyes were red-rimmed. "Tell you the truth, kid, no. What you told me yesterday—I was up all night worrying about your dad. Then it hits me: go straight to the top."

"Your uncle pulled me out of a meeting," said Dr. Hopewell.

"With Mr. Dixon?" said Bobby.

Tori tried to check Jacob's watch. How late was the museum open on Saturdays?

"Dr. Hopewell's a consultant, kid," said Jacob.

"Well, we appreciate you talking to us," said Bobby.

"I'm not sure I do," said Dr. Hopewell.

"You will," said Jacob. "Go on, Bobby. Tell her what you told me yesterday. And Tori too, of course."

Bobby nodded to Tori. "There's going to be a robbery at the museum this weekend," she said, for what felt like the millionth time. "A gang is going to steal the gems from the Desert Sun exhibit."

Dr. Hopewell hooted. "Sure, kid."

Tori felt her ears grow hot. "It's true."

"So you're expecting me to believe that a gang of thugs kicks in the door and saunters up the stairs—"

"They come in through the window."

"What window?"

"On the fourth floor."

Dr. Hopewell took a drag on her cigarette, showing her clunky, gold watch. Tori clenched her teeth. The minutes were shooting by. Were they even on the right track? How much did a museum ticket cost? Could Bobby keep paying for her every time they did anything?

"That's pretty slick," admitted the doctor. "Bypasses the security cams and guards."

"Exactly," said Bobby excitedly. "And they do it on Monday because the museum's closed."

"Use the parade for cover?"

"I guess," said Tori.

The doctor took another drag and blew the smoke at the ceiling, brows creased in concentration. Finally she shook her head. "A job like that would take a dozen men. I would have heard about it."

"I bet it's not a dozen," said Bobby. "You wouldn't need more than half that, I bet."

Dr. Hopewell stubbed out her cigarette and took off her glasses to polish them on a napkin. "That would be pretty small for a job like this."

"I think Bobby's right," said Tori. Surely the article would have mentioned a huge gang.

"Which brings us to another point." Dr. Hopewell put her glasses back on. "How do you know all this?"

"I can't tell you," said Tori.

"And yet, you have pretty detailed intel."

"It's from a reliable source," said Bobby.

Dr. Hopewell lit another cigarette and took a deep drag. "Your dad works at the museum."

Bobby nodded. "He's in charge of the exhibit."

"Is that how you know about the hit?"

"What? Oh, God, no."

"Your father is in charge of the exhibit and you know all about a hit on it, but he doesn't?"

"Well...yeah."

"Doesn't that seem strange to you?"

"I didn't want—I mean—"

Dr. Hopewell balanced her cigarette on the rim of the ashtray on the table. "Look, Jacob, this has all been bags of fun, but I'm done babysitting. Let's go talk to your brother."

"That Boy Scout?" chuckled Jacob. "What for?"

"The Boy Scout is pretty obviously hiding something," said Dr. Hopewell. Behind the tinted lenses, her eyes had gone metallic.

... suspicion quickly coalesced around then-Chief Gemologist Victor Gold, who ultimately served a two-year prison sentence for his role in the crime....

"I read about it," cried Tori. "I found some plans, and I read it. Bobby's dad has nothing to do with it." Maybe.

Dr. Hopewell picked up her cigarette, and inhaled slowly. "Nothing at all?" she said on the exhale.

"Nothing."

"You haven't forgotten anything? Any little detail?"

"That's everything I know. Everything!"

"Ease up there, Doctor." Jacob put a hand on her arm. "If the kids think of anything else, they'll call me. Right, Bobby?"

"Sure. Of course."

"Good enough for you, Doc?"

"Guess it'll have to be." She stubbed out the cigarette and stood. "I won't talk to your brother just yet, Jacob. But it sure looks like I've got some digging to do."

"I'll grab you a taxi."

When they had left, Tori leaned back in her chair, stomach churning. "Damn."

"She is *tough*," agreed Bobby.

"Guess you'd have to be, in her job," said Nichelle.

"What did Jacob say she did?" said Bobby.

"Security at the museum." Tori stood, grasping the handles of the bags. "Which is where we're going *now*."

Chapter 23

Day at the Museum

"This part is exactly the same," said Tori. The Central Park entrance to the Museum of Natural History showcased a statue of a strapping Teddy Roosevelt on horseback, flanked by an equally robust Native American man on his right and an African man on his left. The ensemble radiated testosterone like solar flares.

"My mom has a picture of when they put it in," said Nichelle.

In the lee of the virile tableau, a vendor with a cigarette in the corner of his mouth passed hot dogs to two kids as their father paid in cash. Tori lowered her voice. "Tourists and hot dogs. Gross."

"Gross?" said Bobby.

"I'm a vegetarian."

"You ate chicken last night."

"Your mom was being so nice."

"Then you're not really a vegetarian."

"I'm a vegetarian sympathizer."

"Know what I am?" said Nichelle. "Cold."

"This way." Bobby led them down the steps under the Grand Staircase and through the Members Only entrance into the Theodore Roosevelt Memorial Hall. "We can check your bags at the coat room."

"I didn't know you'd get in for free," said Tori.

"New Yorkers don't have to pay," said Nichelle.

"I don't come here much," said Tori. "Obviously."

"In junior high, I used to come a couple times a week." Bobby waved at a docent, who waved back. "My mom was Sisterhood treasurer back then, so she was really busy. I'd do homework in my dad's office till he was done, then we'd go out for dinner. Oh, bathroom's over there if you need it."

Tori's bags pulled on the skin of her hands, and Bobby's cheerful words roiled her insides. What an easy relationship he had with his dad. She was jealous. He was about to lose it all. She pitied him. What to do with all this information she couldn't share?

"I'll avail myself," said Nichelle. "You know what they say about papaya juice—you only rent it."

"Meet us at the meteorite?" said Bobby.

"Sure." She went into the bathroom, and Tori followed Bobby past the museum shop to the coat room.

"Hi, Jeanette," said Bobby to the lady at the desk.

"Hi, Bobby. Who's your friend?" She wore a white shirt with wide lapels under a dark vest.

"She's from out of town. I'm showing her around."

"Hope you stay long enough for the Desert Sun opening," said the lady as Tori heaved her bags onto the counter. "Bobby's dad has been working on it like a madman."

"I heard." Tori slipped the claim tag in her pocket.

"See ya," said Bobby.

"Later, Bobby. Say hi to your mom for me."

They made their way back to the airy foyer, dominated by a fully assembled T-Rex skeleton as long as an M15 bus. Tori flexed her hands to stretch the red lines creasing her palms.

"The staff is pretty blasé considering they literally work with dinosaurs."

Bobby plucked a museum brochure from a stand and handed it to her as they continued toward the exhibit halls. "Yeah, but those are only millions of years old."

"Not billions." She stuffed it into her back pocket.

"Rookies."

"Fossil-come-latelies."

"Probably need fake IDs to buy dino-beer." Bobby pressed the button at the elevator bank. "So you've been here before? Like, when you were a kid and I wasn't?"

"I think the last time was a fourth-grade field trip." The elevator doors opened, and Tori pivoted to his side, making way for the babbling throng that poured forth. She raised her voice. "With Mrs. Moran."

"You had Mrs. Moran, too?" He held the door for her. "She was old when she taught *me*."

"Now she's ancient." Tori stepped inside. "A diamond in the rough."

A family with two strollers got on. "Press three?" said the mom. Bobby did, and hit four for himself and Tori.

After the family exited, he said, "I didn't want to say this, but—we might not be able to get in."

"Why not?"

"The exhibit doesn't open till Tuesday."

"What?"

"My dad said, remember?"

"No."

"I'll see if I can find someone who knows him."

"I need to get in."

"I know."

"That picture is my portal."

"We hope."

"It better be." Tori chewed the inside of her cheek. This would work. It had to. But would she reemerge back in her apartment, or here in the museum? In 2020, the city was in lockdown. Could she get out of the museum without triggering an alarm? What if she got arrested? If she ended up in jail, could anyone come and get her?

Alarms. Jail. Gems. Home.

"You okay?"

"Great." The elevator doors opened, and they walked out. "For a stranded, homeless time-travel refugee."

"You have me," pointed out Bobby.

"No offense, but it's not enough."

"Understandable." Bobby pursed his lips. "Well. Got any homework for Monday?"

"School's shut because of the coronavirus."

"When it opens, then."

"Um—a paper and a lab report. Why?"

"Look on the bright side. You have forty years to work on them."

Tori looked angrily at him. "You're a riot."

"Just trying to lighten the mood."

"Well, don't. This isn't funny."

"Hey, cut me some slack." Bobby's voice was sharp. "This is hard on me too, you know."

"Hard on *you?* I'm the one trying to get home!"

"You want to know how it's hard on me?" Bobby swung around to face her, and they stopped walking. "You show up in my bedroom, you know where half the stuff in my apartment is, you know things I've never told anybody, you're telling me about stuff that hasn't even happened yet, then *not* telling me half the stuff I ask you about—do you know how creepy that is?"

"Sorry." Tori bowed her head.

"And we're lying to my parents."

"Sorry. Sorry." She stared at the marble floor, clenching her fists.

"They're not stupid," said Bobby. "They'll know something's up pretty soon, if they don't already."

Tori blinked hard. What this boy was telling her was true, but it felt uncomfortably like every time her father had ever yelled at her. Especially lately. "Sorry," she whispered again.

"And then there's the emotional burden." Bobby's voice was quieter.

"What emotional burden?" she muttered.

"I'm still adjusting to the fact that I'm a teenage dad."

Tori giggled in spite of herself, and Bobby flashed her a grin that said, *Mission accomplished.* "Sorry I was a jerk," he said.

"I was probably a bigger one."

"Nah. And I have less of an excuse." He tilted his head at the corridor. "Come on. Let's get you to your magical, mystical, time-travel portal."

They turned a corner. Tori stopped mid-step as her stomach took a short stroll around her interior. A thousand heads stared at her—fleshless heads, their empty eyes glaring atop mouths spiked with jagged teeth. "What the *hell?*"

A woman holding a toddler by the hand looked daggers at her and pulled the child away. No one else seemed bothered by the demonic creatures arrayed throughout the hall.

"Hold your horses." Bobby was clearly trying not to laugh.

"*What are those things?*"

"Skeletons."

"What—"

"Of horses."

Tori willed her heart rate back into double digits. The thousand heads melted into perhaps twenty, held aloft by craggy vertebrae over barrel-like rib cages and spindly leg bones that seemed too thin to support them. Their bleak eyeholes focused on a bronzed mound of mud and bones at the center of the room. A plaque next to it read, "Evolution of the Horse. These bones were discovered in an ancient floodplain, suggesting...."

"Jesus. No wonder Mrs. Moran skipped this part. They look like Satan's nightmares."

"Shh," giggled Bobby. "People will think you're weird."

"They'd be right." She stepped close to one of the skeletons. "Wonder what happened to the rest of the horse."

"Flesh-eating bugs."

"No."

"Yes."

"This place has cannibal bugs?"

"For cleaning skeletons."

"Ewww."

"The bugs eat all the meat off the bones, so—"

"I *said* 'ewww.'"

"It's better than boiling or scraping."

"This is extremely unhelpful."

"Don't worry. They keep them locked up."

"In a super-max prison for cannibal bugs?"

Bobby appeared to consider this. "Metal boxes. But I guess it's the same thing if you ask the bug."

The Harry Frank Guggenheim Hall of Minerals and Morgan Memorial Hall of Gems was vast, crowded, and full of rocks. Nichelle waited by a mammoth chunk of blue-and-green stone that looked like something a gang of excavators might get back to after their lunch break. "Where the telekinetic diamonds at?" she greeted them.

Bobby veered toward the glittering crag as if pulled by gravity. "Have you ever seen this?"

"No." Tori scanned the hall for the new exhibit.

"It's a meteorite." Bobby gazed at it, enraptured. "My dad calls it space junk."

"Is that so?"

"But think how freaking old this thing is. And the chances it would end up on Earth?"

"Astronomical," said Nichelle.

"Right," said Bobby blissfully. "And check out these scales."

"Is he always like this?" Tori asked Nichelle.

"He's your dad. You gotta ask?"

"They show how much you'd weigh on each planet," said Bobby.

"Can we get to the diamond exhibit?" said Tori.

"Weight isn't any more fixed than time or space," said Bobby. "It depends on the density of the surface you're on."

"The diamond," said Tori. "Seriously."

As they approached the far end of the hall, her heart sped up. This was it—her portal, her way home. Goodbye, 1980; hello, 2020!

She hoped.

A banner curtaining the entrance declared, "Timeless Beauty from the Van der Bleek Collection." The O in

"Collection" was a line drawing of a diamond. The inscription, though jaunty, was clear: no one was allowed further.

"Do we break in?" said Tori.

"Probably a very bad idea," said Bobby.

"Got a better one?"

"You're the one who traveled here from a dystopian future, kid."

"Yeah, but I don't know how." She wiped her hands on her jeans.

"You were looking at a picture of it, right?" said Nichelle.

"Yeah."

"Maybe look at this one?"

"Um. Okay." She turned and gazed, unblinking. At the other end of the hall, children shrieked, strollers squeaked, and parents begged everyone to use their inside voices. Finally, she turned away from the banner, wiping her burning eyes. Bobby and Nichelle, having backed out of what they apparently judged to be the blast zone, watched from under the tall windows. "Try touching it," called Bobby.

"Good idea." She had been holding the phone the first time; maybe contact was the missing ingredient. And she was a being of configured energy, right? All she needed was the right prism.

But—what if her personal rainbow never reconverged? What if this sketch of a crystal refracted her out of existence?

She swallowed hard and brushed the picture with her fingertips.

From across the hall, a security guard coursed toward them, his uniform barely containing his muscular body. "Back off," he barked.

Tori leapt clear of from the sign, but Bobby sauntered forward unfazed, Nichelle at his side. "It's okay," he said. "My dad works here. Victor Gold?"

"So what?"

"Well, is Oscar or Claire in today?"

"Don't know, don't care."

"You can ask them—"

"I can, but I'm not gonna," said the big man. "You can come back when it opens, just like everyone else." As he spoke he walked forward, herding them away from the one place Tori needed to be.

"Look, can we—" she said as he walked them through the Hall of Gems.

"Nope."

"If we can just—"

"No."

At the horse exhibit, the guard pulled up short with a sound like a hiccup. He clenched his jaw and jerked his chin in the direction of the exit. "Out."

They left.

◈

"Well, that went great," said Tori. They huddled by the Roosevelt statue, trying to keep their backs to the March wind ricocheting down Central Park West.

Nichelle giggled into her palm. "Did you see his face when we got to the horses?"

"I thought he was just mad at me." Tori could feel her heart whirring. She couldn't tell if she was off-kilter from being in such close proximity with the diamond's picture, or from being yelled at by a museum guard the size of a geological feature.

"Oh, definitely," said Bobby. "But he did *not* like those things."

"Can't argue with him about that."

"Or anything else, apparently," said Bobby.

"We could try again in a few minutes," said Tori. "Hang out in the gift shop or whatever."

Nichelle checked her watch and sighed. "Sorry."

"Your gig?" said Bobby.

"And Katya will kill me if I'm late. However," and she gripped him by both arms, staring into his eyes, "you *will* call me later and fill me in."

"Affirmative, Captain," said Bobby.

"Nice meeting you," said Tori as Nichelle waved over her shoulder and crossed the street. She turned back to Bobby. "So—museum shop?"

He shook his head. "You tried talking to the diamond, and it didn't talk back."

"Even though your geeky friend said it would," she said wearily.

"She's trying to help, you know," he snapped.

"Huh?"

"And so am I."

"I know that!"

"Doesn't sound like it."

This was so confusing. "Then what's next?"

"Back home, I guess."

"You mean give up?" she cried.

"I mean regroup. Unless you have an angle we haven't tried." He set off down the sidewalk. "Don't sweat it," he said reassuringly. "We'll think of something."

Tori's shoulders slumped as she followed him toward the subway entrance. Her cheeks were so hot her vision fogged, and she shoved her sweating hands into her pockets, bumping her phone and the gloves from 2020.

Bobby could say whatever he wanted, but clearly he was out of ideas. So was Nichelle.

Tori was stranded.

Chapter 24

Safe and Secure

Saturday night's dinner was Chinese takeout from The Wanton Wonton. Crisp, white, paper boxes stamped with red pagodas clumped together on the lazy Susan in the center of the table, which the Golds spun to help themselves to rice, appetizers, and entrees. Louise chatted about needing the family car to visit her parents for some pre-Passover shopping, and Victor nodded along so cheerfully that Tori asked him, "Good day at work, Mr. Gold?"

Victor, who was rummaging in a box with his chopsticks, raised an eyebrow. "I didn't go to work today."

Bobby rolled his eyes. "Uh-oh."

"I thought you went to the museum," said Tori.

Victor put down his chopsticks and picked up a fork, which he waggled at her in mock severity. "Are you suggesting that I, a good Jewish poppa—a modern mensch, if you will—would work on Shabbat?"

Bobby turned an anguished face to Tori. "Run. You can still save yourself."

"The Torah tells us, 'Honor your father and mother—'"

"I'm sure Tori honors her father and mother just fine, dear," said Louise, and then looked puzzled when Tori and Bobby burst into giggles.

"Specifically in *Shemot* and *Devarim*," continued Victor, unabated. "However, as the great Rabbi Heschel points out, this is a two-way commandment."

"It is?" Tori reached for the soy sauce. Her family never talked Torah like this.

Victor nodded. "The only one, in fact. A Jewish parent must behave in a way that is honorable, or he is preventing his child—that would be you, Bobby—from being a good Jew. This is why far and wide I am known as Super Jew, the most observant observer of Shabbat." He tipped the carton over his plate, emptying two spring rolls onto it. Replacing the box on the lazy Susan, he gazed at Tori and waved his fingers under his chin as if stroking an invisible beard.

"So you didn't go to the museum?" said Tori, puzzled.

"It is just possible that I went to the museum, which is, after all, open on Saturdays." Victor spoke with great dignity. "It is further possible that I spoke, in a collegial fashion, with a number of my friends who happened to be there, and that as a result, they, who are not Jewish, took certain steps—"

"Worked," said Bobby.

"—to protect artifacts whose safety is in our hands, such that the museum can continue to operate at its best capacity."

"The righteous among the nations," said Louise. "Could you pass the rice, Bobby?"

"So you feel pretty good about the Desert Sun exhibit, Dad?" said Bobby, handing his mother the carton.

"How did you know I was working on that?" said Victor in surprise. "Not that I was working."

"You said so this morning," said Tori quickly.

"Did I?"

"Just before you left," said Bobby.

"Huh," said Victor. "Well, as it happens, I do feel pretty good about it. A few things had me a little antsy, but I managed to convince Security to take appropriate measures."

"What things?" said Bobby.

"What measures?" said Tori at the same time.

"They've really beefed everything up in the past few years," said Victor. "Remember the old alarms, Lou?"

Louise chuckled, holding her hand up to her mouth since she was eating. "So *loud*," she said.

"It used to be that every gallery had a horn," Victor explained to Tori.

"Manually operated," said Louise.

"Which meant that you had to pretty much catch someone in the act, and then hope they would obligingly stand still while you went to cry havoc. Todd—he's our security chief—felt that the system was less than optimal, but he couldn't get the Trustees to fund an upgrade. So he waited till one day when my gallery was exceptionally crowded—I think it was the Cartier exhibit—"

"Bulgari," said Louise. "Opening day."

"—and pulled the lever," said Victor. "And the blast that came out! My God, that sound would have roused an army of the dead, if we'd had one around."

"So it worked?" said Tori.

"Not at all," said Victor.

"This is New *York*, Tori," said Bobby.

"People just kept on with their sightseeing," said Victor. "The locals did what we do best, and ignored the commotion. The out-of-towners followed their lead. They had paid good money to see the jewels, and by gum, nothing was going to stop them. If it had been a real robbery, the thieves would have had to blitz their way through the throng."

"And the guards never responded," said Louise. She and Victor looked at each other, eyes bright with laughter. Tori felt her lungs tighten. The Louise she knew was a widow, an old lady who would never again share a funny story with her husband.

"At which point the Trustees decided that perhaps Todd had a point, and miraculously found the cash." Victor spun the lazy Susan, stopping at a bowl of plastic squeeze packets.

And the Victor Tori knew—well, there wasn't a Victor she knew, because he been dead her whole life. Yet here he was, chatting easily with her as he chose a sauce for his spring rolls.

"They've been listening to him ever since, more or less," went on her dead-not-dead grandfather. "Now we even have a computer! Can you believe it?"

With difficulty, Tori yanked herself back to the present. Which was also the past. "What kind of computer?"

"Honeywell, I think," said Victor. "Why?"

"I was just wondering what it does. For security, I mean."

"It's pretty amazing," said Victor. "If an alarm gets tripped, it sends a message, like a teletype, to the Security Office, and whoever's on duty decodes it."

"Sure beats the old klaxon," said Louise in awe.

"Sure does. Anyone hoping to get past that thing would need advanced technological knowledge."

Tori put down her chopsticks. "It sends a message in code?"
"Sure."
"Why?"
"It's a computer, dear," said Louise. "That's how they work."

"How long does it take to decode it?"

"But that's not all," went on Victor. "There's a camera in every gallery, and the guards can watch it from their office. Every gallery has a dedicated screen, so the whole museum is under simultaneous surveillance." He smiled and shook his head.

"Do they record?" said Tori.

"Does what record?"

"The cameras."

"Record what?"

Be polite. "Everything."

"Everything, every night?"

"Well, yeah."

"That would be an awful lot of film to warehouse, don't you think?" said Victor.

Film. Right. "Well, but in case someone wasn't looking at the right screen when something happened. Shouldn't they be able to go back? Like, to see someone's face or whatever?"

"Huh," said Victor. "That's a good point. I'll mention it to Todd on Tuesday."

"Did Mr. Dixon do anything else, Dad?" said Bobby.

"He hired a new guard—the guy is built like a volcano. Oh, and we've installed the Desert Sun."

Tori choked. "We have?"

"I talked to the Van der Bleeks. They own the collection, Tori. Wonderful people, very generous. It took a little doing, but once I described the museum's state-of-the-art protections, they came around."

Tori stared down at her chopsticks, feeling sick. Bobby glanced from her to his father. "Are you sure that's the best idea, Dad?"

"With our security system? Absolutely." Victor smiled and dug into his spring rolls. "I don't know why I didn't think of it earlier."

Chapter 25

Legend and Lore

〜◇〜

"No *Saturday Night Live* until you straighten your room."

"It's clean," said Bobby.

Louise folded her arms. "Fifteen-year-old boy clean, or mom clean?"

Bobby yanked his door shut. "It's Schrodinger's clean."

Louise's lips twitched, but she was firm. "Tidy it up, or no TV."

Bobby sighed in the manner of a prima donna who has just been informed that her scene was excised from the final cut. "Fine."

"I'll help," said Tori.

"Bobby can clean his room by himself, dear."

"Oh, I don't mind."

"She means," translated Bobby, "that she doesn't want you in my room while I'm there."

"Thank you, Bobby. That was subtle," said Louise. "If you'll excuse me, I'm going to have a cigarette." She turned and walked away.

Tori felt her cheeks flush. "Sorry."

"You forgot, and she doesn't know," said Bobby. "It's cool. Hey, while I'm doing this, you can look up the Desert Sun. Maybe we're missing something."

"How?" Tori itched to Google it, but her phone was a shingle of glass, plastic, and frustration.

"Check the *Americana*."

"The what?"

"Hey, Mom," called Bobby as he stepped into his room. "Can Tori use the encyclopedia?"

"In here," replied Louise. Tori followed her voice into the living room. Louise was sitting on the sofa, waving a paper match in the air to extinguish it. She dropped it into a glass ashtray on the coffee table, exhaling smoke through her mouth, and waved at the bookcase. "Help yourself. Middle shelf by the window."

More than a dozen blue leather volumes stared down at Tori. They were numbered but otherwise identical except for random words stamped in gold-and-black letters at their bases. *Charm-Deluc. Delusion-Frenssen. Freon-Holderlin.* "Um…."

Louise balanced her cigarette in a divot on the lip of the ashtray, and stood up. "What was it you wanted to look up, dear?"

"That diamond at the museum. We tried to see it today, but the guard wouldn't let us."

Louise pulled out a volume and handed it to her. Tori staggered and nearly dropped it. "Whoa. Is this whole thing about diamonds?"

Louise's eyes widened, but she quickly replaced her surprise with an expression that could be bottled as Perfect Hostess. "Well. Let's just look at it together."

Tori joined Louise on the sofa, wondering what she had done wrong, and trying to take only shallow breaths. The stink of smoke beclouded Grandma Louise's breath, clung to her clothes, and poofed up from the cushions when they sat. Did everyone's apartment smell like this?

"An encyclopedia is like a dictionary, only more detailed." Louise took the book onto her lap and flipped through the pages, smoke trailing from her lips. The light from the lamp on the end table made everything look soft and yellow. "You wanted to know about the Desert Sun, right?" She slid the volume over to Tori. The article was over a page long, in double columns interspersed with illustrations.

"This looks great," said Tori. "Thanks, Mrs. Gold."

"My pleasure." Louise cleared her throat. "Tori, I hope you don't mind my asking, but—have you never used an encyclopedia before?"

"Oh, I have," Tori reassured her. "Ours is just different."

"Not the *Americana*, then?"

"No."

"Which one do you have?"

"We don't have it, exactly." Or rather, everyone did, since it was online.

"So there's one at school?"

"Yours is really nice," said Tori. "I'll tell my dad about it as soon as I get home. Do you mind if I read in the dining room?"

"Of course not."

Tori took the heavy volume to the dining room table, trying to ignore the fug of smoke wafting from its pages. That poor book, she thought. Poor Bobby and Victor, breathing this crap in every day, and poor Grandma Louise for not even knowing what she was doing to herself. But it was normal, wasn't it? For 1980? She bent her head to read.

183

> *The Desert Sun is one of the largest diamonds in the world, as famous for its history as for its unusual size and yellow color. The earliest descriptions of the stone center on an area which produces many of the world's diamonds.*

Nothing new here, Tori thought with a sigh. Maybe Wikipedia had used the *Americana* as a source.

"Checking up on my favorite diamond?" said Victor.

Tori jumped. She hadn't heard him come in behind her. "Your fave—oh. Yes, sir."

Victor glanced at the book open before her. "Not a bad little article, if I do say so."

"Huh?"

He pulled up a chair and sat down, pointing to the name at the bottom of the page. *Victor Gold.*

Tori gawked. "You *wrote* this?"

"A few years ago. Publishing is a very slow business."

"Bobby never told me you were a writer."

"I'm not, primarily. But I was pretty flattered when they asked me to pen this particular entry, I can tell you. Are you interested in gems?"

"I am now," said Tori. "Why is this one your favorite?"

Victor smiled, leaning back in his chair. "Do you have a best friend?"

"Sure."

"And she's a little different from, let's say, your second-best friend."

"Of course."

"Every gemstone is unique too," said Victor. "It can take a long time to get to know one and really grasp life's impact on them. They're kind of like people that way."

Tori smiled. "Now I know you're kidding me. Gems don't change over time." Life's impact on a chunk of minerals? As if.

"Don't they?" said Victor. "Life and minerals have been sharing the same planet for billions of years, side by side. It would be a little odd if they didn't affect each other over that span of centuries, don't you think?"

"I never thought of it that way." With an internal click, her understanding of diamonds—cold, inert, eternal—morphed into something far more fluid and dynamic.

"The living and the nonliving certainly seem to be opposites, but they're connected in ways we're barely beginning to understand," said Victor. "Some of those nonliving things are gems, of course. That means each one has its own past, its own process of evolution, that makes it unique. If you combine those natural qualities with the genius of a great craftsman, well, it can take your breath away. Each gem looks different, is cut differently, set differently. They sparkle differently. A beautiful gemstone in a perfect setting is a work of art, just like Michelangelo's David or the Mona Lisa. It's probably why so many have legends."

"Legends?"

"Medieval people believed diamonds had healing properties. People wore them for protection. Warriors thought having a diamond would make them invincible, because of the stone's extraordinary hardness. All kinds of stuff."

"Isn't there one with a curse?"

"Lots. But I think you're thinking of the Hope Diamond. It's at the Smithsonian."

"I heard a bunch of the owners were murdered or killed themselves."

Victor chuckled. "Cursed gemstones are a publicist's stock in trade."

"You mean the stories are made up?"

"The Hope Diamond's are. But not the Desert Sun's. The details get a bit fuzzy, I admit, but I can allow it because it's a lovely story."

"And that's why it's your favorite."

"Sure. The beauty, the mythos—it all comes together."

"I bet you had to do a lot of research for the encyclopedia article," said Tori, glancing at the columns of print.

"I bet you're right."

"Did you ever get bored with it?"

"No," said Victor. "You can never get jaded about gems."

Tori looked at him. "That was terrible. Sir."

"Thank you. And hold on just a moment." Victor left the room, returning to hand her a sheaf of typewritten pages. The paper was crinkly, and she could feel bumps on the back where the typewriter keys had punched it. "So cool," she marveled, running her fingers over it.

Victor laughed. "I'd be more convinced if you read it first."

"What? Oh, right." She smiled, feeling sheepish.

"It's an early draft for the text of the exhibit. You can keep it if you like—Bobby tells me you won't be able to see the show."

"Thanks, Mr. Gold. Mind if I read it now?"

"I'll leave you to do just that." He left, and she pulled off the paperclip to turn the pages.

Stealing Time

But who first discovered this extraordinary gem? Legend states that many centuries ago, a peace-seeking pilgrim suffering from melancholy determined to visit a certain holy place in the hopes of assuaging her sad and restless heart. She packed all the food she had, which was just enough to reach the site and return, and set out on her journey.

Upon reaching the holy place, she found a group of families. A pestilence had destroyed their meager supplies, and babies wept with hunger as their mothers rocked them helplessly.

Moved to pity, the pilgrim decided to give the group all her food, even though this meant she herself would have none for her voyage home. She rushed to gather rocks for a fire pit to cook for them. As she lifted one particularly heavy stone, a hot spring gushed from beneath it, giving forth a scent like cloves and heavenly spices. Drawn by the aroma, the starving families brought their bowls and drank deeply. Their hunger was instantly sated, so they no longer needed the pilgrim's food, though they thanked her for her generosity.

In this moment, the pilgrim realized she could be joyful by helping others. As she made this discovery, the stone that she still held in her hand turned into an enormous diamond, flashing light and rainbows from its golden heart.

The pilgrim sold the diamond to a ruler in a distant land for a great amount of treasure. With this in hand, she returned to the site of the miracle, and built a school for the indigent, and a hostel for weary pilgrims who even to this day come to the remarkable spring to bathe in its waters and drink its scented liquid.

Meanwhile, many thousands of miles away in the desert land, the ruler had his most skilled jewelers cut and polish the diamond. They set the smaller fragments in jewelry, but the largest one stood alone. The ruler named it the Desert Sun. It has been associated with miracles and kindness ever since, being said to protect families and make fortunate the unfortunate.

The American Museum of Natural History is proud to be able to share this remarkable gem with the public for the first time. We hope you enjoy its beauty and brilliance as people all around the world have for hundreds of years.

Tori put down the last page, astonished to find she was crying. Victor had written this, and what was it about? Beauty. Love. Miracles. Not a word about greed or personal gain.

Were these the words of a jewel lover, or a jewel thief? Or both?

The door swung open, and Victor walked in. "Oh, no," he said. "Are you all right?"

"I'm fine," Tori sniffled. She pushed the papers together and handed them to him. "That's a really nice story, Mr. Gold. Is that what you were talking to Dr. Hopewell about?"

"Who?"

"Dr. Hopewell. You said you talked to security today."

"I did." Victor slid the paperclip back onto the sheaf. "But there's no one at the museum by that name."

Chapter 26

Meanwhile, Back at the Hotel

"The first two floors have alarms." Teresa tapped her sketchpad with the eraser end of a pencil. One page held a soft, charcoal rendering of the Hall of Gems; the other, a schematic of the fourth floor of the museum. "You can use that construction shit on the West 77th side to get past them."

"And come in a window?" Gloria sat on one side of Teresa, Mike on the other.

Teresa shook her head. "They boarded them up on that side."

"I guess they fear the criminal element," said Gloria.

"Plus, it's on the other side of the museum from the rocks."

"Any cams?" Maeve tilted her head to look at the sketchbook. She was on the other side of the table, and Teresa turned the book around so it was right-side up for her.

"All over the Hall of Gems," said Mike. "But only during business hours."

"For real?" said Maeve.

A small curl lifted the right corner of Mike's mouth. "That's when people are at the museum, boss."

"Holy shit."

"Gets better," said Teresa.

Mike pointed to the sketch. "All the vitrines have sensors."

"All the what?" said Gloria.

"The glass cases with loot in them."

"Look at you, all talking like a museum guard," she said admiringly.

"Lots of training for the new hires," said Mike. "They even showed me which end of the broom to hold."

"So how is that good news?" said Maeve.

"The sensors get turned off at night too." The curl in Mike's lip blossomed into a full-blown smirk. "What with energy prices being so high."

"Jesus," laughed Maeve.

"And even if they decide to run everything, there's no cams in the staff hallway off the exhibit," said Mike. He and Teresa had scoped it out. Her cover story was she was looking for a bathroom; his, that he had found her wandering around lost and was guiding her back to the public areas. But luck had been on their side, and no one had interrupted their sneak-and-peek.

Teresa tapped the sketchbook again. "So I hide in this closet here, right before closing on Sunday. Mike's already taped down the bolt."

"Watergate style," said Maeve.

"Hell, yeah," said Mike. "We even got our own Cuban burglar." Gloria acknowledged the compliment with a tip of her beer bottle.

"The other guard finishes his round at eleven forty-five. Then me and Mike take out this AC," Teresa pointed, "and let you guys in."

"Love it," said Maeve. "So while we do the smash and grab—"

"—I and Mike take the plywood off a window on the West 77th side, and we get out that way," said Teresa. "Soon as we're in the clear, Mike finds the busted plywood and raises hell."

"Call Barney Miller," suggested Gloria. "He's always so smiley."

"Great work, guys," said Maeve. "Day after, we blow this popsicle stand and get to the Port Authority on 42nd and 8th. No way can we take cabs—from what Snake says, that parade fucks up the entire island, so we hoof it on the subway, but take different trains. Ignore each other at the bus station, got it? No contact, no looking at each other. Nothing to make anyone remember any of us or all of us. We take different busses to get back home, and meet up at my place Wednesday afternoon. Any questions?"

"Yeah." Mike glared at the slight man sitting next to her. "Why does *he* have to be here?"

"He's our wheels." Maeve's shoulder was touching Snake's.

"And the whole thing was my idea," said Snake. "Plus half the planning. If it wasn't for me, you'd still be hitting the place Monday."

"He's a weasel."

"But cute," said Snake. "Girls love me."

"What girls?" said Teresa.

"And how much did you pay them?" said Gloria.

"Dunno, sweetheart." Snake took a pull on his beer. "How much you usually charge?"

Gloria leaped to her feet. Mike's arm flicked, and suddenly he had a blade in his hand, short and dark and evil-looking.

Snake was impressed. "Where were you *hiding* that?"

"I know where I'd like to hide it now."

"Simmer the fuck down, everybody," said Maeve. She half-stood, touching Mike's wrist. Still glaring at Snake, he pulled aside his windbreaker and slipped the knife back into a leather shoulder holster. Maeve nodded at the sofa, and Gloria sat down. Her cheeks were dark with rage, and her eyes glittered.

"Everybody. Listen to me." Maeve looked at the circle of faces around the coffee table. "This here? This is the kind of shit that will tank the whole operation. You don't have to like Snake. You don't have to like anybody in this room, including me. But if you can't work with *everybody* in this room, then we're screwed. Understand?"

"Make him apologize." Gloria clenched her fists in her lap.

"Sorry," said Snake.

"Like you mean it, asshole."

"I was out of line," said Snake. "Sorry, Gloria. See? I said it again."

"All set?" said Maeve.

"No," said Gloria. "I don't want to work with this bastard."

"Makes two of us," said Mike. "Teresa, how about you?"

"Oh, for crying out loud," said Snake. "I said I was sorry."

"You sure are," said Gloria.

"Gloria," began Maeve.

"He can't talk to me that way!"

"I won't," said Snake. "It won't happen again, I swear."

"Like I should believe you."

"Believe it. I need this job."

"We all do," said Teresa.

"I need it more."

"It's all about you, isn't it?" said Gloria.

"Yeah. And that's why you can trust me."

"What's that supposed to mean?"

"Think about it." Snake rolled the beer bottle between his palms. "This all works, and what happens? You all head back to sunny Florida and open your surf shop. Tell everyone you found a—what was it, babe?"

"Silent partner," said Maeve.

"Silent partner, right."

"From another swimwear company."

"Right. Who won't go public about his arrangement with you because of the conflict of interest. Dynamite." The corner of his mouth twitched up. "I forget. Was Cheryl Tiegs involved?"

"Maybe," said Maeve. "We haven't decided yet."

"Either way." Snake set his bottle down next to Teresa's schematic of the Hall of Gems. "Me? If this doesn't work, I'm a dead man."

"Right now, you're a live drama queen," said Mike.

"Stop," said Maeve. "You know who loves a gang that's always fighting?"

"Cops," said Snake.

"Damn right, cops. So are we working together? Yes or no."

"The guy's a shit," said Mike.

"A minute ago, I was a weasel," said Snake.

"I'm with Mike," said Gloria.

Snake gazed at the gang. The gang gazed back.

"That's two against," said Maeve finally. "Teresa?"

Teresa sighed and looked at Gloria, who sat, still tight with rage, on the edge of the sofa. "Don't hate me for this."

"Terri!"

"I need the money."

"Thanks," said Snake. "I always knew you had brains to match the pretty."

"Damn right." Teresa raised her hands in a Time Out gesture and scowled at him. "So before I say yes—if I even do—I got a question."

"Shoot."

"Why should I trust a guy who'd hang his own family out to dry for a job?"

Snake tossed his head back and laughed. "Is that all?"

"Where I come from, family matters."

"Yeah? Where I come from, it's a two-way street."

"What's that supposed to mean?"

"Do you know how many times that prick's hung *me* out to dry?" said Snake. "I did my first hard time because of him. For all I know, he called the cops on me. Or she did. I never found out."

"So now you get to return the favor, is that it?" said Teresa.

"It's not the same thing."

"Tell that to the guy twisting in the wind."

"Puh-lease. I'm not turning him in."

"The cops might see it kind of different."

"He might not even be implicated."

"Wouldn't break your heart if he was, though, would it?"

"Not really, no."

"Sweet."

"It's not that big a deal for him."

"Are you for real?"

"Sure. Nice guy like that, no record, he gets a slap on the wrist. Few months at the most."

"Explain to me again how this isn't hanging him out to dry."

"Okay, then, let's say it's me who gets caught—which it won't be if we get our shit together," he said. "I got two possible outcomes. One is I go up the river. Fuck only knows for how long. Second is, I can't pay No-Name, and next thing you know my new nickname is No-Thumbs."

"You forgot option three," said Teresa. "No thumbs *and* up the river."

"I like option three," said Mike.

"So you see my point," said Snake. "I go away, it's the end of the line. He goes away, it's, like, maybe half a year, max, and he gets to waltz right back where he started, thumbs and all."

Snake collapsed back into his love seat. Wind whistled past the elegant windows.

"I'm in," said Maeve. "Teresa?"

"I guess so," she said reluctantly. "I don't trust him, though."

"After tomorrow night, you don't have to. Gloria? Mike?"

Gloria shrugged. "I don't even have bus fare back to the Village. I'm in."

"You're the boss," said Mike. "But tell him to keep his cakehole shut."

"Think you can do that, Snake?" said Maeve.

"Like the man said," said Snake. "You're the boss."

Chapter 27

Saturday Night Lively

〜 ◇ 〜

"The earlier seasons were much funnier," lamented Bobby. He and Tori were stretched out on the floor of the study, midway through the hundredth episode of *Saturday Night Live*. The boxy TV with its multiple dials had momentarily intrigued her, but when Bobby turned it on she had annoyed him by laughing wildly at a douche commercial that she thought was a skit. The show's cold open, about a séance involving former cast members, had been mildly amusing, but the show had devolved rapidly from there. "Weekend Update" had focused largely on the hostage crisis, but it was hard to see how putting hats on an effigy of the leader of Iran was going to bring anybody home. And an Irish-American senator reading a labored story called "The Biggest Leprechaun" only served to remind her that St. Patrick's Day was coming, which meant the weekend was drawing to a close and she was still stuck in 1980.

"Can you pause it for a minute?" she said finally. "I need the bathroom."

"Yeah, sure." Bobby did not take his eyes from the screen.

"Oh, c'mon," said Tori after a moment during which the show continued unabated.

Bobby's lips tightened as he jumped up to twist a dial next to the screen. The TV grew louder. "Trying to watch here."

"I need to go to the bathroom."

"So go." Bobby settled on the floor again, eyes on the screen.

"It's not even good. You said so yourself."

"Do you mind?"

"Yeah, I do. Just hit pause." What a jerk her dad could be.

"Hit pause on *what?*"

With an internal oops, Tori processed the fact that Bobby had gotten to his feet to adjust the volume. "You don't have a remote?"

"Apparently not."

"Oh. Well, it's this thing that—"

Bobby cut her off. "We don't have a clicker—that's what you mean, right?—but even if we did, there's no way to pause the TV or make it run backwards or forwards or sideways. The only way to watch a show is by *watching* it, which is what I'm trying to do. If you want to make a pit stop, you can wait till the commercial break or miss some of the show."

Dazed, Tori made her way to the bathroom. Imagine having to time your potty breaks around the whims of TV executives. And what about shows with no commercials? Were 1980 bladders made of Kevlar?

And that wasn't the only stupid thing about this decade. The way her grandparents had cooed over the museum's security— a computer with encrypted teletype, cameras that didn't record, guards who ignored alarms—well, it set her teeth on edge just thinking about it.

Was it possible that her grandfather, who was smart enough to write encyclopedia articles and talk Torah over dinner, was really that dense? Or was he a criminal mastermind posing as a charming old duffer? If it was an act, it certainly seemed to have fooled Bobby. She felt sorry for him.

"I feel sorry for her," said Louise.

Tori paused, hand on the bathroom doorknob. The door to Victor and Louise's bedroom was ajar.

"Why?" said Victor. "Seems like a nice kid."

"A nice kid who's being raised by wolves."

Wolves? What did Louise mean?

"What do you mean?" said Victor.

Louise dropped her voice so Tori had to strain to hear. "Everything about her screams of a child who's been alternately spoiled and ignored."

"Nonsense. She's polite enough."

"But the summer camp, the hair—"

Tori tucked her purple streak behind her ear.

"Oh, come," Victor scoffed. "Plenty of kids her age experiment with their looks. And what's wrong with Camp Ramah?"

"Nothing."

"Good, because Bobby would pitch a fit if we told him he couldn't go this year."

Tori winced. By summer, Bobby was going to have problems no camp could solve.

"Camp isn't the only thing we're giving Bobby."

"I'm sure Tori's parents give her more than camp too."

Mostly ulcers.

"You should have seen her this evening—she acted like she'd never seen an encyclopedia before," said Louise.

"She got the hang of it pretty quickly, then."

"I'm serious."

"So am I. She and I had a nice chat about the Desert Sun."

Sure did.

"Don't you see how uneven everything is with her? She's overly polite, she goes to an expensive summer camp but she doesn't seem to go to school—"

"You said you thought her parents were getting divorced."

OMG!

"I still do."

How did she figure that out?

"It's not uncommon these days," said Victor in a tone that said this conversation was well-traveled territory.

"Or else she's a latchkey kid whose mother and father are buying her affections instead of instilling values and education."

Wait. What?

"Have you talked to her?"

What's a latchkey kid?

"You know I have."

Is that like a burglar?

"Talk a little more," he suggested. "Maybe she'll open up to you."

If he really is a crook, then her calling me one is seriously ironic.

"Do you think so?" said Louise.

Go for it, Grandma. Sympathize with the juvenile delinquent from a crappy family!

The phone rang. "I'll get it," said Victor. His shadow fell across the doorway, and Tori ducked into the bathroom, fuming. *A latchkey burglar with no values or education. Great.*

When she came out, still twitching with irritation, Bobby was surreptitiously hanging up the receiver in the study. Tori shut the door behind her, raising her eyebrows.

"Uncle Jacob," said Bobby in a low voice. "He's worried about the Desert Sun."

"He's not the only one," muttered Tori.

"So my dad told him about the cameras and stuff. Then Dad asked him how he knew about the robbery, but Jacob wouldn't give us up." Bobby glanced at his wristwatch. "We don't have to watch the rest of the show if you don't want."

"Why doesn't Jacob just ask Dr. Hopewell? She's the head of security."

"No, that's Todd Dixon."

"Who?"

"Dixon. I've met him a million times."

Bits of the family's dinner conversation floated back to her. *Todd—he's our security chief...Did Mr. Dixon do anything else, Dad?* The skin on the backs of her hands tingled as a series of dreadful tumblers clicked into place, and she ran her fingers through her hair, untucking the purple streak in her distraction.

"What's the matter?" said Bobby.

She lowered her trembling hands. "Your dad didn't know who Dr. Hopewell was."

"Get real." Bobby leaned against his father's desk. "He knows everyone at the museum."

Tori shook her head. "He told me no one by that name worked there."

"You must have said it wrong."

"I didn't." She pushed away from the door and paced in the tiny circle that the crowded study allowed. "Oh, God."

"What's the problem?"

"Bobby," she cried, "if the head of security is Todd Dixon, then who the hell is Dr. Hopewell?"

Chapter 28
Sherlock Grandma

Louise appeared in the doorway, knotting the sash of her bathrobe. "Everything all right?"

"Fine," said Bobby with an anxious glance at Tori.

"Fine," said Tori. Her heart rattled, and her chest clenched tight. *Breathe.* This was terrible. *Breathe, breathe.*

"I thought I heard a shout."

"Something about who's the doctor?" said Bobby.

"That's right."

He waved at the TV. "Sketch about an MD with VD."

"And nurses," said Tori helpfully. *What's VD?*

Louise gave an exaggerated shudder. "Lovely."

Very Dangerous? Violently Delicious?

"It was pretty stupid." Bobby turned the TV off.

I will definitely have to Google that when I get home. Home. Oh, God—!

"It's a far cry from Allen's Alley," sighed Louise. "Ah, well. This too shall pass."

"The earlier seasons were funnier," said Tori. *Sound like 1980, sound like 1980.*

Louise beamed at her. "You know, they film that show not far from here."

"Oh?" *Plus, I definitely said Hopewell's name right.*

"One of my old college roommates works at the network," said Louise. "She gave us a behind-the-scenes tour a few years back, when Bobby had a school project about New York landmarks."

"I know." *How can you say "Hopewell" wrong? Hope. Well. Say, isn't it past your bedtime, Grandma?*

"Oh, did I already tell you? Forgive me—I have a terrible habit of boring people with stories I've already told them before."

"No, no." *Wellhope? I did not say Wellhope.* "Dad told me."

Louise laughed. "Your father seems to have very detailed intelligence about our family."

Behind his mother, Bobby rolled his eyes in a silent frenzy. Tori blushed. "No, I mean—he said they film at 30 Rock."

"Oh, so he knows the nickname."

"We were just thinking about going to bed," said Bobby.

"Well, sure. He's a New Yorker."

Louise's smile dissolved. "I thought you said you were from Massachusetts."

Shit. "I am, but my dad's from New York."

"Oh? What part?"

Shit shit. "Close to here."

"How close?"

Really close. "My grandfather runs a card shop on a side street near Madison Square Garden."

"He does?" said Bobby.

Tori hesitated for half a twinkling. "Yes. He does."

Bobby pursed his lips into a prune shape.

"You know, I don't think I ever asked you what your father does," said Louise.

Tori lifted her chin, pleased to be able to show Grandma Louise she was from a good family with nice parents. "He's a certified information privacy manager."

Bobby gawped, trying to mouth the words "certified information privacy manager." Louise arched her brows. "He's a—what did you say?"

"He helps companies with privacy."

"Oh? How so?"

"He runs a data protection team that creates algorithms for online framework operations."

Bobby buried his head in his hands. Tori said quickly, "And my mom's a lawyer." *That was a thing in 1980, right?*

Usually at this point people would say, "Oh? What kind?" and then they would discuss criminal law versus corporate versus contract while Tori braced for the inevitable onslaught of lawyer jokes. But Louise said only, "I see."

"So they both have, ah, pretty cool jobs."

"And your mother is the one from Massachusetts?"

"Near Boston."

"But your grandfather lives in this area, you said?"

"Mom," cut in Bobby, "it's getting late."

"So this is your father's father we're talking about, yes?"

"That's right."

"I thought you said Bobby is the only other person you knew in New York."

Shit shit shit. "He—is."

"What about your grandfather?"

"What about him?" *Stall, think, think, stall.*

"Tori, you can stay with us any time you want. But if you have family nearby, why didn't you call them?"

Tori resisted the urge to wipe her sweaty palms on her jeans. "He died."

"He did?"

"Died. Did. Yes. Dead."

"When was this, dear?"

"Mom!"

"Recently," gabbled Tori. "Did I say he *runs* that shop? I should have said he *ran* it. I'm still not used to him being gone. Sorry." She turned her head aside, blinking rapidly.

"Well, Mom," said Bobby in the silence that followed, "I think we've all learned a valuable lesson here."

"I'm so sorry dear." Louise sounded genuinely distressed. "Bobby can tell you I do this sort of thing all the time."

"Amen," said Bobby.

"That's okay." Tori lifted her head. "I just—forget sometimes that other people don't know about him."

"If he was an important person in your life, it makes sense you'd still carry him with you." Bobby's mother smiled Grandma Louise's smile, and it caught in Tori's chest. "Well, it sounds like you two are getting ready to call it a night, so I'll leave you to it."

Chapter 29

Finishing up the Interrogation

As soon as Louise had left the room, Bobby sat down heavily and spread his hands in a gesture that in 2020 could only have meant, *WTF, dude?* "Certified information piracy manager?"

"Privacy."

"Next time come up with something more believable."

"I'm not making it up."

"You're not?"

"No."

He rubbed his ear. "Is it a cool job?"

"No."

"So you *were* making stuff up."

"Only the adjectives."

"And that shit about my dad running a card shop." He chuckled, but she only twiddled a loose thread on the cuff of the too-large Mets sweatshirt she was wearing. He stopped. "Tori?"

"What?"

"You made that up too, right?"

"Nope."

"Seriously?"

"Seriously."

Bobby jumped up, outrage propelling him to his feet. "What the hell is my dad doing running a fucking card shop?"

"There's no shame in—"

"Like, baseball cards and crap like that?"

"It's a neat store," she said to her sleeve. "You showed me once."

"If it's such a neat store, how come you won't look at me?"

She raised her chin. "Look, maybe it doesn't happen," she said to the ceiling. "I mean, if we can stop the—"

"My dad's a gemologist."

"I know."

"He works at one of the best museums in New York. In the *world*."

"I know, I know."

"What the fuck happened?"

"Things change," she whispered.

Bobby leaned forward, his usually sunny face grim. "This is my family we're talking about, Tori. This is my life."

"It's mine too!"

"Not yet, it isn't."

"Look, I don't think I'm supposed to tell you this stuff." She had probably said too much already. Her revelations had clearly changed Bobby's understanding of his world, which meant that 1980 was now different, which meant 2020 might be too. Who knew where the ripple effect would end? Any further meddling might erase her from the timeline completely. Or start World War Three, or make it so the Nobel Prize went to Madonna instead of Malala. Who knew? Time travel was possible, so nothing was impossible.

"Just say what happens to my dad."

"I guess running the card shop is the only thing he can do after—" She stopped.

"After *what?*"

Tori clenched her hands inside the sleeves of the drooping sweatshirt. The hell with staying silent. "Who's Hopewell?"

"Answer my question, Future Girl."

"Answer mine first."

"Hopewell's an expert my uncle knows."

"More expert than Todd Dixon, the head of museum security?"

Bobby hesitated. "Well, maybe he wouldn't play ball, so Jacob found someone else. And look, she listened to us, right?"

"She sure did." Tori buried her head in her hands.

"Now what's wrong?"

"What's wrong?" Tori lifted her head, shaking. "Hopewell bamboozled everyone. She's no museum minion. She's a crook, and we told her how to steal the exhibit. I'm sure of it. Oh, God, we were so *stupid.*"

Bobby's face split into a grin as bright as Times Square. "Cool! Now we know who the bad guy is."

"It's not cool, Bobby. She gets away with it."

"How?"

"I don't know—I never finished reading the article!"

"What article?"

"About the heist. It wrecks *everything.*" Tori leaped to her feet, waving her arms at the cheerful office. "This place? It's never the same." Bobby opened his mouth to speak, but she plunged on. "You've got this, this nice life here with your mom and dad and—and Camp Ramah in the summers, and a college fund—and in my world it's gone." She glanced at the study door and lowered her voice, whisper-screaming the rest. "Your dad gets arrested, Bobby."

"No way." He stared, eyes wide.

"It wrecks his life."

"But he can just tell them the truth."

"He does. Nobody believes him. It's a shitshow. He gets fired. He can't work. You get into MIT, and you can't go because your folks spend everything on lawyers, but it doesn't work, it doesn't work—he goes to jail. For *years*. And your mom—"

"What about my mom?" said Bobby sharply.

"She's hooked up to an oxygen tank. Lung damage. Been that way my whole life. She can barely move." Tori's chest convulsed. She drew a jagged breath and then another. Tears spattered from her eyes. "All I can—fucking—recognize about her—here, now—is her smile...."

Bobby looked sick. "What about my dad?"

Tori sat down again, twisting her hands. "He loses all his friends."

"No."

"And his income, from what I can tell. And—and I don't think you ever get over it, because you're always kind of an asshole, frankly."

Bobby sat down, face white. "I am?" he barely whispered.

Tori's stomach writhed, and she swallowed hard before giving a short, hard nod. How many times had she longed to tell her father what a jerk he was, how he devastated her and Adina with his bleak moods and unending criticism? It would feel so good, she had always thought. Instead, she had hurt Bobby.

"But you said we watched *Star Trek* together," he protested.

"I never said I liked it."

"You don't?"

Tori wanted to howl at the ceiling. "No! It's stupid and sexist, and the jokes are crap." She buried her head in the crook of her arm. "I wanted to watch *Phineas and Ferb*. And you wouldn't let me." Her breaths grated in her ears, and the clock on the shelf ticked as though it were connected to a bomb.

"I'm sorry," said Bobby finally. "I mean it. I'm really sorry."

She snorted. Bobby might be sorry, but Bob never was.

"Well—how bad is it?" he said.

Tori lifted her head, glaring. "Bad enough that now, in my world, you and Mom are getting divorced." She swiped at the tears that dripped from her jawline. "When I—came here—she was packing to leave. I'm going with her. And it really *sucks*, Dad."

Bobby folded his arms, hugging himself and breathing heavily. "What else?"

"That's not enough?"

"It's plenty, but there's more."

"No, there isn't."

"You sure of that?"

Tori met his gaze. "Absolutely."

Bobby said, "When you're trying not to say something, you lower your right eyebrow."

"What? No, I don't."

"Yeah, you do. You did it the first night you were here and we were doing dishes, and you did it again in the record store when I asked if the Beatles got back together."

"Fine," she snapped. "I promise not to become a professional poker player."

Bobby looked at her steadily. "What's your name?"

She stared at the window over his shoulder. "Tori. You know that."

"Your full name."

She hung her head. "Victoria."

She could hear him breathing. Finally he said, "You're named after my dad."

"Yes," she whispered.

"So he's…"

She looked up at him. "Yes."

"My God," said Bobby. "Oh, my God."

Chapter 30

Wheeler Dealer

An attendant backed a green Buick into a slot at forty miles an hour, slamming to a halt inches before his bumper and the one behind it mated for life. The sound of screaming tires filled the air.

"Jesus *Christ*, Danny, watch what the hell you're doin'!" bellowed Leo from the office doorway. The concrete crypt of the parking garage surrounded him with its gray walls, gray floor, gray machinery to lift and shift cars. Hell, even their caps and uniforms were gray, and Leo was acutely aware that his hair and mustache had faded to match them. He'd once taken a color photo down here, and people had thought it was a black-and-white.

Danny flashed him a peace sign and slipped sideways between the two parked cars. Good thing he was so skinny, thought Leo. Fat kids didn't last long down here. But should he really have parked that VW Rabbit in that spot? The owner hadn't used it for months. Maybe better to put it more in the rear. What a way to start Sunday morning.

As Danny leaped into a yellow Ford Pinto, thwacking the stick into reverse, Leo realized his phone was ringing. He shut the door and picked up the receiver. "Qwik Parking."

"Yeah, hi. I need my car for tonight."

"No problem." Leo reached for his locator list. "License number?"

"X731664."

"Hold on." Leo put on his glasses and ran his finger down the sheet. The list was alphabetical by license plate, but since their secretary quit six months ago, any new vehicles were penciled in by hand at the end. "Say that again?"

The voice said it again. "Gray Saab," he added.

He sounded impatient. Stressed. Well, weren't they all? Leo's finger stopped on a smudgy line. "Got it. When you need it, boss? I'm backed up here."

"Eight-thirty."

"Tomorrow morning?"

"Tonight."

"Jesus. Can you come in earlier?" Sunday was the worst night of the week, with Manhattanites coming back from ski weekends in the winter and Long Island beach parties in the summer. They all seemed to show up at the same time, double-parking up and down the block, pissing off the neighbors and helping the cops meet their ticket quotas. Plus, tonight marked New York's start on Saint Patrick's Day. There weren't enough tips in the world to make this worthwhile.

"If I wanted it earlier, I'd ask for it earlier."

"It ain't gonna be easy." Besides, Leo had plans, ones that didn't involve green beer. Tonight's game started at 8:00, Rangers versus St. Louis Blues. An 8:30 pickup would punch a big hole in that.

The voice got louder. "How long does it take to find a friggin' car?"

A red Stingray squealed around the corner and up the ramp. "Hold up." Leo put his finger in his free ear and checked his watch. When the car had vanished into what might be daylight—Leo had no way to be sure; might be a total eclipse going on for all he knew—he said, "Yeah, okay. I'll put Danny on it." Danny wasn't a hockey fan. Didn't even care about the Miracle on Ice, which had made the whole damn world hockey fans, including Leo.

"'Preciate it."

"No problem." Leo glanced at the name next to the license number on the sheet. "See you tonight, Mr. Gold."

Chapter 31

Sunday Morning

～ ◆ ～

"Could we tell the cops?" said Tori. It was Sunday morning, and they were back in the study. The sky was smudged with gray, and wind rattled the window. "Maybe we could call in an anonymous tip."

"Forget the cops." Bobby leaned against the desk, arms folded. "Maybe in 2020 they're knights in white satin, but right now they're thugs in blue uniforms. Even if we found any who believed us, they'd just want a cut of the take."

Tori lay back on the sofa, eyes itching with exhaustion. She and Bobby had stayed up late, and what sleep she had scraped from the night had been shallow and restless. "How about your dad?"

"Imagine for just a moment how that conversation would go."

"We could try."

"He already knows about the heist, and all that did was make him install the diamond early so now the crooks can get at it." Bobby sighed and stared out the window, his heavy brows furrowed.

"You're right," mused Tori. "It's right there at the museum."

"Yup."

"Begging to be stolen."

"Yup."

"Or saved."

"Huh?"

Tori pushed herself to a seated position. "If the bad guys can get to the Desert Sun, we can too."

"Now, hold on a minute," said Bobby in alarm.

"We need to rescue that gem."

"So you can get home. I know."

Tori waved away his words. "We don't even know if that would work. I mean, we assume it would, but who knows? You said my time might not even exist. I'm talking about *this* time, here and now."

"I don't follow you."

"When—if—the heist happens, your dad gets blamed, and you and your mom get screwed. So we need to stop it from happening, which means we need to get the diamond somewhere safe."

Bobby's eyes widened. "Are you saying we should steal it?"

"Not in the traditional sense, no."

"What nontraditional sense are you thinking, then?"

"Just take it and hide it somewhere till after the robbery. They can't blame your dad for stealing it if it never gets stolen."

"Forget it." Bobby held up a hand in the manner of one being assailed by too many new ideas at once. "And besides, what about you?"

"Let's talk about you for a minute."

"I'm already home," he pointed out. "Not stranded forty years out of whack."

"A home where a shitstorm is about to make landfall."

"Gosh, you're fun."

"Look. Getting the diamond might help me, but it *will* help you. And you guys matter. To me." She gulped. "So—why not?"

Bobby sat down next to her on the sofa. "So you're saying we should do a preemptive heist?"

"Got a better idea?"

She watched him anxiously. Her father, the anti-shenanigator, would never be up for something so crazy. But what about this kid?

Bobby drew a long sigh. "Usually Sunday nights I do homework and listen to Dr. Demento," he said. "But I guess I can make an exception just this once."

⋽ ◇ ⋼

Not since landing in 1980 had Tori so yearned for the Internet, with its promise of detailed, 3D schematics of the museum, complete with overlays showing conveniently placed (and sized) ductwork. She would even have welcomed a precocious kid clicking madly on a keyboard and barking, "We're in!"

"People do that?" said Bobby. They had moved to the dining room, which gave them a table and the advantage of being further away from his parents, who were still asleep.

"Sure. In movies."

"Oh, so it's like when somebody says to the hero, 'You don't get it, do you?'"

"Or 'You have no idea what you're up against,'" she giggled.

"And the guy who's about to retire—"

"—dies. Or an extra wears a red shirt to beam down to the planet."

Bobby laughed in delight. "Yeah. Or the drunk, divorced maverick cop—"

"—who still saves New York—"

"—or LA—"

"—even though his incompetent boss—"

"—takes his gun and badge!" They said the last part together, racing through the words. Bobby won, but only because Tori was laughing so hard.

"Or how about the crazy Vietnam vet?" he went on. "God, they're all over the place. Did you see *Apocalypse Now?*"

"No."

"It made it seem like being completely unhinged was a prerequisite for serving in the armed forces."

"Or how about anything you hide behind is bulletproof? Trash cans, tabletops, paper bags—"

"Of course, it helps to have a sexy woman with you at the time."

"Who's usually the only one in the whole movie," said Tori. "My mom calls it 'Princess Leia Syndrome.'"

"Huh," said Bobby. "Now that you mention it...."

"Like, how do they reproduce on Tatooine? Seriously."

"How about bad guys who can't shoot straight?"

"You're never safer than in the cross-hairs of a Stormtrooper," agreed Tori. "Wow, you'd think they'd have come up with some new clichés by now."

"Let's talk about it later," said Bobby. "Like in 2020."

"Deal." Tori bent over the brochure spread out on the dining room table. Sadly, it refused to lie even remotely flat, having conformed to the shape of her jeans when she stuffed it in her back pocket the day before. But it had a map of every floor in the Museum of Natural History, and right now that was all that mattered. Post-its hadn't been invented yet, so they had a yellow notepad where Bobby had scribbled "*DS at AMNH—How Get?*" along with Sunday's hours of operation.

"Basically, I figure we pull a Frankweiler." Bobby pointed at two squares along a hallway. "Lie low in the bathrooms till the janitors are done."

Tori considered this. "Won't they clean the bathrooms?"

"Well, we gotta hide somewhere."

Tori scanned the map. "How about the planetarium?"

"That's not bad," Bobby admitted. "The last show on Sundays is 4:30, so they'll probably vacuum it right after the audience leaves."

"So after they're done, we can slip in—"

"And wait till the museum closes. Brilliant!"

"What if someone comes in? Like, after closing?"

"We drop to the floor," said Bobby. "The place is huge. Nobody'll see us. Great idea, Tori."

Tori tingled with pleasure. Her father almost never praised her. "Okay, here's another thing."

"Hit me."

"We grab the diamond tonight. The heist is tomorrow, so it's safe. But then what?"

"I don't follow you, Future Girl."

"Well, either way, it's missing."

There was a pause. "Oops," said Bobby.

"And what if Mr. Dixon or whoever decides to check up on it Monday?" said Tori worriedly. "I mean, *after* the heist we can take it to the cops so they know it's not stolen. But until then—"

"Got it." Bobby pushed back his chair and bolted through the door. Almost before it had finished swinging he was back, sitting down and thrusting a blue Tiffany's box into her hands. "World's best stunt double."

Tori opened the box and took out the massive cubic zirconia replica of the Desert Sun. "You're a freaking genius," she whispered.

"Thanks," said Bobby. "Here's how I figure it. You hold onto this one. When we get to the museum tonight, I'll grab the Desert Sun, because we don't know if you touching it will beam you both back home. Soon as I have it, you put the fake one in its place. Boom! One amazing diamond, rescued from the local scum and villainy."

"Awesome." She folded the map and shoved it back into her pocket, then nestled the fake diamond in its pale blue box. "And what's our cover story for" she lowered her voice "your folks?"

"Oh, that's easy. I'll say we're going to *Rocky Horror*. Nichelle and I go about once a month. Usually Katya comes too. Wish you could meet her. She's super-cool, started a band called Little Bo Shriek. They play at Max's Kansas City and Studio 10, bunch of those places."

This was *so* not her father's scene. "What kind of music?"

"Cross between Patti Smith and Sex Pistols and Blondie. Nichelle does vocals."

"Nichelle?"

"You sound surprised."

"I mean, she mentioned a gig, but she seems so—studently."

Bobby laughed. "She does four hours of homework a night, and three hours of playing with the band."

"Her parents don't mind?"

"They don't ask a lot of questions. And Katya's folks barely know where she is half the time. They split last year. It's like *Kramer vs. Kramer* over there."

"Her last name's Kramer?"

"No, it's a movie."

"Never heard of it."

"It's really big," said Bobby in surprise.

"Still never heard of it."

"Weird what gets passed down or doesn't," mused Bobby. "*Star Wars*, yes; *Kramer vs. Kramer*, no."

"Yeah." Tori became conscious of her own gaps. She could look at this era from her perch in 2020, but she would never know it the way Bobby did. Same city, same apartment, different world. "So your folks don't mind if you go to clubs and stuff?"

He shrugged. "So long as I'm home by curfew, they're fine."

"Don't tell me you're in a punk band too."

"What if I am?"

"No way. Are you?"

"No," he admitted. "But this one time Katya got a limo to drive us to Xenon—that's a club, really popular—and when we got there, the driver got us all in. Jumped the line, didn't have to pay or anything. It was so cool."

"Next you'll be telling me you flashed your fake ID."

"Didn't have to. They never checked."

Her father had a fake ID? What next? "Did they serve alcohol?"

"God, yes. And the music was amazing."

"Amazing," echoed Tori. Which it was, but not in the way he was thinking. "Maybe I can catch them next time-jump."

"That would be great," said Bobby. "Maybe we'll figure out a way to just let you go back and forth whenever you feel like it."

"World's wackiest commute."

"Anyway, we usually crash at Nichelle's after *Rocky Horror*."

"Guess our alibi's all set, then." She stood and stretched. "And we are good to go."

"Hold up, Future Girl. Let's figure out what tools we need." Bobby emptied his pockets onto the table.

"I'm going to go out on a limb and say you can leave behind the eraser and library card," said Tori.

"But the Swiss Army knife is coming." Bobby tossed the knife up and caught it. "Do you have one of these?"

"Of course not."

"My dad gave it to me." Bobby showed her the scuffed, red case. "See those little lines between the cross and the shield? That's how you can tell it's a real Swiss Army knife. If it doesn't have them, it's a knockoff." He slipped it into his pocket. "Maybe I'll get you one for your bat mitzvah or something."

"Don't bother. I couldn't carry it around with me. Not at school, anyway."

"Why not?"

"Probably because of all the school shootings. Which is pretty stupid, because obviously you can't fire a knife."

Bobby blinked. "I'm sorry. Did you just say, 'school shootings'?"

"Yeah."

"School *shootings?* Like, someone just goes in with a handgun and starts firing?" Bobby stared at her, eyes wide.

"Ha! Ha!" said Tori. "No."

"Oh, good." Bobby's shoulders relaxed.

"Usually it's a machine gun."

"Now I know you're bullshitting me."

Tori shook her head. "Swear to God."

Bobby looked at her. "So in 2020, a deathly disease is sweeping the globe, pop culture is recycled from fifty years ago, and people routinely murder kids with machine guns."

"You know what we *don't* have?" flared Tori. "Piles of dog crap on every sidewalk, and rain acid plus rivers that catch fire and that hole in the ion layer that you and Nichelle were geeking out about." She clapped her hand over her mouth. "I'm sorry—I forgot you don't like it when I say that."

Bobby rubbed his ear. "Tori," he said, "what does that word mean where—I mean, when—you're from?"

She lowered her hand. "Geek?"

"Yeah."

"It's a smart person who knows a lot about certain topics. You know, like 'nerd.'"

Bobby giggled.

"Now what?" said Tori indignantly.

Bobby wiped his eyes. "For us, a nerd is a person with no social skills."

"No way."

"And a geek is a carnival worker who bites the heads off live chickens."

"Now I know *you're* bullshitting *me*."

"Swear to God." He chortled, rocking back and forth, his shaggy hair shaking.

"Well, dang," laughed Tori. "No wonder you were mad at me."

Chapter 32
The Things We Carry with Us

～◇～

"I hope this works," said Tori for the fourth time in as many minutes. It was Sunday afternoon, and they were in Bobby's room, packing for their supposed overnight at Nichelle's. Louise had insisted the door remain open, so they kept their voices low.

"Same here."

"God, I hope we don't get caught." The security details Victor had described seemed less laughable now that she and Bobby were planning to bypass them.

Bobby rolled a sweatshirt into a cylinder and squished it into his backpack. "On the upside, we'd be famous."

"Not how I want to go down in history."

"Hey, is the *New York Post* still in print? Or the *Daily News?*"

"I bet you're thinking of the headlines."

"They'd want something snappy and alliterative."

"I was thinking about that yesterday," said Tori. "Imagine what they'd do with the name 'Gold.'"

"Oh, God, yeah. Maybe like, 'This Gold Is No Prize.'"

"'Gold Grabs Gem.'"

"Or 'Gold, Greed—Gotcha!'"

"'Sun Don't Shine after Burglary.'"

"'Bold Burglars Got Stones.'"

Tori shuddered. "I have an idea. Let's not get caught." She glanced at his desk, where he had left his notepad from their planning session. "Dang, Bobby!" She ripped up the top page and mashed it into a ball which she tossed at his wastebasket. It landed on the rim, appeared briefly to consider its options, then fell in.

Bobby made an applause noise into his hands. "She shoots—she destroys the evidence—two points for Team Time travel!"

Tori was indignant. "That was a three-pointer if ever there was one."

"Sez you." Bobby zipped up his backpack. "Hey, did I ever tell you Jacob knows Generoso Pope?"

"Who's that?"

"Owner of the *National Enquirer*. Don't know if he does the headlines, though."

"Sounds like Jacob knows everybody." Which made it all the odder that until two days earlier, she had never heard of him. She frowned at the backpack.

"Sorry," said Bobby. "I know you're not a fan."

"No, he seemed really nice."

"I meant the bag."

Tori half-laughed. Bobby's extra backpack was his *Star Trek* bookbag from elementary school. The *Enterprise* blasted across the back panel, and the sides showed Kirk and Spock beaming down to the latest stop on their interstellar junket. It had the look of something that had come with a matching lunchbox. "No worries. I know you're a stan."

"Who's Stan?" Bobby shrugged his backpack onto his shoulders. "Usually people say I'm most like McCoy."

"Anyway, the one with the tribbles was good." She pulled the zip tab past the intrepid captain and his science officer, and they walked to the front door. Tori looked around, almost tottery with excitement. If their plan worked, she would never set foot in this place again. Or, rather, she would be right back here in a few hours. Or forty years, depending on how you counted; and the apartment would be hers instead of Bobby's. Of course, Bobby would still be there. Well, no. Her father would be there.

She snuck a look at Bobby. What a great kid he was—risking everything for a stranger who didn't even exist yet. A ghost from the future.

If their plan worked, she would never see Bobby again.

"Just a sec." He paused by the front door. "Mom," he bellowed. "We're leaving."

Louise swept out of her bedroom to give him a hug and a kiss. "Have a wonderful time, love. Take a jump to the left for me. Tori, it's been delightful meeting you."

"Same here, Mrs. Gold. Thanks so much for having me." Tori held out her hand, shocked again at the vitality in Grandma Louise's grip.

"Don't forget your toothpaste, dear," said Louise, handing Tori the tube.

"I bet Tori has her own toothpaste at home, Mom."

"Well, now she has more."

"Thanks, Mrs. Gold. It's been a pretty amazing weekend." Tori knelt to open the backpack, laying the toothpaste next to a bulgy pair of socks. She could feel her phone pressing against her leg. If all went as planned, soon she would be back in the land of texts, TikTok, and parents who were older than she was.

"I'm so glad you managed to reach your father," went on Louise. "He's picking you up at Nichelle's tomorrow, yes?"

"Right. We talked yesterday."

"When?"

"While we were out."

Louise puckered her brows. "That must have been awfully expensive, dear."

"Oh, it was," said Bobby quickly. "She had to get, like, five bucks in change. The guy at the bodega was *not* happy about it."

"Sure wasn't," agreed Tori, smothering her confusion.

"She handed him a ten to buy a pack of gum," chuckled Bobby. "And asked for her change in quarters. Ha!"

"Ha!" said Tori. *Quarters for...?*

"Some of these shopkeepers can be so rude," said Louise sympathetically. "You could have called him from here, you know."

Calling! Right, calling. Mental note: I called my dad from a payphone. With quarters.

"That's what I told her," said Bobby. "But she said she didn't want to run up our phone bill with a long-distance call."

Phoning is so complicated now.

"That's very thoughtful of you, Tori."

"No problem." *So I guess the apartment phone works across state lines. Do you have to plug it into a different socket?*

"And your father knows how to get to Nichelle's?"

"We gave him the address and the cross-street," said Bobby.

Louise frowned. "Bobby, I'm fairly certain that Tori can speak for herself."

"We gave him the address and the cross-street," said Tori, because this was apparently what people used in the absence of Waze and Google Maps. She zipped up the backpack and stood, maneuvering its too-small straps onto her shoulders. The bulgy socks, wrapped around the CZ Desert Sun, bumped against the base of her neck.

The buzzer for the front door sounded. "That's Mrs. Shulman," said Louise as she made for the door. "She and I are going to an open house, Bobby—Dad already knows. I do love those fabulous apartments! Have fun, kids. Tori, I hope we see each other soon. Have a good trip home."

Chapter 33

Execution

~◇~

The new plan was better, and Mike knew it.

He had never been crazy about the first approach. Finding investors relied on other people's risk tolerance. Plus, they'd have to pay them back, with interest, and Christ only knew how long that would take or what would happen if they missed a payment. This way the cash was theirs, free and clear.

And now it was all coming together.

The museum floors were only partially lit at night. Mike passed the beam of his flashlight over the *Tyrannosaurus* skeleton. Its ribs flickered, and the enormous skull became a death-mask, glowering in the murk. Mike shuddered. He had seen such eyeless eyes before, staring through the stink of decay in the fuggy jungle air. It got in your hair and your skin and under your fingernails.

It got in your mind.

One day they'd gone back for some wounded. Mike had been in the lead when they breached the clearing, so he was the first to see the wild pigs and the mess they'd made. Even now, more than a dozen years later, if he let his guard down the whole scene rocketed back: the man's face turned toward him, white streaks of bone showing through tattered skin, the mud-soaked Levi's, the boar's teeth grinding on bone, and the maggots bouncing on putrefying flesh with a sound like Rice Krispies in milk.

It had broken Mike into a thousand jagged pieces that never fit back together again. There were always cracks, with sharp edges wounding each other where they touched.

He'd started toking more after that. The smoke filled in the cracks, blurring the fractured margins of what used to be his self, so he could melt back together again.

Only problem was, you couldn't stay high forever.

One day his commanding officer had discovered an Altoids box containing three joints duct-taped to the underside of Mike's bunk, an event that had signaled the demise of Mike's military career. That was in Florida, half a world away from Hawaii, and he had stayed. Then he'd met Maeve and the other girls. Not a bad setup.

He forced himself to look at the *Tyrannosaurus*. Just another big lizard. The teeth were like the gators' back home. Nothing to see here, folks. Move along.

At the top of every hour, Mike punched a clock to record the start of his rounds. He did it again when he finished, then took an OSHA-mandated, fifteen-minute break. Fred, the flabby old fart filling out the other guard uniform that night, started at the bottom of the hour, so one of them circulated every thirty minutes.

Mike ambled upstairs, just another bored security guard pulling a late shift. He could hear his breath and the squeak of his soles on the marble floors. Squeak, squeak, breathe; squeak, squeak, breathe. Jesus, it was quiet.

He shone his Maglite around the Hall of Minerals. Sweep and pause, sweep and pause. Couldn't be too cautious. Couldn't take too long, either.

Stealing Time

Mike had clocked Fred on one of his early circuits. The older guard took every second of his forty-five minutes; the only time there was a bounce in his trudge was when he headed to the staff room for a cigarette break between rounds.

Mike could cover his own round in thirty-seven minutes. He'd timed it twice to make sure. That gave the girls about twenty-five minutes to get in and out, and Mike twenty-three minutes to help them.

～ ◇ ～

The evening of March 16, 1980 was seasonably cold. Temperatures had settled into the mid-thirties, something that in no way deterred the hordes of quasi-Hibernian dipsomaniacs thronging the streets, their judgment withering as their numbers bloomed. The wind swept the sounds of their revelry past the freight entrance to the Sapphire Ribbon Hotel where Gloria and Maeve huddled in the doorway, dressed in black and carrying backpacks. Maeve wore her hair in a ponytail, and Gloria's flounce of curls was held back with a headband and bobby pins. Strapped to the outside of Gloria's bag was a flat, metal prong topped with what looked like a flattened arrowhead. At the other end was a handle, offset like a cakemaker's spatula. Gloria flexed her fingers, willing warmth back into them. The ability to grip was about to get very important. "Think Snake lost the memo?"

"Don't worry." Maeve stared down the side street that was notable for its lack of Snake. "He can't afford to fuck up."

"Now, there's an endorsement."

A gray Saab 900 pulled up, slewing to a stop in a pool of snowmelt as a rat scuttered past its gleaming headlights. Maeve jumped into the front seat, dropping her backpack to the floor. "What took you?" she said as Gloria slid into the back.

"Had to gas up." Snake shifted the car into gear. "The last asshole who borrowed this thing didn't fill it up before returning it."

"When you see him, tell him from me to have some respect for other people's property."

"Next time I look in a mirror," he promised.

"Weird-looking car," Gloria said.

"It's Swedish."

"Is this real leather?"

"Bet your ass," said Snake. "And the gray blends with the night. Perfect for major felonies."

Gloria paused, her hand on the seatbelt she was about to buckle. "You think this is funny?"

"You think it's not?" Snake twitched the steering wheel to avoid a cluster of revelers who had evidently decided that sidewalks were for the weak. One raised a dripping mug to him and shouted, "Begorah, that's some fine drivin', laddie!"

"Ah, Jesus," said Gloria. "He's going to blow the whole thing."

"He'll be fine," said Maeve over her shoulder. "Right, Snake?"

"Sure thing." Snake swerved around a double-parked car to make a left onto the crosstown street through Central Park.

Gloria stared out the window. "Shit, it's crowded."

"And not even the holiday yet," said Maeve.

"Don't tell them that," said Snake.

"There's like a million people," said Gloria. "Someone's gonna see us."

"It'll peter out," said Snake. "There's no bars on Central Park West."

"I don't think they're sticking to the bars," said Gloria.

As if to confirm her statement, a trio of men wearing Kiss-Me-I'm-Irish tee shirts stumbled out of a doorway arm in arm, lifting their voices to the night sky. "*Her eyes, they shone like diamonds. I thought her the queen of the land...*"

"Don't sweat it. New Yorkers never look up," said Snake.

"*Her hair hung over her shoooouuulders, tied up with a black velvet band!*"

"How does anyone drive in this mess?" said Gloria. "We're gonna be late."

"*Before the judge and the jury next morning I had to appear....*"

Snake glanced at the clock on the dash. "I'll have you there in ten minutes, max. Teamwork. Am I right, ladies?"

~ ◇ ~

On his third round, Mike caught up with the other guard, his jacket undone, having a smoke on a bench near the elevators.

"Evening." The older man stubbed his cigarette out in a sand-filled ash can and stood, extending his hand. "Fred."

"Mike." Mike shifted the Mag to his left hand so he could shake Fred's chubby, nicotine-stained fingers.

"Welcome aboard, son." Fred's tie was knotted perfectly, bisecting the crisp, white shirt that stretched over his drooping belly. His gray hair was combed straight back from his forehead. "Heard they hired you pretty quick."

"Got a kid down in Florida, and I'm a little behind."

"Been watching you make your rounds," said Fred. "You're pretty careful, aren't you?"

"Was in the military," Mike said. "Guess old habits die hard."

"Military, eh?" Fred looked him up and down. The younger man was about four inches taller, and though they probably weighed the same, on him it was all muscle. "What branch?"

"Navy. With the SEALs."

"No kidding? I was in the Air Corps myself."

"Oh?"

"Yep. Two years."

Mike looked down on him. "I did ten."

"I was in the big one." Fred stood so straight and tall that he almost reached Mike's chin.

"So was my dad."

Fred darkened. "Smart guy, eh?"

Mike said nothing. Fred folded his arms. "Son, this museum has twenty-six buildings, forty-five permanent exhibition halls, a planetarium, and a library. Did they tell you all that in orientation?"

"Yes, sir."

"It has over thirty million specimens," plowed on Fred. "Plants, animals, fossils, you name it. People come from all over the world to see what we have here."

"Yes, sir."

"Good," said Fred. "Glad you understand." He turned on his heel and left.

When his footsteps had faded, Mike unhooked his walkie-talkie and raised it to his lips. If Fred had looked closely, he would have noticed that the radio was bigger than his, and had a knob on the side for changing frequencies. Also that it came from Radio Shack. "Base to Closet."

A voice fizzed from the speaker. "Yeah?"

Mike clenched his jaw. "Say 'Go ahead.'"

"Jesus, Mike."

"Base to Closet."

The response was the verbal equivalent of an eye roll. "*Go ahead.*"

"Stay put till I get there."

"You know I can just open the door, right?"

"Yeah, but don't. Fred's got a hair across his ass. I'll make sure he's gone."

"Cool."

"Say 'Roger that.'"

"Whatever."

"Clear." He snapped the radio back onto his belt and walked out of the hall.

Chapter 34
Trust the Time Traveler

◈

"You literally know your way around this place in the dark," said Tori as they crept through the gloom-drenched museum. She rubbed her neck, which had developed a crick as they waited in the planetarium till the last janitor had turned off the last light and left for the night. They hoped. Bobby had provided distractions: granola bars and water for dinner, stories about school and camp for entertainment. Now the fake Desert Sun had slipped down inside his old schoolbag, and she shifted her shoulders to keep it from poking her spine.

"Blindfolded with one hand tied behind my back," said Bobby. "But keep your voice down."

"Right," she whispered.

Bobby stopped by a diorama of ostriches defending their eggs from jackals. "Don't whisper," he said in a barely audible murmur. "It carries. Just talk low."

Her dad was a good guy to be breaking and entering with. "Where's the stairs?" she said, matching his undertone.

Bobby pushed open a door, and they headed up. Tori's hands twitched on the banister, leaving a sheen of sweat. Every shadow housed a dozen monsters, and every squeak of their sneakers screamed like a klaxon. She wished she could swivel her head all the way around, like an owl.

Bobby pulled open the door for the fourth floor, and for the second time in two days they stepped into the Harry Frank Guggenheim Hall of Minerals and Morgan Memorial Hall of Gems. The only light came from the tall windows, and shadows lapped the centerpiece of blue-green meteorite. The last time they had been here, thought Tori, the place had been full of parents, strollers, kids, and daylight. Then, they had entered lawfully; now, their presence was illicit. She swallowed. Did this make them bad guys? Because really, what kind of lowlife would be here in the middle of the night like this?

"You give the signal?" said a woman's voice.

Tori and Bobby leaped behind the stone chunk.

"Soon as Fred takes his millionth cigarette break." A man's voice, closer.

Bobby and Tori locked eyes. They had heard him before.

"When's that?" said the woman. Closer. Tori's stomach jostled her tonsils.

"Ten minutes. Guy's a walking nic fit."

"Any chance he made us?" A pair of shadows slithered along the base of the meteorite.

"Hell, no. He's dumber than these rocks."

She chuckled, and the shadows slid away.

Tori counted to fifty. The shadows did not return. She looked at Bobby, who let out a ragged breath. "That was close," he said in a voice as soft as the shadows.

Tori brushed her hair out of her eyes. Her fingertips felt cold where they touched her forehead. "I am *not* cut out for a life of crime."

"This isn't crime. More like derring-do."

"But not the legal kind."

"Fair point." He stood up and peeked around the edge of the monolith. "Did that guy sound familiar to you?"

"Yeah."

"Is he from the future?"

"Past."

"Oh, God. Another time traveler?"

"Our past. He's the guy who threw us out yesterday."

"That's not half as exotic." He held out his hand to help her to her feet.

"It's still a problem." Tori pulled herself up. "He's going to signal someone."

"And let them in."

"Then they grab the gems."

"And run."

"Told you," said Tori.

"Trust the time traveler." Bobby gave a tremulous smile. "The cardinal rule of science fiction."

"And listen to your daughter."

"Next heist." He paused. "Hold on. I thought the robbery was supposed to be Monday."

"So did I."

"Maybe you being here threw the whole time-space continuum out of whack."

"If it's busted, maybe I can get home through one of the cracks."

"Here's hoping."

"So now what?" said Tori.

"Go for help. Command center's downstairs."

She shook her head. "The place is crawling with crooks."

"Two isn't crawling."

"He said he was giving a signal," she pointed out. "Could be a lots more coming in."

Bobby rubbed his ear. "Shit."

Tori agreed, though she didn't say so. "We have to get help without showing ourselves."

"Inside ten minutes."

"Less, now."

Bobby brightened. "He said Fred was finishing up his round."

"So?"

"We can leave him a note. Fred, I mean."

"A note?"

"Yeah." Bobby dug into his backpack and pulled out a notepad and a pen.

"A *note?*"

"Got a better idea, Future Girl?"

Tori thought of the dark halls and the voices and the signal for a sudden uptick in the local hooligan population. Her knees were shaking, had been since they dove behind the rock. "Guess not."

Bobby clicked the pen open. "Fred," he began, writing as he spoke.

"Good start."

"Possible malefactors on fourth floor. Hall of Gems at risk—"

"Possible what?"

"Bad guys."

"Why don't you just say bad guys?"

"Malefactors sounds cooler."

"What if Fred didn't ace his SATs?"

Bobby shoved the pad at her. "You're so smart, you do it."

Tori scowled as she balanced the pad on her knees. "Fred," she began.

"Good start."

"There's…a…gang…on…the…fourth…floor…."

Bobby peered over her shoulder. "You're *printing?*"

Tori felt her ears go red. "So?"

"So it looks like a first grader wrote it."

"No one uses cursive anymore." She bowed her head over the pad, digging into the paper with the nib of the pen as she wrote.

"He's gonna think this is a prank."

"Oh, and your fake cop talk was going to save the day?"

Bobby watched her crafting each letter. "Jesus, this is slow."

"It goes faster when you're not nagging."

"Just use cursive."

"No."

"Why not?"

"Leave me alone."

Bobby stared at her. "Oh, my God."

"Look, just—"

"You don't know *handwriting?*"

"I can read it," she protested.

"You can read it?"

"Sort of."

"Can you write it?"

"Sort of."

"*Sort of?*"

"Printing's quicker."

"No, it's not."

"It is for me."

"Only because you don't know cursive."

"I said, no one uses it anymore."

"So everybody just takes half an hour to print everything?"

"Everything's keyboard now. It's faster than—this." She waved the pen in disgust.

"So what happens if you don't have a keyboard? Like, say, now?"

"You're always bugging me about my handwriting!"

"No, I'm not, because apparently you don't have any."

"You know what I mean. You—"

"And stop blaming me for stuff I haven't done yet!"

Tori ripped out the sheet of paper and crumpled it up, shoving the pad at Bobby. "You do it, then."

"Fine." Bobby wrote in swift strokes. "'Fred. There's a gang on the fourth floor. The other guard is one of them. They're going to steal the Desert Sun.'" He looked up. "Okay?"

"Sure," she grumbled, looking around the dusky hall. "Where do we leave it?"

Bobby snapped his notebook closed and slipped it back into his pack. "Staff room. That guy said Fred's headed there for his cig break—we can slide it under the door."

Tori peered around the edge of the meteorite. "I hope you're right."

"Me too."

A white beam sailed through the murk. "Mike?" said a man's voice. "Who you talking to?"

Tori's heart leaped. Her guts plunged. Her feet bounded after Bobby as they bolted from the Hall of Gems.

"Fred?" Another voice, ahead of them.

Bobby's head snapped from left to right. Tori whipped around so they were back to back. If this was their last stand,

241

they'd go down fighting. Feeling wobbly, she grabbed the knob on the nearest door for support.

It swung open.

Whoa!

She seized Bobby's sleeve and heaved them both into the closet, keeping one hand on the inside knob so they wouldn't be locked inside.

She needn't have bothered. In their panic, neither of them noticed that the latch bolt was secured with duct tape.

Behind them in the Harry Frank Guggenheim Hall of Minerals and Morgan Memorial Hall of Gems, a portly, middle-aged man shone a flashlight onto a scrumpled leaf of paper.

Chapter 35

Shadow Dancing

Maeve cinched her backpack strap around her waist. The side of the Museum of Natural History facing West 77th Street was swathed in scaffolding from the sidewalk to the edge of the roof. The snow from earlier in the week had long since slid to the ground, and the night sky beckoned. "Ready?"

"Kidding me?" Gloria grinned.

"On my count, then. One—two—hey!"

Gloria had leaped onto the lowest crossbars and was spidering her way nimbly up to the second floor, where wooden planks made a walkway. Maeve followed, her movements strong and deliberate.

"Remember the three points of contact rule," sang Gloria from overhead.

"I know." The tubing was cold, and rust gritted under her palms.

"One hand, two feet, or two hands, one foot."

"I *know*."

"Part of you always needs to be actually touching the scaffolding."

"Oh, shut up." Maeve half-laughed, focusing on her next grip.

"Important safety tip, boss." Gloria squatted by the opening in the platform as Maeve's head and shoulders emerged.

"Hell, yeah." Maeve pulled herself through the opening and sat, her feet dangling through the hole. "We're the friggin' OSHA of the underworld."

"Damn straight." Gloria slipped behind her and buzzed up the ladder that led to the next platform. Maeve stood, blew on her hands, and followed.

~ ◇ ~

Fred huffed up to Mike just outside the Hall of Gems. "You think this is funny?" His Maglite's beam made jittery patterns in the air as he gestured.

Mike stepped into the light. "Whoa. It's me, Mike."

"Don't I know it." Fred held up a wrinkled paper. "What's the big idea?"

"What are you talking about?"

"This!" Fred shook the paper at him.

Mike took it. "Mind getting that light out of my face?" Teresa was hiding behind the archway at his back. In two minutes, Maeve and Gloria would be at the window. Timing was crucial.

"This isn't how we do things here, son." Fred lowered the flashlight.

Mike read the note, his face expressionless. "Looks like a little kid wrote it."

"Or a big kid."

"What's that supposed to mean?"

"Maybe they did practical jokes in the SEALs, new guy, but not here." Fred spat the words. Mike felt his breath with each syllable.

"I didn't do this." He could almost feel the seconds ratcheting up.

"Then who did?"

If he was late, Snake would never let him forget it. "Like I said, probably some kid."

"Sure, sure. Because the place is crawling with kids at eleven o'clock Sunday night."

"I meant earlier. And the janitors missed it."

"The custodial staff are professionals, kid. They know what this place is, even if you don't."

"What's that supposed to mean?"

Fred stood as tall as he could, which wasn't very. "Working here isn't just a job. It's an honor."

"So I hear." Mike tensed his shoulders. "Mainly from you."

"If you don't get that, you don't need to be here."

"Look, I need this gig," said Mike in alarm.

"Should have thought of that before you got all funny."

"This wasn't me." The false accusation was unsettling. Mike was much more used to denying things he had actually done.

"I'm gonna write you up."

"Wait," began Mike. Last thing they needed for tomorrow was this jackass telling the cops the new guy had been acting weird the night before.

"Forget it. You had your chance." Fred pushed past him.

Teresa leaped from behind the arch and smashed her flashlight down on the old man's skull. The crump of metal hitting bone reverberated in the hall.

Fred collapsed.

Gloria and Maeve stood on the highest platform of the scaffolding, almost level with the lip of the red tile roof that sloped up to meet the night. Gloria leaned against the railing and waved at the gray Saab on the street below. "Hi, Snake!"

A voice crackled from her backpack. "Hi, gorgeous. How's the view?"

"Wow," said Gloria. "I didn't think he could see us from down there." She reached into the bag and clicked her walkie-talkie, which matched Mike's. "Come on up and see for yourself."

"Not big into heights, sweetheart."

"Ah, give it a try. We've got a bird's-eye view."

"A beautiful chick like you can fly. I'll stay on the ground, thanks."

"Radio silence till we bag the rocks," said Maeve, pulling two coils of rope from her bag.

"Gotta go." Gloria tossed her radio into her backpack and took out a small hammer. Next, she detached the tool with the offset handle. She slid the flat, hooked head under a broken shingle, wiggling it about until it caught on something, then hammered vigorously on the bend above the handle till the tool jerked loose.

"How long is this gonna take?" said Maeve.

"Not long. They only ever have two nails to a shingle." She slid the tool under the tile again.

"Does it have to be a broken one?"

"Nope. Just happened to be there." The tool snagged again, and Gloria hammered on it until it slid free. Its anchoring nails severed, the tile slid toward her with a rasping sound. She caught it and set it at her feet.

"So we're doing them a favor, taking out this broken shit," said Maeve.

"That's right. They should be thanking us." Gloria set the cracked slate down on the platform and slid her tool under a new one. Snag, tap, break, pull, snag, tap, break, pull, repeating the process till she had cleared away an opening that revealed a lattice of stout, wooden cross-members. "Your turn."

While Gloria put away the hammer and strapped the slate ripper back on her pack, Maeve tied each of the ropes to the newly exposed rafter before knotting the free end around her waist. She tossed the second rope to Gloria, who quickly did the same. "Ready?"

"Bet your ass."

Cords trailing behind them, Maeve and Gloria bounded up the roof. Slate tiles clacked under their sneakers, and the cold, March air swept across their cheeks and their blazing eyes.

~ ◇ ~

"What the fuck?" said Mike.

'You're welcome," panted Teresa.

"I woulda got this sorted."

"He woulda wrote you up."

"Now we've got a body to deal with."

"We almost had a paper trail to deal with." She knelt by the older guard and tilted his soft, floppy head toward her cheek. "Anyway, he's only sleeping."

"Good." Mike jammed the note into his pocket. "Stash him. I'll let the girls in."

At the edge of the roof's downslope, Gloria and Maeve grabbed their lines, tightening the slack. Turning their backs to the vast, airy expanse of the museum's inner courtyard, they dropped from sight.

The rush was fantastic. This was what they'd been leading up to, thought Gloria, their whole time in New York. Every recon trip, every strategy meeting, every wild and crazy party at the Sapphire Ribbon Hotel featuring them rappelling down the side of the building and landing on balconies five flights below. Once they had even crashed another party: Maeve had descended with a wineglass clenched in her teeth, and when an astonished waiter goggled at her, she'd handed him the goblet and said, "Refill, please."

None of which had gotten them the investors, the funding they needed for their surf shop in Florida. What that smarmy jerk Buell had said was true: Maeve the Wave might be famous in the Sunshine State, but that didn't cut it up here in the Big Apple.

Well, screw it. There was more than one way to strike it rich. In the racing darkness, Gloria's face glowed with triumph.

Teresa grasped Fred's collar and heaved. He slid a quarter of an inch. "Jesus, he's fat."

"Should have thought of that before you cold-cocked him." Mike crouched behind Fred's supine form and shoved him to a seated position.

"Gonna have tea and cookies with him?"

"Shut up," suggested Mike. He gave the unconscious man a bear hug and rose, lifting both of them to a standing position. "Straighten his knees for me, willya? And take his radio." She did so. Maneuvering to the front, Mike jammed his back against Fred's chest, grabbed the guard's wrists, and pulled up on them till he had the old man halfway over his shoulders. He tugged Fred's arms down and close, bending forward slightly.

"I think he likes you," said Teresa.

"Just get the closet door."

Mike lumbered down the hall, Teresa nipping ahead of him. She stopped at the closet, one hand on the doorknob. "Should tie him up," she said, ever the professional.

Mike shifted his shoulders, letting Fred thump to the floor. "With what?"

"Tape, moron."

"You got tape, moron?"

"Thought you had it."

Mike gestured at the closet with his chin. "I threw it in there when I fixed the lock."

Teresa flung open the door and shone her flashlight inside.

～ ◇ ～

"This is it," said Maeve. Her foot nudged the metal box poking from the window, its bulk supported by metal struts. "Best security system in this lousy burg about to get fucked up by a hundred-dollar AC."

"Fantastic," panted Gloria. They waited on either side of the unit, swaying in the darkness, their raw hands gripping the ropes.

"Where's Mike and Terri?" said Gloria presently.

"They'll be here."

"They're late."

"Mr. Military Time? No way."

"He's late, I tell you. I checked my watch before we came down."

"Then they're coming," snapped Maeve.

Gloria looked up at the looming bulk of the museum, then down at the pavement. "What's taking them so long?"

"I don't know," admitted Maeve. Her arms shook.

"Did we get the wrong window?"

"No," grunted Maeve.

"Shit," cried Gloria. "What if they grabbed the rocks and ran?"

"Shut *up*."

The thrum of traffic rolled over the roof in waves. Dogs barked; sirens harmonized with a sozzled, a cappella rendition of "Danny Boy." But near at hand, the only sound was the rasping of the two women's breath.

"Maeve," said Gloria, "I can't hold on much longer."

⁓ ◇ ⁓

Teresa played her flashlight across the closet floor. Just outside its dazzling beam, a sneaker nudged a small, gray item forward. The second sweep of her light illuminated a roll of duct tape by the threshold, its free end scrunched. "Got it."

STEALING TIME

"Give it." Mike took the roll and slapped a strip of tape over Fred's mouth before binding his wrists. Teresa held open the door, and he rolled the unconscious man inside.

Chapter 36

Good Team

"Oh, my God."

"They didn't see us."

"Obviously."

"Oh, my God."

Tori and Bobby jammed themselves against the rear wall of the closet as far as their backpacks would let them. The only light came from the gap under the door, which barely illuminated the inert form of the guard at their feet. He gave a sound like a cross between a sob and a moan, but he did not move.

"Is he dead?" whispered Tori.

"Not if he's making noise." Bobby squatted, fumbling at the unconscious man's waist. Tori heard a click, and the room was flooded with the blue-white blaze of the guard's light. "Hold this." He thrust it into her hand, and she shone it on the guard. His eyes were shut, and the back of his head was dark and sticky. Bobby made as if to grasp the old man's shoulders.

"Wait," said Tori.

"What?"

"Fingerprints."

"Seriously?"

"Yes." She jammed the flashlight under one arm and dug into the pocket of her jeans.

"Our prints must be all over the museum," protested Bobby.

"Fingerprints out there are different from fingerprints on a knocked-out guard in a closet. Ah, got it." Smiling in triumph, she pulled a scrunch of latex gloves from her pocket.

"Man, you are one prepared girl."

She handed him the wrinkled mitts. "We'll wipe down the flashlight and doorknobs when we leave."

Bobby did not put them on. "What about you?"

"I don't exist for another twenty-five years," she said. "You do. So right now you're important to protect, not me. And don't get all mushy, because I'll deny I ever said it."

Smiling, Bobby pulled them on. "Gloves and all. You're like Quincy, M.E."

"Is that good?"

"Yeah."

Tori felt her cheeks grow warm. "It was your idea."

"It was?"

"You gave them to me. Because of the coronavirus."

"Shows we're a good team." He bent over the old man. "Shit. It's Fred."

"You know him?"

"No." He pointed to the nametag on the uniform.

"Thank God," said Tori. "I thought we were about to have a poor Yorick moment."

"This is the guy they were talking about," said Bobby. "If they already got to him, the rest of the gang must be here."

Tori felt a cloud of frozen feathers drift down her spine. "We have to get out of here."

"After we take care of him." As gently as possible, Bobby peeled the duct tape from Fred's mouth. The guard's lips

253

formed a slack O, and his eyes stayed shut. Bobby gently pushed his shoulder so he lay on his side. But as soon as he took his hands away, Fred rolled onto his back. Bobby pushed again, but again the limp body flopped back to its supine position.

"What are you doing?" said Tori.

"Rolling him onto his side so he doesn't choke on his vomit."

"Is that a thing?"

"Yeah."

"Gross."

"Not a good epitaph," he agreed. "We need to prop him up."

Tori set the Maglite down on its base so the beam went straight up. "Shouldn't we untie him?"

"Right." Bobby took his knife from his pocket and pried open a blade. "Can you hold him so I don't slit an artery?"

Tori squatted, holding Fred by one shoulder and supporting his head as Bobby sawed at the tape. Fred's arm flopped free. "Nice job."

"Thanks." Bobby closed the knife and dropped it back into his pocket. "Maybe we can prop him against the wall?"

As quietly as possible, they shoved aside the mops and buckets, and, with a certain amount of grunting and heaving, they shifted Fred to the wall and positioned him on his side, one shoulder against the wall, one arm under his head like a pillow.

"Let's leave the flashlight here," whispered Tori. "He'll need it when he wakes up."

"Good idea." Bobby rubbed the Maglite clean with his tee shirt. He slid it under Fred's hand and turned it off. Tori opened the closet door.

Chapter 37
The Gang's All Here

~◇~

Something buzzed like a dentist's drill. Metal squealed on metal. Tori stopped, hand on the knob. The door was open by a hairline, and in the syrupy light oozing through it she could see Bobby beside her as they both strained to hear.

"Ready?" said a man.

"Lower." A woman. The duo from the Hall of Gems. They grunted with exertion. A gust of cold air swept under the closet door, followed by gasping and the squeak of shoes on stone.

"Jesus, Mike, what took you so long?" said a new woman. "You left me and Gloria hanging. Like, for real!"

Tori bit her lip. She'd heard that voice before too. Somewhere.

"Isn't Teresa supposed to be taking down the plywood?" This speaker was new. Must be Gloria, who had been kept hanging. Bobby held up four fingers, and Tori nodded, breathing shallowly. Four crooks so far. Her hands were damp, and her knees shook.

"We got made." Mike.

"What? How?" said the new woman.

"Read this."

"Oh, shit," breathed Bobby.

"Oh, shit," said the woman.

"It looks like a little kid wrote it," said Gloria. "One who doesn't know how to write real good yet."

"There's only two kids who know about a job here tonight." The first woman's voice was tight as a fist. "And one dirtbag who knows them."

"But Maeve," protested Gloria. "You said he wouldn't—"

"I was wrong, okay?"

"Never did like that asshole," said Mike.

A blitz of static filled the hallway. "Snake?" barked Maeve. "Listen to me, you—hey!"

"I'll take that," said Mike.

"Give it back!"

"No."

"Gimme my goddamn radio, Mike."

"What are you going to say to him?"

"To put his head between his knees and kiss his ass goodbye, because in about ten minutes I'm gonna knock his teeth so far down his throat he'll have to spit 'em out single file."

"And then he'll sit around waiting for us to show?" Mike sounded mildly curious.

"We don't have time for this," snapped the woman named Teresa. What was it about her and plywood? "We're behind already."

"Plus, we need him to get back to the hotel," said Gloria. "Don't we?"

"Yeah, we do," said Mike. "Unless you wanna call a cab to the scene of the crime."

A second buzz of static filled the air, and a voice. "Hey, doll. You called?"

257

Bobby gasped. Tori stiffened. And Fred said, "Inggghhhhaww."

"Did you hear something?" said Gloria.

"Ready for pickup? Damn, that was quick, gorgeous," said the crackly voice. Bobby shook his head as if he could jerk the sound away. Tori stared at him in a funk of misery.

"Hhhhaaagggghhhh," said Fred.

"Heard what?" said Teresa.

"It sounded like it was coming from over there," said Gloria.

"Ghghghghgghaaaohmy*head*," said Fred.

Tori flapped her free hand at Bobby in a gesture that said, "Make him shut up or we are *dead*." Bobby squatted by the prostrate guard and patted him awkwardly on the shoulder. "Shh," he whispered.

Fred half-rose, flailing his free arm and knocking over two mops. "Damn Krauts," he yelled. "They got me." Then he vomited with a noise like every toilet in Manhattan flushing in concert.

"Now don't tell me you didn't hear *that*," said Gloria in triumph.

"Gimme your radio, Terri," said Maeve. "Snake? Listen close, because you're about to hear what happens to snitches and their rugrat sidekicks."

The closet door jerked open. Framed in the opening stood a lithe woman dressed in black, her hair pulled back in a ponytail. Her free hand held a walkie-talkie. Her jaw was rigid, her eyes slits.

Instantly, Tori realized three things.

One: Maeve was Dr. Hopewell.

Two: she was mad.

Three: really mad.

Maeve plunged into the closet, landing squarely in the splash of Fred's vomit. Her feet shot out from under her, and she slammed to the floor, tobogganing into his recumbent form. His nerveless limbs flopped about her in a zombie embrace that she struggled to escape. Scrambling to his feet, Bobby knocked over a pail full of mops. Maeve made a sweeping grab for him, but he skidded past her. She screamed into her radio. *"Snake!"*

"Bobby!" yelled Tori at the same moment.

"Run!" cried Bobby. *"Run!"*

They bolted out of the closet, almost colliding with the burly security guard and two women who, like Maeve/Dr. Hopewell, were dressed entirely in black. An air conditioning unit lay at their feet; above them, an empty rectangle opened onto the night, letting in cold air and the distant sounds of wannabe-Irish revelry. A short woman bounded at them and grabbed their backpacks. As though they had rehearsed it a thousand times, Tori and Bobby flexed their shoulders and slipped out of the straps before pelting down the hall to freedom.

"You goddamn fart pipe." Fading behind them, Maeve's voice was a cataract of acid. "You freakin' Judas, you goddamn ratfink flopdick. I don't know what your goddamn game is, but those kids are gonna be sorry they ever played it. And when we're done with them, we're coming for you."

≈ ◇ ≈

The lone figure in the Saab stared in horror at the walkie-talkie in his hand. "Maeve? Maeve. Babe, listen to me."

The radio was silent. He tossed it aside, burying his face in his hands, the kids' voices juddering in his ears.

How had everything gone so wrong?

Snake lifted his head and flexed his thumbs, marveling at their perfect obedience to him, even though they were vibrating like a tympanum at a heavy metal concert. He imagined red-hot pain jetting up his arms, his screams mingling with No-Name's laughter.

No!

Waves of bleak terror rose from his gut, buffeting him. He tried to gasp, and could not. It was alive, this fear. It would consume him.

No.

The boy's cry. His terror.

The kids. The gang. The job. One person was at the heart of that Venn diagram.

Somehow, it was his fault.

Bobby needed him.

"Shit," he said to no one. "Shit, shit, shit."

With a moan, he flipped up his collar, opened the door, and stepped out into the night. Sick at heart, wishing he could blame someone else but knowing he couldn't, Jacob Gold, aka "Jake the Snake," bent but purposeful, strode toward the museum.

Chapter 38

Ten Million Possibilities

"Jesus, are you okay?" Gloria leaned into the closet, wrinkling her nose at the stink of vomit.

Maeve staggered out, still clutching Teresa's walkie-talkie. Her ponytail was askew, and bits of Fred's dinner clung to the seat of her jeans. She glared black fire at her gang. "Don't say a fucking word."

"Course not." Amusement shimmered in Mike's dark eyes.

"And what the hell's that?" Maeve shot a dirty look at the two backpacks that Teresa still clung to stupidly.

"The kids left her holding the bag." Mike's glee deepened.

"I didn't see you stopping them, Studly Do-Right," snapped Teresa. Mike's cheeks flushed, and the light in his eyes went bleak. Teresa dropped the bags to the floor and wrenched them open, rummaging inside. She lifted out a lump of socks, and a fist-sized crystal tumbled into her hands, scattering flecks of light and color.

"It's the Desert Sun!" cried Gloria.

"Like we needed more proof there's another gang," snarled Maeve. "What else they get?"

Teresa set the bauble on the floor and ran her hands through the bags again. "Just toothpaste and shit."

"Then the rest of the loot's still waiting." Maeve slapped the walkie-talkie into Teresa's hand, and held out her palm to Mike.

Wordlessly, he relinquished the radio he had taken from her. She clipped it to her belt with one hand while yanking the elastic out of her hair with the other. Her chestnut waves fell about her shoulders as she tossed her head to get the part in the right place. "Listen up. We have one chance to rescue this shitshow, okay?"

"Right." Teresa stood, surreptitiously wiping the radio on her jeans.

"Sure," said Gloria.

"You're the boss," said Mike.

"Damn right." She took a deep breath. "I and Gloria will get the rest of the rocks. Teresa, you clear the window. None of that's changed. And Mike, you grab the little punks. Clear?"

"Clear," said Mike.

"I don't get it." Gloria scooped up the radiant crystal and dropped it into her bag. "Why would Snake plant the kids here? What's his game?"

"Don't know, don't care. But we can use them to keep him in line."

"Don't worry." Teresa's jaw was clenched. "They won't get past me again."

"Forget it, Terri. You're on plywood detail." Maeve pulled her hair back with both hands and snapped on the elastic. "Meet you at the window in ten."

"I can't get that crap off by myself," protested Teresa. "Those sheets are huge."

"Get started. We'll help you when we get there." She looked at the circle of expectant faces. "What are you all waiting for? Go!"

As Teresa left the hall and Gloria and Maeve turned toward the Desert Sun exhibit, Mike raised his walkie-talkie to his lips. "Base to Snake. You wouldn't like her when she's angry."

※ ◇ ※

"Did you hear—"

"Shut up."

"That was—"

"I said, shut *up*." Bobby's shoulder bumped against a wall, and he stopped running. His hands clenched and unclenched at his sides, and his face creased. He whirled and pounded the wall with his fists, then collapsed against it with his head in his arms, his back quaking. "God *damn* it."

Awkwardly, Tori patted his shoulder. He flinched, and she dropped her hand. "You okay?" she said.

"That was Jacob," he mumbled.

"Yeah."

Bobby lifted his head. His cheeks were splotchy, and his eyes shivered with tears. Tori had never felt as sorry for her father as she did now. Had she ever felt sorry for him, or was this the first time? "Yeah," she said again, softly.

"He called her 'gorgeous,'" Bobby went on wretchedly.

"I heard."

"He knows she's here."

"I know, I know."

"And he—used us—he used you and me—to tell her—how to—" He squeezed his eyes shut and rubbed his forehead with a shaking fist.

"I know," whispered Tori. "We told them everything."

Bobby did not answer. His breath made mewling noises deep in his throat.

"They're looking for us," she said, almost apologetically. "We gotta keep moving."

Bobby set his mouth in a line and pushed himself away from the wall. "This way."

"Where to?" Tori turned to follow him.

"My dad's office. Lock ourselves in and call the cops."

"Thought you said they were crooked."

"Got a better idea?"

They dogtrotted down a flight of stairs to a door marked "Museum Staff Only." The hallway was dark and windowless. As they stepped in, Bobby pulled a miniature flashlight from his pocket and turned it on, keeping his fist over the bulb. It shone through his gloved hands, and the dim, red glow was enough to illuminate the words "Victor Gold, Ph.D." on a door halfway down the corridor. He turned the knob and pushed.

The door stayed shut.

Heart thrumming, Tori pointed to a number pad above the knob. Bobby moaned. "I don't know the code."

"How did you think we were going to get in?"

"It's always open when I'm here with my dad."

"Is there another phone?"

"Sure." Bobby sounded exhausted. "One in every office."

Tori glanced at the line of locked doors receding in the shadows, then back at the keypad. "Bet this is hackable."

"If we had a hacksaw."

"Don't need one. Watch my moves." Grinning, she punched in 72779673.

"What's that?" said Bobby.

"It spells 'password.'" She turned the knob.

The door stayed shut.

"Thanks, Dr. Feynman," said Bobby.

"Who?"

"I'll tell you later."

She scowled at the recalcitrant pad. "It's the most common password."

"For what?"

"I'll tell you later."

Bobby glanced up and down the hall. The scarlet murk of the flashlight shining through his fingers made him look like an anxious Star Wars creature. "What's the second-most common password?"

"This." She punched in 123456. Again, the door refused to budge. She rattled the knob in frustration. "Shit. You do it."

"I already told you, I don't know the code."

"Then figure it out!"

"Figure it out? Do you know how many possible combos there are?"

"No, but I bet you're about to tell me."

"Ten to the power of N," plowed on Bobby. "N being the number of digits. So that's ten *million* possible—"

"Just give it a shot," she begged. "Before Jacob and his buddies get here."

Bobby lifted his hand to the pad and stopped, his fingers inches away. He shook his head. "I don't...."

"Come on," she begged. "You know your dad. What would he use for a password?"

Bobby's hand dropped to his side. "I don't think I know anything about anyone."

"Well, get ready to learn, kid," said a deep voice.

A switch clicked. Fluorescent lights buzzed to life. In their flickering glow stood Mike, glaring hot as a volcano about to blow.

Chapter 39
Nothing He Would Not Do

Tori jumped. Bobby dropped his flashlight. "How'd you find us?" he gasped.

"'My dad works here. Victor Gold?'" recited Mike. "Jesus, kid, you made it so damn easy." With appalling effortlessness, he grasped Tori's arm, lifting her to her tiptoes. A short, fat blade swept before her eyes in a way that said he could make it do whatever he wanted.

"Bobby," she whispered, *"run."*

"Wrong, kid." Mike tightened his grip, sending a blaze of pain from her shoulder to her fingernails. "Do exactly what I say. Got it?"

Without moving her head, Tori locked eyes with Bobby. He stared at her in a paralysis of horror, his face blanched. Even his lips were pale. "Anything," he gasped. "I'll do anything."

There was nothing he would not do for her, Tori realized in shock.

And nothing he could.

Mike thumped her back to the floor, still clutching her arm. "This way." He turned to the exit, but halted when he saw Bobby stooping. "What's that?"

"My flashlight."

A smile slithered across Mike's face. "Leave it."

Puzzled, Bobby stood, leaving the light on the floor. Mike glanced at the boy's hands. "Gloves? That's adorable. Watch a lot of cop shows?"

"Huh?"

"Drop 'em."

Mystified, Bobby stripped the gloves off his hands and let them fall next to the flashlight on the threshold of Victor's office.

"That'll give the cops something to think about." Mike gave a dark chuckle and hustled them up the hallway.

Tori groaned inwardly. *Suspicion quickly coalesced around then-Chief Gemologist Victor Gold....* She craned her head at the awkward angle necessary for looking at the big man. "If you let us go, we'll tell everyone you saved us."

"No."

"You could be a hero."

"I've been a hero. Didn't pay enough."

"But—"

He tightened his grip, and she gasped with pain. The sobs she would not cry scorched her from the inside.

"So," said Bobby cheerfully, "were you in 'Nam?"

"What makes you say that?" said Mike.

"Kind of everything," said Bobby, glancing at him. "But mainly you said you'd been a hero, so—"

"Shut up, kid."

Bobby shut up till they were halfway up the staircase. "Where are we going?"

"To see my boss."

"Dr. Hopewell?" said Tori.

Mike gave a dark chuckle. "Doctor. Sure."

They reached the first landing. "She's with the Desert Sun, right?" said Bobby. He pushed on the door. "This way."

"Cute. We're going how we came."

"This hall bypasses the security cameras."

Mike snorted. "And you're being so helpful all of a sudden because why?"

"I don't want you to hurt my girlfriend," said Bobby. Tori gurgled, and when Mike looked at her she ducked her head.

"Awright," he said. "But no funny stuff."

Bobby opened the door. As they stepped over the threshold, green floor lights flared, and skulls sprang into view—bilious, leering skulls with hollow eyes and jagged teeth, floating in the darkness. Mike screamed, thrusting his knife at the horrors. Tori yanked free of his suddenly slack grip, and she and Bobby bolted past the horse skeletons and into a long, dark hallway.

"How did you know?" she gasped.

"They freaked him out by daylight," he panted. "So I was hoping."

"You're a genius. What now?"

"There's a phone booth—" Bobby pitched to the floor. A slender figure in black leaped onto his back and twisted his wrist up toward his shoulder blades till he cried out.

"Mike!" shouted Teresa.

A white ray reeled on the marble floors and walls. Mike lurched toward them, eyes wide and forehead glittering, brandishing his Maglite as though its shaft of radiance could protect him. Teresa smirked. "Taking the scenic route?"

"Turning off the lights," mumbled Mike. "Energy prices are a fucking nightmare."

"Meanwhile, I'm doing your job for you." With her free hand, she dug a roll of tape out of her pocket, and yanked the last strip off with her teeth. "Just remember, kids: silence is golden, but duct tape is silver."

Chapter 40
Victor Vanquished

~◇~

Louise and Victor had stayed up late to watch *American Film Institute Salute to Jimmy Stewart*, a special hosted by Henry Fonda and featuring Grace Kelly and Frank Capra, among others. When it ended at eleven, Victor rose with a contented sigh and turned off the television. "Ready for bed?"

"Very." Louise spoke through a yawn. "Did you reserve the car?"

"The car?"

"For Tuesday? I want to take Mother Passover shopping."

"Ah, yes. Before the best macaroons are gone," said Victor.

"It's well-known that Elijah won't come to a seder with inferior macaroons."

"Maybe that's why he never shows up when we host."

"Anyway, did you call the garage?"

"I'll do it now." He ambled over to the desk and picked up the phone. "Evening, Leo. Oh, Danny, is it? This is Mr. Gold. Can you have the car ready for Mrs. Gold Tuesday morning? Any time after morning rush hour is fine."

"Ah—I guess so," said the voice at the other end of the line.

"Any problem?" said Victor.

"Oh, no problem. I'm just surprised you want it again so soon."

"Soon? We haven't used it in over a month."

Danny hesitated for an awkward moment. "Mr. Gold—you have it right now."

"I made him check." Victor was slumped at his desk. "It's gone, all right."

"But how?" said Louise.

"He said I picked it up a few hours ago."

"Which you obviously didn't."

"No, but someone who knew our name and the license number did." Victor raised his head, and he and Louise locked eyes.

"That cheap, two-bit thug," she said.

"Now, hold on. We don't know he did it."

"You didn't even have to ask who I meant."

"He always tells me if he wants to borrow it. And—I always say yes."

"He never even fills up the tank when he's done with it."

"This makes no sense," said Victor.

"It makes worlds of sense. Mr. Gold called for the car; Mr. Gold took the car. I wonder how often he's done this without our knowledge or permission."

A siren screamed outside. The hairs on the backs of Victor's hands prickled like tiny knives. "Where's Bobby?"

"He and Tori went to see *Rocky Horror*. Why—what?"

Victor was shaking his head violently. "They only show it Fridays and Saturdays."

"I thought it was an extra screening for the long weekend."

Victor sat back, relieved. "Right. Probably getting worked up about nothing." He reached for the phone book. "I'll call, just to make sure."

"Bobby has the Playhouse schedule in his room." Louise left the study and came back with a flyer, her eyes wide. "You're right. There's no show listed for tonight."

She read him the number. Victor dialed, spoke briefly with the box office, and hung up, his face drawn. "You're sure he said *Rocky Horror?*"

"Positive. He said they were going with Nichelle."

He handed her the phone. "Call her parents."

"Well, if either of them calls, would you give us a ring? It doesn't matter how late. Yes. Right. Thanks." Louise hung up, glaring at Victor. "Nichelle has a 'gig.' She's not with Bobby, and Bobby's not at *Rocky Horror.*"

"Oh, God."

"Call your brother."

"Now, let's not jump to conclusions," protested Victor.

Louise snorted. "He steals our car the same night our son lies to us and disappears. Do you really think that's a coincidence?"

"He would never do anything to hurt Bobby," whispered Victor.

"Then please call him *now* so he can explain that to you."

Victor dialed. The phone rang. And rang. And rang. He hung up, bowing his head. Traffic thumped outside. "What could Jacob want from Bobby?" he said finally.

Louise spoke as if every word hurt. "The Desert Sun."

"No."

"Victor, listen to me. He told you someone was after the diamond, but he wouldn't say who."

"He was helping me."

"Then he asked about the security for it. And you told him."

"That doesn't mean he...." His voice trailed off. "But what about Bobby?"

"Bobby knows that museum better than anyone who isn't actually on staff, and Jacob knows it."

"No." Victor shoved his chair back, as if to escape her words.

"If he puts our son in danger—"

"He wouldn't do something like that. Not to Bobby."

"Tori," said Louise suddenly.

"What about her?"

"If she's involved with something illegal? Think what happens to runaways in this city." She took a deep breath. "My God, if he harms that girl, I will—!" She stormed out of the study.

"Where are you going?" called Victor.

"I'm searching Bobby's room. And so are you."

◊

"Need any more proof?" said Louise bitterly. They stared in horrified fascination at their reconstruction of the paper Tori had torn up. *DS at AMNH—How Get?*

Victor's shaking finger pointed at the familiar handwriting. "Desert Sun."

Stealing Time

"Yes."

"And—today's hours for the museum."

"Yes."

"You don't think." Victor cleared his throat. "Bobby wouldn't do something like that."

"For Jacob?" Louise looked up at him. "Or to help Tori?"

He shuddered. "I'm calling Todd."

A brief conversation with Todd's family babysitter revealed that Mr. Dixon and his wife were out enjoying an Irish a cappella concert and could not be reached. She promised to have him call upon his return.

"I'll try the command center at the museum," said Victor. He dialed the number. The phone rang. And rang. And rang.

⁓◇⁓

"Call the police," said Louise.

"With their track record? Not unless I can reach Serpico personally."

"Then what?" cried Louise. "What else is there?"

Victor marched to the hall closet and pulled on his coat. "I'll go to the museum. If Jacob's there, he'll listen to me. And if Bobby's with him—"

Louise folded her arms. "You'll never get a taxi."

"Subway, then."

"Would take an hour at least. And what will you do once you get there?"

"Then I'll—I'll—" Victor stopped, one arm in his sleeve, and stared at Louise with tear-shattered eyes. "What can we do?" he burst out. "Bobby needs us."

Chapter 41

Smash and Grab

~◇~

Maeve stopped at the doorway to the exhibition hall, eyes alight. "Ready?"

"Hell, yeah." Gloria's smile sparkled in the dusk.

Moving as fluidly as a swell on the ocean, they dropped their backpacks to the floor and unzipped them, pulling on gloves and grasping ball-peen hammers. They glided through the exhibit, smashing and grabbing. Flakes of light fell through the air, and glass crackled under their feet like sand. Gloria's bag sagged under the weight of stones. Maeve lifted a necklace from its case and let it slide through her fingers in a stream of luster. She felt as though she were breathing fire instead of air. Every moment of her life had brought her to this very second, this flash of perfection, and she laughed with savage joy.

Gloria crashed her hammer down on the largest case, and it shattered in a luminous cloud. "Hey—what's that?"

A series of grunts sounded in the hallway, followed by a gasp and the sort of crash one does not want to hear when speed and silence are of the essence. Maeve dropped the necklace. "Abort."

"Is it those kids?"

"I said *abort*, goddamn it!" Maeve dropped her sagging backpack to the crook of her arm, hoicked it shut, yanked it onto her shoulders, and churned toward the doorway like a speedboat, hammer clenched in one hand.

"Now, ladies, is that any way to greet your old pal?"

Maeve whipped to a stop, her sneakers kicking up a froth of broken glass. "Sonofabitch."

"Missed you too, babe." The slight figure stepped out of the shadows, mouth lifted at one corner as though listening to a joke no one else could hear. A light danced contemptuously in his dark eyes, but his knees shook.

Gloria sucked in her breath. The other two stared at each other across a yard of space, unmoving. Beyond the museum, seven million human beings were sleeping or drinking, fighting or singing, reading the *Daily News* or using it to catch drips as they painted their rent-controlled apartments; but in the midst of this vital swirl of activity, two people who scant hours ago would have placed their lives in each other's hands glared at one another with a rage that only betrayal can birth.

Maeve spoke first. "Mike was right about you."

"Maybe I was right about him."

"Get out."

"Not till I get what I came for."

Maeve's shoulders tightened under her drooping backpack. "You can forget about your share for this job, asshole."

"Done." Snake spoke with barely a tremor in his voice. "Take the damn rocks. I don't care."

"I thought you were going to wait for us in the car," said Gloria.

Snake chuckled as he sauntered over to her. "That was plan A, kid."

"How did you get in?"

"Same way you did," he replied, and for the first time she saw that his knuckles were bloody and his knees were scuffed. Shoving past her, he plucked the luminous stone from its cushion and tossed it from hand to hand. It blazed with the flame-glow of stars being born, of the laughter that overcomes darkness, of time and eternity whirling in an unending dance. Gloria thought of the crystal nestled in her bag, and realized that whatever else it might be, it was not the Desert Sun.

Jacob's eyes widened with appreciation. "Damn, that's enough carats to choke Bugs Bunny."

Maeve leaped to his side and swiped at the jewel, but he yanked it out of her reach. His smile was dangerous. "Where are the kids, Maeve?"

"Give me the fucking rock."

"This thing is made of time. Or so my brother tells me."

"Let him have it," said Gloria. "We got plenty already."

Maeve shook her head. "That's the one we came for."

"Compressed time, man." Jacob lowered his hand, still gripping the precious stone. "Can you dig it?"

"Maeve—"

"Thing about time is, it's the only thing you can't make more of."

"We got as much as we need," said Maeve.

"Maybe not as much as you think," said Snake.

"He's right," said Gloria. "We gotta move."

"I'm not leaving without that thing."

"You don't have to." Jacob tossed it again, and it wheeled through the air, scattering fire in the shadows.

Maeve's eyes glowed like black embers. "Nothing's free with you," she spat.

"True."

"What do you want?"

"Just that one little thing," said Jacob. "Or two, since I guess his girlfriend's with him."

"I don't know where they are." Maeve's jaw was tight.

"Then you better figure it out pretty quick, babe."

"Gimme that rock."

"No."

"Do what the lady says, you dumb fuck," said a deep voice.

All three heads swiveled toward the doorway. Teresa, smirking, held Tori by the arm. Next to her, Mike gripped Bobby in one massive fist. The boy's wrists were bound in front of him, and his eyes were wide and glassy. Mike's other hand held a knife, its blade at Bobby's throat.

Chapter 42
Rise of the Desert Sun

Tori stared at the unreal tableau. Empty display cases, broken and gaping like mouths with their teeth punched out. Maeve and another woman, both dressed in black and glaring like hot iron, bracketing Bobby's Uncle Jacob. And everything seeming to float in a star-cloud of broken glass.

Jacob nodded at Bobby. When he spoke, his voice was mild. "Just out of curiosity, kid, what the fuck are you doing here?"

"Playing Hardy Boys," said Mike. He jabbed his knife a little higher, forcing Bobby's head to what must have been an uncomfortable angle. The boy gagged. "You know this punk?"

"My nephew."

"Guess stupid runs in your family."

"Not our shiningest moment," admitted Jacob. His fist was at his side, and between his fingers Tori could see facets of an enormous solitaire. Maeve was looking from it to Mike; so was Gloria. Tori thought, *That thing is what everybody wants.*

"Then I'll use nice, short words," said Mike. "Get out."

"Soon as I have the kids."

The diamond is why we're all here.

"Hey!" barked Maeve. "Who's giving the orders?"

The knife was tight in Mike's fist, his eyes tight on Jacob. "I'll let 'em go when we're in the clear."

If I get it, I can bargain for Bobby's life.

"Other way around, Mikey."

"No."

"Then no deal."

Maeve whirled to face Jacob. "Do what he says."

"Forget it, babe."

That guard's still unconscious. No one else knows we're here.

"We don't want the kids," said Maeve. "Just the rocks."

"And I don't want the rocks. Just the kids."

"Yeah? How's that gonna work with No-Name?"

"I'll worry about him later."

She scowled. "Know how I can tell you're lying? Your lips are moving."

"Not this time, gorgeous." Jacob's smile never wavered. "Leave the kids, and I'll take the fall."

"Like hell."

Outside, clearly audible through the broken window in the hallway, above the ever-present blur of traffic, a siren sounded.

"I already called the cops," he went on.

"You don't have the balls," said Maeve.

The siren grew louder. Gloria gasped, and her face blanched like a star extinguished. Maeve panted, shoulders heaving. "You—goddamn—prick-weasel—"

"I love it when you talk dirty to me."

"Maeve," cried Gloria. "We have to go."

"After all the work we put in? Fat chance."

"Just leave the gems on your way out," said Jacob. "And the kids, of course. Was I clear enough about that?"

"So you can walk away with the loot." Teresa's mouth was right by Tori's ear, and her voice was uncomfortably loud.

"So I can tell the cops I was alone," said Jacob. "Hard to do if the rocks are gone."

The sirens grew louder till the shadows pulsed with sound. Gloria stumbled, pushing through Mike and Teresa. "No, no, no—I can't—" She ran down the hallway, her eyes alight with tears.

"Gloria!" cried Teresa.

"Damn, she seems shook up," said Jacob

"You shit," said Teresa. "She's on probation. They catch her, she's done." Her grip tightened, and Tori winced.

"Is that so?" Jacob seemed intrigued. "How inconvenient. Because my guess is as soon as she sees the inside of the pig wagon, she'll sing like a soprano at the Met."

Maeve whirled on him. "Sonofabitch. This is your fault."

Jacob's eyes dropped to his clenched fist. "Yeah. It is."

How can I get it away from him?

"Hold up." Teresa frowned at Maeve. The sirens had stopped.

"Oh, hey," said Jacob, lifting his head. "Is that the sound of a squealer being taken into custody? I think it is."

Bleak silence filled the room. Maeve looked out the windows, and turned slowly back toward Jacob. Her breath made a restless sound, and a flame flickered at the back of her eyes, growing brighter and clearer as she spoke. "When…did you drop the dime on us?"

"Let's see." Jacob rubbed his chin with his free hand. "I think it was right after you called me a ratfink Judas flopdick."

Teresa spoke up. "You didn't have time."

"It was a short conversation, sweetheart."

"There's no phonebooth where you parked."

"There is unless they moved it in the past ten minutes."

She shook her head. "It's on the other side of the block. Woulda taken you ten minutes there and ten back, plus however long you took to squeal, before you could even start to climb up here." In her excitement, she loosened her grip. Tori tried to breathe normally. *I can do this. I can get that diamond and save Bobby.*

"So you're lying," said Maeve.

"Don't hurt my feelings like that."

"If you told the cops about this job, they'd be inside the museum by now."

Timing has to be perfect.

Jacob tossed off an airy laugh. "Look, ladies—"

"This is on you, Maeve," thundered Mike. "If you'd of listened to me—"

"Who runs this gang, you or me?" flared Maeve.

"There's only one way to end this." Mike shoved Bobby forward. The boy gasped, wide-eyed.

"Hey, man, relax," said Jacob. A shimmer of sweat stood out on his forehead.

"Don't try to smooth-dog your way out of this one," snarled Mike. He tensed the arm holding the knife. "Know what happens to double-crossers? Their families get hurt."

"Stop," cried Jacob. He held up his hand, and on his palm the enormous stone glistered. "Take it. Just don't hurt the kid."

"Damn right, I'll take it." Mike's lips pulled back, and his teeth showed. "Soon as I'm done with this little turd."

"Then have fun finding it," said Jacob. He pulled back his arm and threw.

The Desert Sun rose above the astonished group, trailing coruscating rainbows in its wake.

"Get it!" yelled Maeve.

Teresa lifted her head to follow the arc of the soaring diamond. Tori stomped on her feet. Tiny bones crunched.

Teresa screamed and dropped Tori's arm. The star-colored gemstone spiraled overhead, shedding pinwheels of light and time. Tori stumbled toward it, hands outstretched. *Grab it—save Bobby—*

Mike hurled Bobby aside. The boy hit the floor hard, and rolled over with his head cradled in his arms. Mike lunged at the gem.

So did Maeve.

And Teresa.

Jacob launched himself upon them. Tori heard the sound of flesh striking flesh, and guttural gasps as teeth and knuckles and bone slammed together. Time stretched and collapsed.

The diamond shot over her head landed on the floor, lustrous in the saturated shadows.

Mike blasted out of the scrum of bodies. Jacob grabbed at him. Maeve pushed herself up on one elbow, striking viciously at his knee. Jacob screamed and fell, and Tori saw the flash of a hammer in Maeve's hand.

Mike leaped at the stone. Still on the floor, Bobby twisted to one side and kicked it toward Tori. She slid headlong across the smooth marble, hands outstretched. Her fingers curled over it.

"Tori, *run!*" screamed Bobby.

But Tori could not run. She could not stand. The Desert Sun burned in her hands. Time dripped from her fingers. Brilliance streamed into her veins, protons and moonglow soaring through her plasma. A wave of spitting light hit the ceiling and coursed down the walls in searing bands of color. Radiance swirled from the heart of the diamond, taking shape and forming visions that Tori understood in the way of a dream.

Her apartment.

The printer in her dad's study, spewing papers around the room like falling leaves in Central Park.

Her bedroom, with her father at the closed door.

A gray sidewalk, lifeless except for her mom, who was scurrying toward the front door of their building, shopping bags banging against her legs, her face tight with fear.

The undulating images pulled on Tori, merging with the magnificent glow that filled her every corpuscle. She was made of light, and light was made of her. She slid into the whirl of iridescent warmth and memory.

"Oh, crap," she thought as 1980 dissolved. "I hope Bobby's okay."

Chapter 43
Let's Do the Time Warp Again

The walls buckled. The floor pitched and rolled, sending plumes of broken glass aloft. Sparks of blue and green, gold, cerise, and chartreuse, hung in the air and clung to the walls, blazing like living opals. Mike crouched low, rigid with terror, eyes sweeping the room. "Grenade!"

"Flashbang!" cried Maeve as she struggled to her feet.

The exhibit hall shuddered to a stop. The sparks dimmed. In the shadow-drenched doorway, a wavering figure appeared, listing and unsteady but determined. "Freeze," grumbled Fred.

"Oh, *shit*," said Teresa.

In the next four seconds, several things happened.

Maeve, Teresa, and Mike hurtled toward the doorway. Fred held up a hand to stop them. The hand, being vastly outnumbered, did not last long against the stampede. It and its owner were hurled aside, and Fred slammed into the doorframe with a bone-jarring jerk, falling to one knee. As the torrent of footfalls and cursing swept down the hallway, he pulled himself up and stumbled after it. "Freeze!" he begged. "Freeze!"

Two shadows lay on the marble floor, dark and still as onyx. One of them moaned and half-rose, crawling to the other. A fumble, a click, and blades shone in its hand.

Bobby whirled around, his bound fists landing like a mallet on Jacob's cheekbone. The knife clattered to the floor as Jacob whipped back, his hands flying to his face. "*Ow!* It's me, kid."

"I know," snarled Bobby. He kicked, pushing himself away from his uncle.

Jacob glanced at the doorway, then back at Bobby. "Gimme your hands."

"Come and get them." He drew back his doubled fists for another strike.

Jacob sighed. "We don't have time for this, kid."

"Screw you."

Jacob picked up the Swiss Army knife he had dropped when Bobby hit him. Miniature scissors poked from the case. "Your hands," he repeated. "Unless you wanna chew through that stuff."

Bobby hesitated, then lowered his fists. Jacob snipped through the duct tape, and Bobby yanked it off, glaring. "I hate you."

"Me too." Jacob clicked the scissors back into the knife and slipped it into his pocket. "Let's get out of here."

Bobby stared at the exhibit hall with its tall, dark windows and its glittering field of slivered glass. "Where is she?"

"Your girlfriend? Probably bolted during the fireworks."

"She wouldn't."

"Seems she did. Say, what the hell was that, anyway?"

"And she's not my girlfriend."

"Whoever she is, she's smart enough to cut and run." He turned toward the door again. "Coming?"

"No."

"Bobby, this is fucking serious. We gotta get out of here."

"Then you go, since that's so smart."

287

"Not without you."

"Yes without me."

"Jesus, Bobby—"

"She might come back." Bobby crouched on the spot where Tori had been. A lemon-sized stone lay on the floor, and he stretched out his hand to it.

"Don't touch that!" Jacob kicked the stone aside.

Bobby jumped in surprise, losing his balance and almost falling. "Hey!"

"Crime scene." Jacob was almost panting. "You want the cops thinking you were in on this?"

Bobby stood, wiping his hands on his jeans and glaring. "Anyway. I'm staying here till they show up."

"Which they won't unless someone calls them."

Bobby blinked. "But you said—"

"I lied."

"How did you know there was going to be a siren right then?"

"That was a little luck and a lot of improv, kid."

"Holy shit, Uncle Jacob—"

"Right now we're still lucky, so let's use it."

Bobby stared at the spot that no longer held Tori. "Forget it."

Jacob stepped close, blocking his view. "Bobby, listen to me. We need to call the cops. Right now, the girls are climbing out of the museum, and Mike's going to meet them later—"

"How do you know?"

"Because I planned this job."

Bobby glowered at him. "You are such an asshole."

"Alternatively, they might come back for the rest of this shit. So let's *go*."

Scowling, Bobby strode out of the exhibit hall, Jacob limping in his wake.

"Slow down." Jacob was breathing hard.

"You said to move."

"I've had better days, kid."

Bobby stopped at an emergency light, and his eyes widened. Jacob's cheeks were scraped, one eye was swelling shut, and a smear of blood darkened his upper lip. "You need a doctor."

Jacob shook his head and kept walking. "Need a cop more."

"Maybe the guard will catch them." Bobby fell in beside him.

"Maybe angels will shoot out of my ass and sing the national anthem."

"Why are you so in love with cops all of a sudden?"

"Because Maeve and her crew couldn't pour water out of a boot with the instructions on the heel. They can shake a punch-drunk rent-a-cop, but not New York's finest. They're gonna get caught, and when they do they're gonna spill, so I need to call the cops right now."

"Why?"

"I'll explain later."

Bobby followed him, staring angrily at the floor. When he looked up, they were at Victor's office and Jacob was punching numbers on the keypad.

"My dad told you the combination?" said Bobby in surprise.

"You're kidding, right?"

Bobby sagged against the wall. "Then forget it. There's literally millions of possibilities."

"Yeah, but only one of them is your birthday." Jacob turned the knob, and the door opened. "Coming?"

Bobby stared stupidly at the keypad and shook his head with silent fury as he stooped to pick up the things Mike had made him drop.

"What's that?" said Jacob.

Bobby clenched his fist around the items. "None of your business."

"Show me."

"No."

Jacob stood on the threshold of the office and frowned. "Listen to me, kid. We have a very small, very closing window to control just a little of what happens after I call 911. One thing that will definitely happen no matter what is the cops will search you. So if whatever's in your hand is gonna push you deeper in the shit, tell me now."

Bobby glared, then winced as the action irritated a bruise forming under his left eye. He held out his hand.

Jacob's eyes widened. "Holy shit, kid, are you trying to make juvenile delinquent of the year?"

"We were trying to stop the robbery," mumbled Bobby.

"And you had to bring a burglary kit?" Jacob snatched everything from him, shaking his head. "Flashlight, I guess that's okay. Seems pretty benign. Knife?"

"Bar mitzvah present from my dad."

"Marginal. And the gloves definitely gotta go." He rubbed his chin. "Burn 'em? Nah. The stink is too obvious."

Bobby scrabbled at him. "Give them back!"

"Hey!" Jacob whisked his hand away. "Calm down, kid."

"She gave them to me!" shouted Bobby.

Jacob glanced up and down the hallway, jamming the gloves into his pocket and holding open the door with his free hand. "We'll talk inside."

"Do you think she's okay?" said Bobby as he closed the door behind himself.

"Likely." Jacob reached for the phone. "The gang won't want a hostage now—it'd slow them down. So as long as she sticks to the shadows, she's copacetic."

"Then why call the cops?" said Bobby.

"Because Maeve and Gloria's bags were bulging with boodle, as the press might say. Cops like to know these things, along with stuff like where the gang's staying locally, and where they live in Florida. Do me a favor and lock the door, okay?" He took his finger off the button and dialed. "Hang tight, kid," he said as he hung up. "They'll be here in a few."

"There's a back way out." Bobby shifted toward the door.

"I said hang tight."

Bobby stared at him. "If I get busted, my mom will kill me."

"If you bolt out of here at the wrong second, the cops will kill you."

"No, they won't."

"Someone runs out of a crime scene in the dark? They shoot. It's 1980, kid. Time to get tough on crime, unless you haven't heard."

"But they'll arrest you."

"I'm counting on it."

"Why?"

"Get there first, lower my sentence."

"How?"

"Last one to sing has the least to say, kid. I'm gonna tell the cops everything I know about the gang before the gang tells the cops everything they know about me."

"Seriously?"

"Kid, I am gonna roll on them like an explosion in a ball-bearing factory. But first, we gotta settle this." He pulled Bobby's belongings out of his pocket, and tossed the boy his flashlight. Bobby caught it with one hand. "Like I said, that seems pretty benign. Lots of kids have 'em. But can you explain these gloves in any way that doesn't make it look like you were robbing this place?"

"I told you," Bobby almost whispered. "Tori gave them to me."

"When?"

"Tonight. So I wouldn't leave fingerprints."

"Tonight, here?"

"Yeah."

Jacob sighed deeply. "She gives you latex gloves in the middle of a B&E. Want to explain that to the fuzz?"

Bobby blinked and looked at the floor.

"Me neither. So if you'll excuse me, I'm gonna take my last leak as a free man."

"Are you serious?"

"As a heart attack. Prison toilets are skeevy, man."

Jacob listened at the door, then opened it a finger's width while bracing it against his foot. He peeked up and down the hallway, then, satisfied it was empty, strode into the men's room three doors down from Victor's office, holding the gloves. A moment later, the sound of flushing filled the hall, and he emerged empty-handed.

Bobby was leaning against the wall, hugging his elbows. He looked at his uncle. "Uncle Jacob?" His voice was small.

"Yeah?"

"Are you going to jail?"

Jacob passed a hand wearily over his forehead. "Yeah."

Stealing Time

Bobby swallowed. "For how long?"

"Few years. Most likely."

Bobby looked at the floor and took a ragged breath, and another, as though something were tearing deep inside of him. Jacob stood next to him. "It's okay, kid," he said quietly. "I'll see you on the other side."

Chapter 44
New York City, Monday, March 16, 2020

◊

Tori sat up on her bed, gasping like a weekend warrior in the New York City Marathon. She lifted a hand to brush her hair from her sweat-soaked cheeks, but her fingers were transparent, made of shadow and memory. She tried to scream, but only a gurgling bleat came out. Luminosity reeled around her with a fantastic rushing noise, painting angles and shapes. She could see through her flesh to the cheery yellow of her bedroom walls—

Bobby's bedroom walls are white.

—with its posters of *Hamilton* and Billie Eilish, looped over with fairy lights.

Where's all the nerd crap?

Her palms grew firm, then her fingers, and finally her nails. The room gave a final ripple—

Buffering?

—and stopped. Tori drew a tattered breath. She could feel her heart thumping in her chest, not swirling with eddies of present and past. Her legs shook, and her now-solid hands were wet. She wiped them on her shirt.

Her Wonder Woman tee shirt from the Gap.

She was still in 1980!

Oh, shit.

A knock at her door. "Tori?" said Bobby.

STEALING TIME

"Come in," she said miserably. The diamond had been their last shot, and all it had done was jet her across town.

Her father threw open the door and bounded across the room to clasp her in a bear hug. "Welcome home," he whispered.

"Dad?" She pushed away and stared up at Bobby's kind, funny eyes looking at her from her father's middle-aged face.

"Good to have you back, kiddo." His gray hair was neatly combed, his figure trim.

Tori stepped back, taking in the room with her colors, her posters, and her clothes poking from the closet door. "Home?"

"It's 2020."

"2020?"

"And I see you still have a side hustle as an echo."

She ran her hands through her hair, tucking the purple lock behind her ear. "You knew?"

"Took a pandemic to make me forget it." He pulled out her desk chair and lowered himself into it. "But then I saw all that chromatic stuff melting under your door, and a sound like a hurricane and an opera had a baby, and I was like, 'Wait—is today the sixteenth?' So I knocked, and, well, obviously you just got back." He nodded at the shirt.

She plopped down heavily onto her bed, a concession to her still-teetering knees. "It worked."

"Sure did. Were you just at the museum?"

"Yeah." She looked around again. White sunshine streamed through the window, but the usual sounds of New York—traffic, horns, shouting—were absent. She took a deep breath, pulling 2020 into her lungs. "Wow."

"How you feeling?"

"Like I have the worst jet lag ever."

"Want a glass of water?" His heavy brows knitted with worry.

"Nah. If it's like last time, I'll get over it soon enough." She grinned at him. "Did we stop the heist of the century?"

"We did." He smiled Bobby's smile.

"Then what happened?"

"After you left?" He drew a deep breath. "Well, the cops came."

"Uh-oh."

"Jacob called them."

"Seriously?"

"Seriously. Turns out he owed money to some pretty unsavory characters. Between that and the gang suddenly wanting him dead, a holding cell must have looked pretty good."

"You were *arrested?*"

"Him, very much so. Me, no. The first cop took one look at us and said," her father's voice deepened and took on a depthless Brooklyn patois, "'What kind of assclown uses a kid for a human shield?'"

"Omigod."

"Then he goes, 'Call his mom. We ain't doin' nuttin' till we talk to her.'"

Tori jerked upright, eyes wide. "No."

"Yes."

"That is *so* much worse."

"Oh, God, yes. Made for a hell of a college essay, though."

"You—went to college, then."

"MIT class of '88."

"Congratulations, Dad. That's awesome."

"Thanks. The acceptance letter might have been when my folks forgave me."

"Ouch."

"Very ouch. The cops took me and Jacob down to the local precinct—say, did you know the back of a cop car doesn't have door handles?"

"I did not."

"Well, now you do. Anyway, my parents got there...it wasn't pretty."

"I bet."

"My mother never forgave Jacob."

"What happened to him?"

"He landed on his feet, more or less," said her father with a trace of bitterness. "His kind generally does."

Tori made a mental note to Google "Jacob Gold," now that she was back in the land of the Internet. Her fingers brushed the phone in her pocket. Phone! "So I just went poof?"

"Oh, God, if only."

"What do you mean?"

"You disappeared, all right. The problem was, so many people had seen you. Me, my parents, Jacob, the gang...and then suddenly, there you weren't. How could I explain I was pretty sure you'd gone back to a place that didn't exist yet?"

"I never thought of that."

"So I just kept telling everybody I didn't know where you were."

"Did they believe you?"

"Would you?"

"Guess not."

"And it was a high-profile case, so the cops kept asking and searching. Of course they never found you, so eventually you were...declared dead." He swallowed, and his voice was suddenly scratchy. "Just another kid who disappeared from New York back then."

"Hey, are you okay?" said Tori in concern.

He looked at her with tear-bright eyes. "It was the worst day of my life."

Tori stood up and touched her father's shoulder. It was shaking.

"I cried like a baby," he went on. "Your grandmother too...God, it was awful. She thought you were a runaway, you see, so when you disappeared she blamed herself for not taking better care of you that weekend, letting you know you mattered.... Then, years later when your mom was expecting and we found out we were having a girl, Grandma Louise suggested we name the baby after my friend who vanished all those decades ago."

Tori's head was awhirl. "So I'm named after...me?"

"What can I say?" Her father spread his hands.

"Waitaminit." She held up her hand. "So my whole life you've known I was me from back then?"

"Not really, no."

"But you just said I was named after me."

"The day you were born you were just a baby," he said. "Then you were a toddler, and then a little girl."

"That's the usual sequence, isn't it?"

"My point is, I didn't know if you were going to be the Tori I knew from back then, or just some kid with the same name."

Tori inhaled as the import of his words sank in. How do you raise a kid you might already have met? She imagined him watching his child for a decade and a half to see if she was the girl from forty years ago—no, wait, to see if she would turn *into* that girl from forty years ago—but that girl, the Tori from 2020 who went back to 1980, had grown up with a different Bobby as a father, one who hadn't known her from before. So he was a different person, which made her a different person, since she'd grown up with him. No, wait—she'd grown up with cranky Bob and his weight of misery. But then what about the Tori who had grown up with this dad instead? Had the two of them meshed on her return flight? She squeezed her eyes shut. "My brain is going to go kablooey."

"It's a lot to take in," he agreed.

"You seem okay with it."

"I've had time to sit with the idea."

"Fifteen years."

"Or forty, depending on how you count. Anyway, I watched you grow into smart, funny, tough you. Then last summer you got the purple hair, and I started to think the odds were pretty good you were in for some time travel."

"Why didn't you tell me?"

"I can't believe I'm saying this, but would you have believed me?"

"Not at all."

"Also, I thought there were some things about your future that I shouldn't share with you."

She giggled. "That's fair."

"I thought so." He smiled something like Bobby's smile, but softer, a mix of Bobby's and her father's. She realized with a shock that both of them were proud of her.

"So I'm named for Future Girl, after all those years of being named for your dad." She shook her head. "That's going to take some getting used to."

"You can talk it over with him."

"With who?"

"Granddad. He and Grandma should be here shortly." The spark was back in Bobby's eyes, and he looked as though he might cackle. "Nichelle and Katya—did you meet her? So much to catch up on! We were all in high school together, and they got married as soon as it was legal. I was best dude. Anyway, Grandma and Grandpa flew in from Greece yesterday—"

"They did *what?*"

"Caught the last flight before the airports all shut. Took a little doing, I can tell you."

"What the heck were they doing in Greece?"

"I guess in your previous life your grandparents weren't working with Syrian refugees on Lesbos."

Tori felt dizzy again, but this time it had nothing directly to do with time travel. "No. No, they were not."

"I took your advice and got Grandma Louise to stop smoking."

"No way."

"Way. She's very perky."

"What else do they do? Tough Mudder competitions and senior pickleball league?"

"No, they had to give those up after your grandfather got his knees replaced."

"So what about Nichelle and Katie?"

"Katya. They're over at your grandparents', helping them to pack to come over here."

"Say what now?"

"I mean, my folks are pretty spry for their ages, but we thought it would be best if they stayed with us for the next couple weeks, till this coronavirus thing dies down. Your mom would have been happy to pick them up, but Nichelle and Katya have that big car, what with all the guitars."

"So...wait, where's Mom?"

"Probably has some other shopper in a headlock over a roll of toilet paper."

Tori felt a lightness in her chest. "So you guys aren't splitting?"

"Oh, God, no."

Tori punched the air. "That's *awesome!*"

"I think a lot of things are going to be very different from what you remember," said her dad. He hesitated. "One in particular."

"What?" said Tori warily. He looked so serious all of a sudden.

Bob rubbed his ear and took a deep breath. "It's about my parenting skills."

Tori blushed. "Oh."

"I believe you used the word 'asshole.'"

"Sorry." Tori stared at the carpet. Just when she was starting to think things would be different, her dad went and picked a fight.

"No, no." He touched her on the shoulder, and she looked up. "*I'm* sorry. I made you unhappy, and I feel terrible about it."

"You do?" And then she remembered she was talking to Bobby as well as her dad.

"I do. And I've been waiting a long time to apologize."

Tori wanted to laugh. She wanted to cry. Instead she said, "Forget it. That wasn't you. That was someone else."

"Who you helped keep me from becoming."

She gazed at him thoughtfully. "You're Bobby."

"I'm also your dad."

"True." She chewed her lip. "Jekyll *and* Hyde."

"Wow. Was it that bad?"

"No, no," she said hastily. "I'm just thinking that you're both these guys, and it's weird."

"It is that."

"We're in uncharted territory."

"Again."

"Kind of a thing with us, isn't it?"

"Does seem to be," he agreed. "But we got through it last time."

"That was a weekend," said Tori. "This is a lifetime." She was conscious of fifteen years of memories pulling on her like a parachute after a jump. She studied his face. It was the face of someone she had known for a long time, ever since he was her age.

"Think we can figure it out?" he said.

"Yeah. You're really different now."

"Thanks?"

"I mean—"

"Forget it," he chuckled. "I'm just messing with you. And look, while we're waiting for everyone to get here, why don't you walk me through what happened back then? Forty years ago, I mean."

"You were just telling me all about it."

"Sure, but I've forgotten parts. It was a long time ago." He smiled. "And you know, I was only a kid."

Epilogue

New York Times, Obituary Section

Jacob Gold, Noted Jewel Thief, Dies at 73

Jacob "Jake the Snake" Gold, a convicted thief connected to one of the biggest jewel heists in New York City history, died July 21 at his home in Manhattan. He was 73. The cause was heart failure, according to his brother, Dr. Victor Gold.

Mr. Gold was a gambler and petty thief who operated on the outskirts of New York's vast underworld in the 1960s and seventies. His life of crime was unremarkable until 1980, when he confessed to having helped plan and execute the theft of the Desert Sun, a storied diamond that was the centerpiece of a display at the American Museum of Natural History, where his brother, Dr. Gold, was chief gemologist. The daring theft took place over St. Patrick's Day weekend and made front-page news nationwide. The diamond and all other jewelry from the ransacked exhibit were recovered within 48 hours, thanks largely to Mr. Gold's detailed information regarding his accomplices, the notorious Hopewell Gang, led by Maeve "the Wave" Hopewell, a semi-professional surfer from Florida. Mr. Gold's voluminous testimony also helped convict the gang, all of whom served prison sentences for their roles in the heist.

Mr. Gold was taken into custody at the scene of the crime, along with his juvenile nephew, Robert, the son of Dr. Gold. The following day, however, he was released when Generoso Pope, the owner and publisher of the *National Enquirer*, secured his bail and paid him for a multi-part exclusive about the heist. (Mr. Pope, by then a resident of Florida, flew to New York expressly for this purpose, betting correctly that the escapade would make for a publishing bonanza.) The colorful story was serialized in subsequent issues of the tabloid, with stories focusing on the mechanics of the heist, the colorful characters involved, and the disappearance of a teenage girl who had been present at the scene. This last installment was the most popular, owing perhaps to Mr. Gold's suggestion that the child was a space alien with purple hair.

Persistent rumors stated that Mr. Gold used the monies provided to him by Mr. Pope to pay off shadowy figures to whom he owed considerable sums.

Although Mr. Gold cooperated fully—some would say enthusiastically—with the authorities, his central role in the robbery, combined with his criminal record, led to his conviction and a sentence of three years in prison.

Shortly after his release, a lucky hand at poker won him the proprietorship of a small shop that sold baseball cards and other sports paraphernalia. He renamed it Gold's Diamonds to reflect his claim to fame. Apparently tiring of a life of lawlessness, Mr. Gold ran the shop without incident from 1984 until his death.

Mr. Gold borrowed his brother's car the night of the heist, resulting in Dr. Gold's briefly coming under suspicion as a possible accomplice. However, Lucas Van der Bleek, the wealthy philanthropist who owned the Desert Sun and other pieces in the exhibition, came to his defense, stating, "We cannot judge individuals by what their families do. I have known Dr. Gold for years, and he is incapable of anything dishonorable." An internal investigation confirmed Dr. Gold's innocence. He was later quoted as saying that Mr. Van der Bleek's public show of support was instrumental in saving his reputation from possible association with the crime.

Jacob Gold was born on Jan. 23, 1935 in New York City to Sidney, an organizer with the International Ladies' Garment Workers' Union (ILGWU), and Frieda (Feldman) Gold, a women's suffragist and factory worker. Mr. Gold attended Brooklyn College for one year before being expelled for paying a classmate to take an exam for him.

In addition to his brother, Mr. Gold is survived by his sister-in-law Louise, and their son Robert.

THE END

A Word of Explanation

If you visit the American Museum of Natural History and meander into the Halls of Gems and Minerals, you will notice right away that they are on the first floor, not the fourth; and that they are windowless, not windowful. In short, they are radically different from the Hall of Gems in *Stealing Time*. So what's up with that?

On October 29, 1964, surfer and surf-shop owner Jack Roland Murphy, nicknamed "Murph the Surf," broke into the American Museum of Natural History along with two accomplices. Their target: the Star of India, a 563-carat sapphire, one of the most valuable jewels in the world at that time. The gang entered the Hall of Gems, then on the fourth floor, by climbing through one of its windows, which had been left open for ventilation purposes. Once inside, they found that all of the burglar alarms were broken; and they did not encounter any guards. (We swear, we are not making this up.) The gang made off with the Star of India and many of the other gems—a hoard worth millions of dollars in today's money. They were caught within two days, and in their mad scramble to implicate each other they revealed the locations of many of the gems, including the Star of India. Much of the treasure was never recovered, however, and the museum responded by moving the Hall of Gems to the first floor and getting rid of all the windows. Thus it is to this day.

When we set out to write this book, we changed Murph the Surf into Maeve the Wave, and invented the fictional Desert Sun as a stand-in for the Star of India. We also put the Hall of

Gems back on the fourth floor, as if the 1964 heist had never happened. Everything else is an accurate depiction of New York in 1980, or as close as we could get.

Thanks for reading this far—we hope we made it worth your time.

Visit us a stealingtime.net

Acknowledgments

Creating a book takes readers, proofreaders, editors, and more: a literary village. We would like to thank the denizens who made *Stealing Time* possible.

Every writer needs a ruthless editor. Ours is Michael Marano, and we are grateful for his insights.

Every book needs beta readers. Ours are Lilly Clair Colón, Nathaniel Findlay, Kara Hatalsky, Nyosha Homicil, Blair Nelson-Peterman, Lily Novak, Allyson Walker, Alex Webb-Hackl, and Bryn Zilch. Thank you for helping us make sure that Tori, Bobby, and Nichelle rang true.

Every book presents its own set of challenges, and *Stealing Time* is no exception. For shining a light on historical obscurity, the prize goes to John Barelli, former head of security for New York's Metropolitan Museum of Art and author of *Stealing the Show: A History of Art and Crime in Six Thefts*. Mr. Barelli's depth of knowledge is matched only by his generosity, as was evident when he graciously answered all our questions about museum security in the 1970s and '80s.

Jonathan Campbell, architect and high school classmate, led Tilia on a merry canter across the rooftops of Boston one winter afternoon, then later showed her how a slate ripper works; Maeve and Gloria would have had a much tougher time without his specialized knowledge. Jim Bickford drew on his military career to give us specs on what kind of walkie-talkie Mike would have used the night of the heist. Ace investigative reporter and mystery writer Hank Phillipi Ryan was lavish with specifics about what a journalist might do and say to get a quote out of a reticent subject. Kit Aikin provided some key details about *The Rocky Horror Picture Show*, and Bobby's subterfuge was all the more compelling for it. Former federal prosecutor Karl Colón was his usual unstinting self when it came to explaining just what kind of legal quagmire we had gotten our characters into, and what we—and they—might do about it. Bruce Coffin, retired homicide detective turned mystery writer, answered many more questions about police procedure past and present. He also provided proof that one can in fact flush rubber gloves down a toilet. Fellow writers Joanna Schaffhausen and Dale Phillips scoured the manuscript for typos. Paul Michaels designed the website: www.stealingtime.net. We're also grateful to M.J. Rose and Ann-Marie Nieves.

Other thankworthy folks include William Vodrey, Jay Chalnick, Tess Vigeland, Tom Sturteveldt, Jordan Smith, the late Calvin C. Hernton, Jonathan and Naoko Goldberg, Robyn and Leon Specthrie, Lisa Birnbach and Michael Porte, Jonathan and Joan Birnbach, and of course Maks and Naomi Birnbach.

Norman would especially like to thank his wife, Deborah, for her support, and their children, Ben, Fischer, and Rebecca, for inspiring parts of the book.

Tilia would particularly like to thank Doug for formatting the manuscript; Nate, for selecting the font and insisting on standard ligatures; and Elwyn, for reading the book and finding typos that we would have sworn weren't there. The three of them comprise the best family/support system/cheering section a writer could ever hope to have.

Special thanks to Taxi, our tireless muse. We would be lost without you.

About the Authors

Tilia Klebenov Jacobs is a bestselling novelist and short story writer. She serves on the board of Mystery Writers of America-New England, and is proud to say that HarperCollins calls her one of "crime fiction's top authors." Tilia has taught middle school, high school, and college, as well as classes for inmates in Massachusetts state prisons. She lives near Boston with her husband, two children, and pleasantly neurotic standard poodle.

Norman Birnbach is an award-winning writer who has published over a hundred essays, op-eds, short stories and articles. His work has appeared in *The New York Times, The New York Times Magazine, The Wall St. Journal, Chicago Tribune, Miami Herald, San Francisco Chronicle, McSweeney's Internet Tendency, New York Magazine, The Magazine of Fantasy & Science Fiction,* and *Militant Grammarian.* He has also studied gemology at the Gemological Institute of America (GIA). *Stealing Time* is his debut novel. A native New Yorker, he lives outside Boston with his wife, three children, and dog, Taxi.

Tilia and Norman met when they were students at Oberlin College.

Made in United States
North Haven, CT
06 March 2025